The Vindicated Man

A Novel by

G.K. Beatty

The First Book in the Barton Anderson
Series

Chiselbury

Chapter One

"Well, Smoke, another day, another piss-ant town!"

That was the un-inspired thought that ran through the mind of Barton Anderson as he rode past the weather-beaten city limit sign that proclaimed that the name of this spot in the road was "Dog Creek, Kansas". Even the name of one of these small specks on a traveler's map was a good indicator of what one could expect. Especially if one spent more than 10 minutes in such non-essential, God-forsaken towns. That is the theory Barton held to, after traveling through countless such places of no repute. Barton had said many times that if a town's name contained creek, branch, hole or gulch, or the part of an animal's anatomy like leg, foot, back, then you just needed to get your business done and get the hell out as soon as possible. He had found that ignorance and impatience are not a good mixture when it comes to social interaction, and they usually led to the reality of bleeding, bandages, and bail. He would sometimes share with younger men who would be striking out on a quest for income or adventure: "don't start any conversations that take more than three sentences to finish", "never ask what they think or what their opinion is, because that may give them the impression you actually care what they think", and "never brag on their kid, horse, gun or anything that might cause them to go on a sad memory trip and waste the biggest part of your day."

"If you want to make a living telling people stuff, then get a job as a politician or a reporter, otherwise, just shut up and get your work done" was the Anderson motto, which was one of the few that he lived by. He did not know if it had worked for anyone else, but it had kept him sane and above ground so far.

As they strolled into the heart of no-where, Barton patted his long-time travel companion on the neck and he said, "Smoke, you know how this works. If this goes as planned, we will both find something to drink, and eat, and be on our way. If not, then I better not have to call your name twice to get both of us out of here". Smoke whinnied as if to say that he was aware of the situation and was ready to hold up his end of the situation.

Barton surveyed the surroundings and observed the usual structures that he would find in most stops along his journeys, no matter how small or insignificant: a saloon, a general store that doubled as a post office, a jail, and a church. He had formed another mental reality of life after encountering many such locales—these establishments were essential to any place where human beings were staying more than one night. Each structure represented the main characteristics of the people who had dropped their bags here and never picked them up again. The church represented those who cared, who tried to do right, may mess up from time-to-time, but would try to make it right. The saloon reflected people who could care less, one way or the other, at that given moment, just give them a few minutes of unwind and they will go back to whatever they do. The jail was the proclamation of those who did not care at all, who were motivated by nothing, except the church people and the saloon people had something they wanted, and the jail people had made bad choices to get those things. As for the general store, it was the place that supplied whatever all the townspeople needed to be who they were, and to do whatever that entailed.

So, for this day, Barton would start this visit with the people of the saloon, because if you need information for your quest, that was the best place to be. People in a saloon seem to be chattier and more willing to share their knowledge of things, without having to spend a lot of time establishing a relationship or a trust. Barton was not here to form long-lasting friendships that would result in swapping letters and correspondence. He just needed what pieces of a puzzle he could get to help him better navigate the trail he was traveling, to get to the result that he was looking for. The services offered in a saloon seemed to put people in a state-of-mind to talk fast, think slow, forget faster. And, for now, that was what Barton needed the most, and that was what he would pursue the earliest.

Smoke walked up to the hitching post, like so many that this horse had spent his days at. There was a water trough there, so that would take care of Smoke's basic need for a while. Barton would have to go inside to find what he was looking for, so he gently pulled his leg over the saddle, the rifle, and the rope and dismounted. No sooner had his boots hit the ground, a sound came out of the saloon that caused Barton to pause, take a deep breath, and check to see if his revolver was loose in its holster.

"Hey, you stupid girl, I pay you to work, not talk! I'll knock some sense into you if you don't understand. I expect you to keep your mouth shut and your feet moving! Shut up or you will be sorry...." came blaring out of the front doors of the saloon in a voice, and language, that had not been to the local church in a long time, if at all.

Barton had hoped that this would be a quick stop for information, wet his whistle and move on down the road to the next place that might give him the pieces he needed to put together a plan to continue his course. But already he knows from the vocal barrage that he has heard that there is a potential mess to step into if he doesn't glean this watering hole quickly.

As Barton slowly pushes his way through the old, battered swinging doors, his eyes scan the premises slowly, because one missed truth could mean this day becoming entangled with other people's character flaws, or them just having a bad day.

He had learned, when it comes to reading a room, that you check first for situations where there is more than one person in a spot. He had previously learned that one-on-one situations are easily controlled, but the extra person in a situation is always where unexpected trouble comes from. This joint wasn't big enough, or important enough, to be a gathering place, especially at this time of day. So, everyone was here alone, except for two old gentlemen in the right rear corner who seemed to have a card game going on. From their friendly banter, they wouldn't pose any problems and would be the first place he would engage for local news and gossip. As for the rest of the joint, Barton counted five people: the bartender who looked like he would rather be somewhere else, the barmaid who looked like she had been somewhere else, a young man staring into his beer hoping it had the answers he was looking for, a man in a shirt and tie who probably works at the general store. And at the end of the bar, still ranting and raving was the loudmouth that Barton heard riding up to the saloon, who was still verbally assaulting the barmaid for some perceived bad work habit.

The two old card players in the back corner was where Barton would start his search for any information that would help his current venture. As an act of respect, he would not interrupt their game or conversation, but would just pull up a chair to the table and watch. He knew that their reaction would tell him if this would be valuable time spent or a waste of time. They would either invite him to join them or tell him to get lost.

Grabbing a chair at a nearby empty table, Barton slid it over to where the two old gentlemen were engrossed in a life-or-death battle of cards— even though Barton noticed the stakes were 30 to 40 matchsticks in the center of the table, and there was a box of matchsticks nearby just in case the wagering got really serious. and more were needed.

"I've got a pair of queens and a pair of sevens, " the old gentleman with the bushy mustache proclaimed. "Beat that!"

His card partner, clean shaven and square jawed, leaned forward in his chair, slowly spread his cards across the table and said, "Well, if I am not mistaken, a full house of kings and threes will run your sorry hand out of town, every day. I win... again!"

As the victor pulled his bounty of matchsticks

to himself, Barton noticed the one with the mustache as he stood up, reached across the table, and grabbed his victorious partner's wrist. He growled, "You cheatin' old coot, I ought to kill you, right here in front of everyone!"

Barton's first thought was that he had misread these two old gentlemen passing the day with an innocent game of cards. How did he sit down in the middle of what should have been a quiet card game, but looks like it could go south in a serious way? Barton quickly slid his hand down his right side to the leather strap that held his Colt revolver in its holster, and he slid it off the hammer just in case he needed to take control of the situation.

As Barton's fingers slid around the handle, the old man with the mustache sat back down in his chair and bellowed, "I ought to kill you! But my gun's at home, and by the time I go get it, I won't be mad anymore and you ain't worth the wasted trip!"

Both men laughed out loud, gathered the cards up to play another hand, and Barton slid his fingers from the handle of his gun; relieved that, for today, this confrontation will take a back seat to dealing the cards and continuing the competition.

"Did we scare the crap out of you, boy?" The question coming from under the bushy mustache as both men chuckled at the newcomer. The one with the square jaw explains that it's all part of the game. That someone must get mad or the game gets boring after a while. Barton takes a deep breath and sits back in his chair, pretending that his hands are shaking, and says, "All I know is I was hoping this town had a good undertaker." Now, both men are howling with laughter, pleased at the effect their act seems to have had on their new acquaintance.

"If you can get those hands settled down, would you like to join us?"

Barton has the invitation that he had hoped for, the one that would hopefully build a conversation, so he answered, "You guys play for pretty high stakes, hope I don't lose my horse before I get out of here."

Both old guys laughed again, and ol' square jaw observed, "Will, I think we have a smart-ass here!"

"Well, Jack, we always said the world needs more smart-asses!"

Barton now knows names, which helps make any questions or conversations more personal. Will, the one with the mustache, is the more jovial of the pair. Jack waits for his moments but can be just as cutting with his humor. Barton will play each one according to his strengths and comfort areas.

"Seeing that you are a stranger, grab the box and count you out 40 or so matchsticks. Let's get this game started", Will said, with a big grin on his face as he started dealing the cards. "And keep your eyes on that old, wrinkled coot there, cause if he is winning, then you know he's cheatin'!" Barton had a feeling that his luck with the cards was going to be minimal with these two characters. But he was hoping his luck at retrieving details would shine today.

The conversations during the first few hands were focused on the cards and what they were holding. The barmaid came by the table, asking if the old gents needed refills and if Barton wanted something to drink. Barton thanked her and said he would take a mug of the coldest thing she had, and he would pay for whatever his card partners were having. His new friends thanked him as the girl headed back toward the bar to retrieve their orders.

"Seeing that it's not the picture-like scenery around here nor our sparkling personalities that brought you through this part of the country, what does call you to our fair town?" Jack finally asks.

Barton knows that how he answers this will either open the door to the conversation he needs to have or will bring this interaction to a rapid close.

"I was actually hoping to find someone that I have been looking for, for some time," Barton answered. "I had heard that he had been through this area, and I figured he might have stopped in here for supplies or a cold one."

Now, Will gets involved in the conversation by asking, "This fellow a friend of yours?"

"Not really a friend, just someone who I need to talk to about a family matter,"was Barton's reply, still trying to keep the conversation easy and simple. "Some unfinished business that needs to be tidied up!"

At this point, the card game slows down and

the conversation starts to pick up as the interest of the old men in Barton's quest also finds new momentum.

"What's this fellow's name?" Jack inquires as he gets back into the conversation. The card game is now an afterthought, as interest in their new friend has brought interest into an otherwise boring day.

"Coy Newton is his name. He goes by Rough House sometimes, depending upon how long he stays in one place. He may have come through here in the last month or so," Barton answers.

"Coy Newton, Coy Newton, Rough House Newton..." Will rolled the name around in his memory. "I don't recall anybody by that name coming through here, do you, Jack?"

Barton could tell Jack had already started racking his brain for any details that might put this discussion at a different level and bring forward any intrigue to this new experience, in a town where new experiences are few and far between.

"I can't say the name is ringing any bells for me either," Jack replied. "What does he look like? Is there anything about him that would set him apart from everyone else and make a person remember him?"

Barton knew that if there was any information that he needed in this town, there was a chance that these two gentlemen will have it, or would know where to get it. Barton started explaining that Newton was a big man, 30ish, rough and unkept, didn't talk much unless he was drunk or

9

mad, was missing three fingers on his right hand and was the kind of person you just didn't care to be around anymore than you had to.

"Missing three fingers on his right hand, eh?" Will inquired and then added, "Not much of a chance you are looking for a piano player then, are you?"

Barton didn't need to lose this interaction to humor, so he focused back on Jack's interest. "He, mainly tries to pick up spending money by finding ranch work, farm work. Something that he doesn't have to stay long at. He also is not beyond resorting to stealing to finance his daily needs and beating a quick retreat out of wherever he is. Either way, he seems to wear out his welcome rather quickly. What are the chances your local law would have any thoughts on him?"

Will responds with a half-laugh and answers, "The sheriff here hasn't had a thought in a long time, mainly because he was killed almost a year ago and no one has stepped forward to take his place. U.S. marshal rides through every couple of months to check on things or use the jail as a stop-over if he is traveling with a prisoner. I guess we just don't pose a threat to humanity to rate another lawman."

Now, Jack is resting his chin on his fist as if to help him think clearer, and then yells out to the barmaid, "Becky, come here when you get a chance!" Jack turns back to Barton. "She might know something. She sees a lot and hears even more when she is working in here, which seems to be always."

Becky, whose hard life makes her look older than her twenty-nine years, comes over, carrying a tray with Barton's mug of beer and a coffee pot for the old men's refills. She sets down the tray and explains that she is working as fast as she can, thinking that her patrons are not satisfied with her effort. But Jack assures her she is doing fine, knowing any complaint would get a physical response from the loudmouth at the end of the bar who happens to be the owner of this saloon. Jack lets her know that he just wanted to ask her something. Becky perks up as she doesn't have many people needing something from her except for something else to eat, to drink, or for company.

"Well, Jack, what is it that you think I can help you with?" She smiled as if she was the most important person in the room, at least for this moment.

"Becky, in the last few weeks, have you seen a gruff, unfriendly, loner come through here? He'd be a big guy, missing three fingers on one hand?"

Becky turns her head and looks out the front window, like the answer or something that would shake her memory might be out there. She shares a thought, "There are a lot of large, rude, dirty guys that come through here with the cattle drives, so those aren't the ones that make impressions in a place like this, a place that will serve anyone that has the money to pay for the goods. But a stranger missing three fingers would definitely leave a mark on your mind, that's for sure."

11

Will, growing impatient that the card game has now taken a back seat to the banter between the other three, growls, "Girl, do you know anything or not? Have you seen anyone like what they are describing or not?"

"Yes sir, I have."

Her response brings Barton to the front of his chair, for this is the first positive sighting that he has heard of, or at least the first chance of a sighting that he has had in two weeks of travel.

Now, Barton's focus is to make sure she understands the question, and that she is not just trying to 'fit in' to someone else's conversation, hoping she finds worth and relevance on this day.

"Miss, you think you have seen a person such as this in the last three or four weeks?" Barton asks. Not threateningly as to cause the girl to be intimidated, but firmly, to let her understand the seriousness of his search.

"Yes, sir!" replied Becky, looking at Barton with a look, hoping to sell her honesty. "He was in here a few weeks ago, came in with some of Asa Givens' ranch hands. Funny, each time he came in with them, he didn't sit with them; didn't sit with anyone, really. He always sat near the front door, drinking his drink and looking out the front window like he was expecting someone to show up or something. He just sat there, drinking and tapping the remaining two fingers on his right hand."

Barton's mind is racing, and his heart is, too. He knows that a couple of weeks' time is not that long, as Newton will usually stay at a place a month or so before he wears out his welcome or gets into serious trouble with the law.

Suddenly, Will sits up in his chair, like he has been hit with a lightning bolt of revelation, and asks, "Becky, I wasn't here, but was this guy the one that broke that chair across that drunk cowboy's back and grabbed his head and beat it against a table until six or seven guys finally pulled him off? Dang, near killed that cowboy, from what I heard!"

"That's him!" Becky is now fully involved in this telling of facts, which seems to have captured the attention of everyone at the table. "That's him, the cowboy didn't mean any harm, he just walked up behind the big man, startled him, and old two-fingers jumped up, grabbed the cowboy and started wailing on him with a chair. Then started beating his face into the table before anyone knew what to do. The first couple of guys who tried to save that cowboy got flung across the room like corn-husk dolls. It finally took six to loosen the big man's grip. By then, that cowboy was bleeding out of every hole in his head, and a couple of openings he didn't have when the evening started. Funny thing, old two-fingers walked over to his table, finished his drink, and walked out the door like nothing had happened. We haven't seen him since that night. And no one is sorry about it because that guy isn't right in the head!"

Will was sitting there, shaking his head with a puzzled looked on his face. Then he asked, "I know the owner of this joint keeps a twelve-gauge sawed-off under the bar. Why didn't he pull it out and stop it before it got so out of control?"

Becky looked around to make sure her boss couldn't hear her, and then she softly answered, "He was watching the whole thing like he was enjoying it."

"Any idea where the big man went, what direction he went in?" inquires Barton as he tries to bring the conversation back around to the job that still needs to be finished here.

"The last I heard, he went by Asa Givens' ranch, picked up his stuff, and rode hard up the north road. Where he went from there, is anyone's guess.", Becky shared. "Good riddance to him. He was eaten up with bad news ready to happen; everyone was afraid of him.

Barton turned back to Jack and asked, "You think this Asa Givens could be of any help? How would I find him and talk with him?"

Before Jack could answer, Will took a big breath and let out a long, "Ooooh boy! Whew! Ooooh boy!"

Jack looked Barton in the eyes with a look that seemed to make the next words very important. "Son, finding where Asa Givens is, at any given time, is not a problem, he owns everything north of town for the next fifty miles. In other words, you can't miss where he may be if you go in the right direction. But the truth is, no one talks to Asa Givens unless you are family or crew, and if you are one of those, you still aren't guaranteed a conversation with him."

Barton is confronted with a new challenge, but

will try to find a way around it as he has been around Jack enough to know this man can be trusted, at least in Jack's interpretation of the situation.

"When was the last time either one of you talked with Mr. Givens?" Barton asks his card partners, hoping one had an in-road to the next step in possible information.

Jack responds first. "I have lived here over thirty years and I have never spoken to him, never met him, couldn't point him out if my life depended on it. The man just doesn't have a big desire to socialize with anyone, I mean anyone!"

"Heck, I have lived here longer, and the only person I know that has seen him in the last ten years is Doc Allen. And that was the time when Asa was bit by that rattler. Asa sent one of the ranch hands to town to fetch Doc. The old man wouldn't even come to town for his own sake. Doc said Asa was near death, but he was too mean to die. Doc said he wouldn't be surprised if the snake crawled off and died after getting a mouthful of Asa," Will said with a chuckle.

Barton was starting to get restless and said, "I guess I will just have to ride north and introduce myself to this Asa Givens. He seems to be the next stop I need to make to keep my search going. Thanks for your time and the card game, but I have to be going while the sun is still up."

As Barton started to rise out of his chair, Jack put his hand on Barton's arm, as to stop him for a moment. Barton didn't let anyone put their hands on him and his first instinct was to knock Jack's hand off. But he saw an expression on Jack's face that told him that this old man had some last words to share, in case they never saw each other again.

"What's on your mind, old man?" Barton asked Jack.

"Just that you might want to dig around town a little more. The bridge on the north edge of town is where Asa Givens' land starts. And on that bridge is a sign that warns everyone that trespassing will not be tolerated and all violators will be shot on site. There are a few people who had the same thought as you are having right now and have never been heard from again. Is finding this man that important?"

"If it wasn't, I wouldn't have taken the time to come to your little town. Simple as that!"

Just as Barton stood up, again thanking his card partners for their time and help, Barton flinched as he heard flesh hitting flesh, then heard the sound of something landing on the floor behind him. When he swung around, his hand already on his sidearm, Barton saw Becky laying on the floor with blood running from her mouth, her jaw already turning color, her eyes unable to stay open. The brutish saloon owner was standing over her with his big hand drawn, ready to land another vicious blow as soon as Becky could come to her senses enough to stand up.

"I told you, you whore. I don't pay you to talk and make friends; I pay you to keep the booze moving and the money picked up. You're just good for nothing trash and I'm going to teach you a lesson that might just stick in that hollow head of yours," the saloon owner bellowed, in a voice that could be heard out in the street again.

"You didn't need to do that, you just didn't," pleaded Will as he started to reach out to help the wobbly Becky as she struggled to make sense of where she was and what happened.

"Shut up, old man, or I'll put you on the floor next to her. Do you want to keep her company, you stupid ol' fool? Do you want the blood slapped outta your mouth?" The owner is now louder and bolder by the lack of action from anyone else in the room.

Barton's mind was racing a mile a minute. He needed to go, but Becky's situation could not be left to find its own solution. He was pretty confident that this burly bully wouldn't see the error of his ways and calm down. Barton, within seconds of Becky hitting the floor, remembered being in a similar situation in another town, and he just hoped that his next move, and its result, would be satisfactory to all involved. Barton slid his hand from his Colt, reached over and picked up his empty beer mug and proclaimed, "Hey, I want another cold one before I go. Get me one!"

The saloon owner, still standing over the bleeding, dazed Becky, had a look of confusion, and then annoyance, on his face when he responded, "Hey moron, can't you see she is a little busy bleeding to wait on you, right now?"

Whatever smile Barton may have had on his face to try to diffuse the situation is now gone. His eyes have narrowed as to focus on the object of his

17

attention, and he informs the gruff bully, in front of everyone, that "I wasn't talking to her, I was talking to you, fat man!"

With that proclamation, Jack and Will slowly get up and move out of the corner, as to get away from the perceived commotion that was getting ready to present itself. The saloon owner rolls his large hand into a fist, and while taking a step toward Barton, asks the question that will put this confrontation into a higher emotion, "You're asking me to get you a beer? Exactly what do I look like to you, you crap-for-brains?"

With the beer mug still in his hand, Barton calmly responds, "You look like someone who knows every sheep in this area by their first name!"

The gasp that went out across the barroom from the patrons still there seemed to help the loudmouth realize what Barton had just accused him of, and rage flew up inside the big man. Immediately, he stomped with both fists balled up toward Barton. Barton felt the wind off the bar owner's ham-sized fist, as it missed its mark and sailed over Barton's head. The big man's weight carried him past Barton just enough for Barton to land a blow against the side of the big man's head with the beer mug. The mug found its mark, shattering from the full force hit and knocking the bully to his knees. While his adversary was still in a vulnerable position, Barton grabbed the big man by the hair of the head and drove his knee into the saloon owner's nose, sending blood splattering over the stunned man's face.

"Bleeding is not so funny now, is it, fat man? Especially when it's your own blood?" Barton asks softly; never raising his voice, never losing control of his emotions.

Everyone in the bar is stunned. No one has ever confronted the violent nature of the saloon owner. No one has ever put this big man, literally, in his place. Every eye was on Barton as he made his next move against his wounded and reeling foe. Barton knelt on one knee next to the big man, still holding him by the hair of the head, pulled his head backward to where his chin was sticking up in the air. Calmly, the tall man removed his Colt.45 from its holster and placed the seven inch, blue-steel barrel underneath the bleeding man's chin. Then he shared some vital information with the saloon owner, drawing the man's ear next to Barton's mouth and whispering. "If I ever hear of you hitting this girl again, or I hear of you hitting any girl again, I will come back to this piss-ant town and I will kill you. Do you understand me? Do you understand that I will kill you and not give a tinker's damn while doing it?"

The big man mumbled something, and Barton pressed the barrel tighter against his chin and asked one more time, "Do you understand what I have just said?"

"Yes," said the saloon owner.

"Yes, what?" inquired Barton.

"Yes, sir!"

"Do you believe I will come back and kill you?"

"Yes, sir!"

Barton slowly lifted himself to his feet, placed

the revolver back in its holster, wiped the beer and blood from his hand, checked to see if Becky was going to be ok, and headed for the front door. No more conversations were needed. He wasn't in the mood for it and the rest of those there had enough to talk about for days. As Barton reached the front doors, Jack met him there.

"Are you going to Asa Given's ranch?" Jack softly asked.

"Yes, I am. I didn't come this far to give up on what I am looking for. And what I need is probably to be found there," replied Barton, walking past the old man's extended hand and his effort to say goodbye.

Jack, not understanding why his act of sincerity was ignored, still offers a last note. "You be careful, young man. And, in case things don't go well, and you become another missing visitor to the Givens' ranch, what name do we give the U.S. marshal when he is filling out his report?"

Barton turned to go out the door, not wishing to lose any more time with useless chatter or complicate the encounter by revealing his identity. But he turned back to the old man, because his question was an honest one and one of someone who was truly concerned—and his name may be needed in such a case.

"Anderson, Barton Anderson!"

He heard them gasp as they heard it. Becky dropped her tray when she heard it. The busy chatter in the saloon stopped after the patrons heard it.

Jack, simply, responded, "Ohhhh, my Lord!"

Barton walked out the doors to where Smoke was waiting. Barton swung his leg over the saddle, told Smoke "Let's go", nudged him with the heels of his boots, and they headed north.

As they rode past the front of the saloon, Jack was standing on the porch. The old man yelled out one last question as the tall man on the dark gray horse rode by, "If you find this Coy Newton, are you going to kill him?"

Without turning around, Barton responded, "Very good chance I will."

And with that, Barton and Smoke rode away.

Chapter Two

What makes a man's heart suddenly grow cold? What makes a man's soul go suddenly dark? Where there had been laughter, love and kindness; is now a void of anything that can be given, anything that can be shared with others, anything that would make people cherish the thought of being around him, and him around them. What can make a man have no reason to live, have no reason to look forward to what a day may bring, having no desire to be more than you have to be? There are things that can turn a man into a cold, empty chasm. Just living until the day the sun doesn't come up again, and not caring when that day comes. This is what happened to Barton Anderson, that day in October, one year ago.

Barton had lived in Smithview, Kansas his whole life. Grew up to be a respected citizen, a ranch owner, married to the girl of his dreams, and father of two growing boys. He worked hard, would drop what he was doing to help someone else, was always the first to give when a need was brought forth, and would listen to anyone with a broken heart or broken dream.

Barton had played a major part in helping Smithview grow after the railroad decided to put a livestock depot right outside of town. Barton hadn't been to college, but always had a hunger to read and know things. People turned to him when the town started getting bigger, asking advice on all subjects and he, usually having an answer, the ability to get an answer, or knowing someone who might know. He had been approached more times than he could remember about running for a political position, sitting on a committee, or becoming a partner in a new business venture. But Barton liked his life. He enjoyed the pace of being a rancher, and he loved raising a family with Jenny.

Barton and Jenny had been a couple ever since fifth grade. They were always together at the dances, at the fairs, at the church socials; and they always talked of the life that they were now blessed to live. The ranch wasn't big, about 500 acres that Jenny's dad gave them as a wedding gift. They always kept 200-300 cows, rotating out a hundred or more each year to the cattle market in Topeka. New spring calves always kept the herd fresh and growing. Barton would also tend 50 or so horses on the ranch, mainly because he always loved horses and would send a few to the local Army fort when the need was there. The military always came to him first for his honest reputation was respected all around that area. He could have been bigger, richer, and more powerful, but that was not the dream he and Jenny had all those years. What he had was everything he wanted.

As for family: Adam, age ten, and Seth, age six, were Barton and Jenny's whole world. As a family, they worked together, played together, and went to church together. They were hardly ever seen without the other three. And since Jenny's dad,

Nate, had his stroke and was limited physically, Barton built a room onto the main house and moved him to the ranch, where they could watch after him, let him live around those who loved him. Family life just couldn't be any better, ranch life couldn't be any better. But Barton could never have known what was coming.

Barton and Adam were working on a section of fence in the north corral on the ranch, a place Barton used to gather livestock instead of driving them all the way back to the barn.

"Daddy," Adam said with an inquisitive tone, "look over there. That dust cloud looks like it's being kicked up by a lot of riders riding hard."

Barton responded, "I think you are right. Looks like they might ride right past here!"

And that is what the riders did, because it was a posse being led by U.S. Marshal Lyndon Tomes. He had dropped by the ranch house, looking for Barton, and Jenny had told him where to check. As the riders came closer to the corral, Barton could see by the look on his face that Marshal Tomes was in a hurry for a reason. Something had happened that called for fast action and quite a few men. It was hard to make out what Marshal Tomes was yelling, but when he got close enough to be heard, what he was saying let Barton know that fixing the corral fence would have to wait for another day.

"Bank robbery, Barton. Bank robbery!"

The marshal had barely stopped his horse when he started filling in Barton with the details. Five men had stopped in the Smithview bank, didn't even bother to wear masks, because they weren't planning on leaving any witnesses. And they didn't. By the time the thieves were riding out of town, the banker, two tellers, two customers, an unfortunate by-stander and the town constable were all dead. And, about three thousand dollars was taken, most of which was railroad payroll, which had just arrived the day before.

"I was riding through town and had to stop by the blacksmith to have a shoe tightened on my horse. I heard the gunfire, grabbed my rifle off my saddle, and ran toward the shooting," Tomes said, quickly trying to get his story told, as he knew time was of the essence. "I got a couple of shots off as they were riding away; may have hit one. But I was trying to get to the constable to see if he was still alive, and did he know who they were?"

"Was he able to say anything before he died?" Barton asked.

The look that came over Marshal Tomes' face told Barton that what the constable said was not something that the marshal wanted to hear at that time, or anytime, to be honest. But it was a fact and would have to be dealt with, and it would not be easy.

"Angus Ford!" The marshal sighed, hoping that this news wouldn't cause him to lose Barton as a member of the posse.

"Angus Ford, have you heard of him?" Barton searched for the reason for the marshal's measured response.

Marshal Tomes shook his head to the

affirmative, and replied, "He's a bad one, Barton. He is beyond bad. I have read posters on Ford. Killing is as natural as breathing to him. He is so evil that Hades probably wouldn't even have him. A couple of months ago he, and probably this same gang, killed fourteen people during a country church service in Whitesville. Those people lost their lives for the offering of eight dollars and some change. And then Ford burned the church down with all the victims still in it, including three children. Three lawmen have lost their lives trying to put this devil in jail or in the ground. I hate to ask you. I know you are a family man, but will you ride with us?"

Barton looked around at the other eight men in the posse. He knew them all from ranching, church, and from town. He saw from their expressions that they were counting on him joining up when they volunteered. They knew Barton was level-headed and was the best shot in the area, especially with his Henry rifle, which Jenny had given him one year after sewing and baking to raise the money. Marshal Tomes had asked Barton to join him when other incidents had risen, and the marshal had noticed that men seemed to be easy with following Barton's example. The marshal knew he would never have to worry about Barton panicking, running or wasting time or shots.

Barton turned to Adam, and said, "Son, take the wagon back to the house, tell your momma I will be back in a couple of days, don't forget the two cows getting ready to have calves and don't get into it with your brother, while I am gone. Can you do that?"

"Yes sir, Daddy!"

Barton thought it was a good thing that he had brought Smoke with him to fix the corral. Smoke wasn't one much for just hanging around the barn, especially when he could see Barton and the boys going off to work or on some adventure together. So Barton would put Smoke's saddle in the back of the ranch wagon and let him tag along. Smoke wasn't a horse. He was considered one of the family, and Barton had said that the dark, gray horse was an "extra pair of eyes" around the place. Nothing got past Smoke and he had this high-pitched whinny he would let out when the horse had questions about a situation. Barton trusted his life and his family with this horse, and in moments like this, he would be thankful to have his friend underneath him.

"Marshal, how much of a head start does Ford and his gang have on us?" Barton inquired as he put on Smoke's saddles, checked the cinch strap on his saddle, and the saddle bag for rifle cartridges and the canteen for water.

"I figure, timewise, they have a two-hour or so head start, but if I did hit one of them, that may slow them down. If they are dragging a wounded man, that may help us cut into their head start maybe in half by sundown. If we can ride steady until then. And Ford doesn't know that there was another lawman in town when he rode out, so he won't be expecting a posse to be organized this quickly," Tomes answered, sounding like he was trying to convince himself more than he was the others.

Barton got on Smoke, and the hunt began. Marshal Tomes said that the robber's tracks out of town showed they were heading north. Barton, trying to put himself in the mindset of someone needing to escape but also needing to provide himself cover in case he was caught up to, figures that going west or south out of Smithview wouldn't be smart because the land in those directions was flat and wide open, offering no alternatives other than to ride hard for 100 miles until you, eventually, get to some foothills. To the north, there were woods and hills, but also the Rams Head River, which would be full and swift this time of year, and might be too dangerous to try. Barton's mind figured that somewhere north of Smithview they will probably turn east and head toward the mountain range, known as Heaven's Hills, which would offer the cover of higher ground, forest areas, rock ledges, water, and game to sustain one until it was safe to come out and re-supply at one of a few small towns beyond that area.

"What are you thinking, Barton?" Marshal Tomes yelled over the sound of hooves running at a steady pace on the hard ground.

"I wouldn't be surprised if these tracks take a turn to the east, in a few miles, just wouldn't be surprised at all." Barton shared his hunch with his co-riders. The others seemed to be encouraged, and even relieved, that Barton seemed to be working on a plan even though there was a U.S.

marshal leading them. This was why Marshal Tomes would be glad to have Barton with them. He just knew that men would follow the tall man on the dark, gray horse.

As Barton expected, the tracks took a turn toward the east, about twenty miles north of Smithview. Tomes smiled and was not surprised that his friend's gut feeling was right on the money. But in the back of the marshal's mind, even if catching up with this band of thugs was going smoother than predicted, it's what will have to be done and what was waiting for them that was occupying the lawman's mind since they left the Anderson ranch.

The marshal was concerned about Angus Ford and his gang getting to Heaven's Hills and establishing a stronghold in the trees and rocks. It was a certainty of them being impossible to flush out without sustaining heavy damage and casualties. The outlaws would have the high ground and would have the advantage of being able to see the posse coming, as the posse would not have a sure idea on where their targets were until they heard the report of their guns firing or the smoke rising after the shots were taken. By that time, the sun could be going down and they could be under serious fire and sustaining multiple hits. The marshal yelled at Barton as they rode of his concerns and did Barton have any ideas to, hopefully, help even the odds a bit? Ford had four hardened outlaws on his side of things while the marshal had two railroad workers, a gunsmith, a freight hauler, a couple of lumber mill hands, a rancher, a saloon sweeper, and a retired schoolteacher in his troop; not exactly a group that would put enough fear into Angus Ford to throw down his guns and give up. Tomes had left two of the constable deputies back in Smithview to, hopefully, bring some order to the chaos that had broken out after the robbery and the slaughter of innocent people.

"Marshal, if they have a wounded man, and depending on how far they had to ride this morning to get to Smithview before the holdup, we may have an advantage of fresher horses and healthy riders," Barton explained. "But if we get to Heaven's Hills after the sun goes down, there is no way for us to confront them in the dark. We won't have any idea where they are. We will have to wait until morning. That will have given them and their horses the time to rest up, and we will have lost whatever edge we had. If we alternate between running the horses and walking, and if we water our horses from our canteens instead of stopping at the watering hole between here and Heaven's Hills, then we may arrive minutes after they do instead of an hour or more behind them. And they could be too busy getting their camp set up to notice us coming. It's about the only approach that we have that gives us any chance at surprising them, and apprehending them without paying too steep a price—man or horse wise."

The marshal shook his head to the affirmative as he kept rolling the plan over in his head. "I like it. I will tell the others while we are walking the horses. That water hole you were talking about is about thirty minutes ahead of us. Heaven's Hills is another hour beyond that. I will also make sure every rifle is loaded up and each man has reloads handy. I have a feeling once we catch up with them and the shooting starts, wherever you jump off your horse will be where your cover will be until it's over, one way or another."

Tomes waited until they were ready to walk their horses. Then he went to each rider, never stopping or getting off their mounts, and explained what the plan was. Each man seemed to be in agreement, except John Moor, the retired teacher. Moor was concerned about him and his horse, not being the youngest in the posse, and they might not be able to sustain the non-stop ride without a break at the water hole. Tomes, realizing that the continual trek forward was the only option they had to have any chance of confronting Angus Ford and his group, told Moor that if he was sure that he and his ride would need a break, then he could pull out of the posse, do what he needed to do at the watering hole, and try to catch back up with them as fast as he could. John Moor seemed relieved at the marshal's suggestion and it was then that Tomes wondered if the old former teacher should not have come in the first place.

Up front of the posse, Barton can see a little way just ahead of them the small stand of trees that was the sign of where the watering hole was. It was just a spot out in the middle of a flat, clear area. A traveler would find a few trees to provide shade in the daytime, a few rocks to provide a

31

place to sit, and a source of water amazingly coming up out of the ground at all times of the year. Barton's father-in-law, Nate, once said that it was a place that God had put there just for fools who were off course and had no clue where their next drink of water was coming from.

Elston Saltsman, one of the mill workers, rode up beside Barton and started to make a case for stopping at the resting place. "Anderson, I know about the plan, and I know we should stick to it, but the thought of a cool drink of water and giving my butt a break from this saddle, well I just think that—"

By the time Barton turned to see why Elston didn't finish his thought, the tall man on the dark, gray horse heard the delayed sound of the rifle firing and saw the blood pouring from Elston's chest. The mill worker never knew what hit him. His life was over upon impact as the right side of his chest was torn open, his life-giving fluid rapidly leaving him as he fell backwards from his horse.

"Get down! There is someone bunkered down at the water hole!" yelled Barton, as he was pulling his rifle out of its sleeve and sliding off Smoke all in one motion. He grabbed Smoke's bridle bit, twisted it hard and in a downward motion, and Smoke knew this meant to lie on the ground. The horse knew, because this was the thing Barton would make him do for the kids at the church picnic, except his owner wasn't laughing this time, and there weren't any kids.

Kaboom! Kaboom!

Two more rifle shots rang out and Tomes

yelled that John Moor, the old schoolteacher, had been hit.

Kaboom! Kaboom! Kaboom!

The rifle assault continued at a regular pace. By now, everyone was off their horses and laying as flat as they could, in a prone position, ready to return fire. As soon as they knew what to shoot at.

"Just start shooting into the grove of trees, hopefully we will get lucky enough to hit something, or at least let them know we are still here!" barked Tomes as he tried to crawl to old man Moor to see if he was still alive.

"Barton, anybody hit over your way?" asked the marshal as he continued to watch for muzzle flashes or gun smoke as the shots continued, only stopping long enough to reload. At least, that was what Tomes was guessing.

Barton answered, "Saltsman is gone. He won't be sitting in a saddle when he goes home."

Tomes bit his lip, concerned that this trip had already taken its toll upon his band of volunteers. Counting himself and Barton, his posse now had 8 members. His advantage in numbers of living bodies was dwindling.

While Barton was carefully placing his shots strategically around the trees and rocks of the watering area, the rest of the posse was firing haphazard and as rapidly as possible. Barton knew they were scared, and he knew how they were feeling. It was just he seemed to be able to keep enough sense about him to have a strategy to his gunfire. He also had enough sense about him to realize that the consistent pattern of a rifle being fired one shot at a time could mean there was only one shooter in the trees and rocks.

"Hey, Marshal," Barton shouted over the sound of all the rifle fire going off. "I think there is only one person that has us pinned down out here!"

"Yeah, I kind of got that feeling, too. If there was more than one, the sound of gunfire would be more erratic and rapid. We can't just lay out here and wait for them to run out of cartridges. The sun is going to be going down in a little while and then we are going to really be hurting. We've got two dead. Mark Miller's horse has been hit and if there is only one in the trees, then the rest of the gang is still on the run, getting further away from us!"

Barton didn't hear anything that the marshal said after he made the announcement that "two were dead." That meant that old man Moor, who had taught Barton and his boys, would go home across his saddle the same way that Elston Saltsman would. Smithview is minus two good citizens, and he is minus two good friends.

Marshal Tomes yelled out the name of each of the remaining posse members and so far, no one else was hit, just shaken up. He told each man to stay down and stay where they were and try to shoot into as many places as they could. If they couldn't hit who was shooting at them, then maybe they could slow the shooter down until he could think of something.

As Tomes was taking inventory of his remaining posse, Barton was thinking about the situation and what could be done to remedy their current position. First, Barton whistled to Smoke. Three short, high-pitched sounds. It caused the horse to stand up and take off in the direction they came from as hard as he could. Smoke would continue running until the sound of gunfire was not as loud. This was something that they had worked on together in case Barton was working on the ranch and encountered outlaws, renegade Indians, Ganchezes, or any other assaults where he would need to take cover and keep the horse safe. As Smoke ran away, he whinnied, and the other horses seemed to take that as a signal to join him. So, they did, and with that feat, transportation out of this area was secured if anyone survived to get out of there.

As for the posse, there were still eight of them left, and possibly just one shooter in the watering hole area. How could that be used for their advantage?

There would, surely, be casualties if they all rushed the trees at the same time. What if the shooter isn't in the trees but behind one of the rocks over by the water hole? The shooter could pick off two or more if they headed in the wrong direction.

"Hey Barton, you got awfully quiet. Are you ok?" the marshal asked with a nervous tone in his voice.

"I am thinking. My mind can't do two things at one time, especially when someone is trying to take my head off with a rifle. And to top it all off, he hasn't even introduced himself yet. Kind of rude don't you think?"

The marshal appreciated Barton's attempt to lighten up the rest of the men, and Tomes especially was grateful that Barton was working on a resolution to their situation. Time was running. Any gang members who were not here were getting further away, and the marshal was tired of laying in the dirt, hoping and praying that the next shot from the trees didn't come too close in his direction.

"Barton, was you any good at arithmetic in school?" the marshal strangely asked.

Barton was stumped by why the marshal needed to know this information, especially at a time like this, but he also knew that the lawman wasn't much for foolishness. So Barton decided to go along with the inquiry.

"I did alright, thanks Mr. Moor and a couple of other schoolteachers. Why do you ask?"

The marshal waited a couple of seconds and then answered, "Because I have an idea, and whether I survive this idea will depend upon how sharp you can work the numbers involved."

"What are you talking about, and what do my math skills have to do with getting a shooter out of that grove of trees?"

The marshal quickly started his inquiry. "How long do you think it takes to fully reload a Henry repeating rifle?"

Barton thought for a second, and then shared that it would "take twenty to twenty-five seconds if you didn't fumble around with the cartridges too much." Seeing that he owned a Henry, Barton was trying to picture himself doing it and counting the time until he finishes, in his mind.

"Ok, how long would it take for a man to run one hundred yards over level ground?" Tomes continued with his testing of Barton's knowledge of timing.

"I would say around 30 seconds or so, depending on age, health, and if a person was carrying anything." Barton was now starting to figure out what the marshal was contemplating doing, as he figured they were about one hundred yards from the grove of trees by the watering hole.

"I could probably run it in twenty to twenty-five seconds if I take my boots and my coat off." Which was Barton's way of volunteering for the task.

Before the marshal could respond to Barton, another offer came from Jason Nash, a young man who had a successful gun shop in Smithview.

"Marshal, I am the youngest one here and outside of Mr. Anderson, I am probably the best shot here. I am willing to do whatever it is you are thinking about!"

The marshal quickly put all thoughts of anyone besides him taking any risks on this day.

"I appreciate the offers, but I am the one with the badge and the one in charge." Tomes then shared what was on his mind. "If I am correct, the shooter is shooting sixteen times before there is a break to reload. It sounds like he has a Henry, so that means he is reloading 44 rimfire cartridges into it. If Barton's calculations are correct, and it takes thirty seconds to run one hundred yards, then he will be loaded and leveling the gun on me before I get to him. But, if all of you fire continually in his direction, you may rattle him enough to gain those extra few seconds I need to get into the trees. From there, I will have a better chance of locating him, and hopefully, stopping him."

Before anyone can respond or protest to the marshal's plan, the shots from the trees start again. This time one finds a target in Mark Miller, whose horse was wounded in the original attack. Mark lets out a painful groan from a wound in the lower leg but assures the marshal that he can still shoot.

"That's it," proclaims Marshal Tomes, as he reloads his rifle and makes sure his Colt is loaded as well. "We are not wasting any more time laying here getting picked off one at a time. The time is now, get ready! When I get up and start running straight to the grove, unload on the trees and rocks!"

Upon counting sixteen shots from the trees, the marshal jumped up and ran straight toward the trees. He knew that he couldn't try to zig or zag as the posse needed to know what line he was running so that they would know what lines they could shoot in. The bark and leaves were flying through the air, and sparks were dancing off of the limestone rocks as the seven men poured bullets ahead of the marshal's path.

Tomes was trying to run toward the front of the trees and keep an eye on the rocks in case the shooter had been there this whole time. He was past the water hole and almost to the first tree when he saw movement to his left. His instinct caused him to fall to the ground and roll, making himself a smaller, more difficult target.

The first shot from the reloaded shooter hit the ground and ricocheted off a tree root. Tomes heard the second shot while lying on his stomach as it whizzed over his head. The marshal felt a searing pain in his right arm as the third shot found its mark. Tomes lost his rifle as his grip was weakened from the impact and pain of the entry of the bullet into his arm. He can't get up off the ground and run for cover as one arm is bleeding and useless. The other arm is frantically trying to remove his Colt from its holster, which is made almost impossible by his being right-handed, his holster being on his right side and having only his left arm and hand available at this time.

Tomes rolls over on his back, reaches across his body, works the pistol out of its holster, and rolls back over onto his stomach in what seems like one continuous motion. It feels more like minute, and not seconds for him to locate the shooter, who has now stepped out from behind the tree that he had been using for cover and is now standing there, twenty feet away, with his rifle pointed straight at the marshal. Tomes thought it was funny that his last thought before he was to die was that he was right about the outlaw shooting at them with a Henry rifle.

Kaboom!

Tomes didn't feel an impact, didn't sense any new pain. He didn't feel any bleeding on his person other than the blood that was still oozing from his arm wound. All he saw was the shooter jerking backwards, bouncing off a tree and falling to the ground. The marshal realized the shot didn't come from in front of him, but from behind him. Tomes rolled over, steadied himself on his left side, and there he saw a sight that caused him to throw his head back in relief and gratefulness. Standing fifty yards away, feet spread wide, a wisp of gun smoke still rolling from the end of his Henry rifle, was the tall rancher—Barton Anderson.

When he saw the marshal go down, Barton jumped up and ran toward the action as hard as he could. As the shooter stepped from behind the tree, Barton knew he had only seconds to save his friend, and that would not be enough time to line up the sights on his rifle to insure an adequate hit. No, this was going to be all muscle memory and instinct from all those times of standing behind the barn and target practicing on boxes, tree stumps, and old lumber. Barton never imagined that those simple practices would come in handy when the stakes were real and a lawman's life was in the balance.

"Are you ok?" Barton asked as he ran to the marshal and grabbed his good arm and helped him up.

"No, I am not ok. I am shot, bleeding, and my arm is burning like Hades itself! But all in all, I could be worse if not for you. And for that I am beholden to you and that Henry rifle. I will have to remember to thank Jenny for giving you that," replied the marshal.

By now, the rest of the posse, except for Mark Miller, who was resting his wounded leg, is running up to the two men. All of them glad that the marshal is alive and that they were too. Barton just listened to their chatter as he started tearing the marshal's sleeve, applying a bandage made from a handkerchief, and trying to get the wound cleaned and the bleeding stopped.

While Barton continued to dress Tomes' wound and the others talked among themselves, reliving the facts of the last half hour, Marshal Tomes heard a movement behind them and realized that the shooter had been wounded, not killed. The lawman, still with his mind on the duty that had not been fulfilled, walked over the wounded outlaw. Barton was still trying to dress the wound as Tomes walked. The marshal kicked the rifle away from the bandit, checked the outlaw for any other weapons, and then softly, but sternly, inquired, "What's your name, boy?"

The outlaw looked up at Tomes, and with a weak voice, replied, "Paul, Paul Hanley!"

The marshal inspected the young man's wound: the bullet from Barton's rifle had hit him right below the middle of his chest. From the looks of the blood-soaked coat, and the blood that was on the ground, it would only be a matter of time before this law breaker's life would be over. Tomes also noticed that the young man had a wound on his back, just under his left shoulder. It was an older wound and had started bleeding again. Tomes realized that this was probably the rider that he had shot at when the outlaws were leaving the bank in Smithview. Angus Ford had cold-heartedly sacrificed this one by leaving him behind without a horse or a hope, so they could get away and put more time between themselves and the posse.

"Paul, I am not going to lie to you," the marshal started. "It doesn't look good for you. As a matter of fact, if you have anything you would like to say or share, you had better get to it. You can't undo what harm you have done in your life, but the Good Lord might take it into consideration if you wanted to help anyone else from having to suffer at the hands of your friends by telling us where they are headed. Are they headed east, to Heaven's Hills?"

Paul, who was now starting to gasp more than breathe, looked up at Barton, who was now down on his knee beside the young man, trying to find a way to comfort the boy's last moments of life. "Sir, I know I will be in Hell before the sun finishes going down. That's my reward for the choices I have made. I ain't deserving of any comfort or consideration from any of you, and I am pretty sure I ain't getting none from the Good Lord when that time comes. But I do know that Angus Ford showed me no mercy when I needed it, so I don't owe him nothing. He and the rest ain't headed for Heaven's Hills. They are headed back to Smithview."

"What did you say, boy?" was the shocked response of Marshal Tomes, as he grabbed the coat of the young outlaw and pulled him closer.

"What are you talking about? What do you mean they are going back to Smithview? Why are they going back to Smithview?"

There was no response, and the marshal's shock and frustration caused him to tighten his grip upon the young man's coat, as if that would cause the answer to come.

Jason, confused by the marshal's actions and by Barton's lack of a re-action, kept inquiring. "Why isn't he telling you, Marshal, why isn't he telling you?"

Barton gently placed his hand upon Tomes' fist, squeezed it to break its grip and removed it from the boy's coat, and then shared the fact that the marshal already knew, but didn't want to accept. "He's gone, He has no more to say."

Barton laid the top of his hand across the eyes of the young man and gently pulled down, closing Paul's eyes one last time. They didn't have any idea of what to do with the boy's body, for he didn't live long enough to share any information as to where family might be. But Barton knew that somewhere, there may be a mama and a daddy that had prayed for a wayward son to come home, parents who had hoped for a long time for a reunion. He felt they, at least, were owed an explanation why their boy had never ridden up the lane. But the posse, at least, had a name. As Barton thought of plans for the young man's remains, Marshal Tomes was trying to think of plans for the rest of them.

"How things can change in just a short amount of time. When we got to this water hole, they were the ones with the wounded rider and tired horses, and we were catching up with them. Now, here we stand with two dead, two wounded. Angus Ford has a two-hour lead on us, and it will be more, depending on how long it takes us to round up our horses!"

As soon as the marshal finished his quick appraisal of the situation, Barton turned to the west, whistled long and loud, and within moments, a familiar sound of rapid hoofbeats could be heard heading in their direction. On a normal day, with the sun going down, it would have been hard to see the dark, gray horse approaching them. But luckily, there was a full moon starting to come out, and it was easy to see Smoke's mane flying in the wind of the swift pace he was moving. Smoke slowed down just enough to make a turn around Barton; close enough that Barton could reach up, grab the saddle horn, and let Smoke's momentum pull him up into the saddle all in one well-timed movement.

As Barton put his rifle back into its sleeve that was attached to his saddle, Tomes stepped in front of Barton and Smoke, grabbed Smoke's rein and bellowed, "What do you think you are doing? We are going to need help rounding up the horses, getting the dead and wounded mounted, and figuring out what to do with that boy's body."

"I don't have time to argue with you, marshal!" Barton had an edge to his voice, one that betrayed a worry in the tall man's mind.

"Bury the boy, catch the horses, let Arnie Proffitt take care of the bodies and Mark. Being a freight hauler, Arnie will know how to strap them on the best and will be strong enough to keep three horses moving together with one hand. He can take his time coming back. The rest of you come as fast as you can, when you find your horses and get mounted."

"What do you think you are going to be doing during all of this?" asked Tomes, hurting from the pain in his arm and concerned that Barton was determined to leave them behind.

"That boy said that Angus Ford was headed back to Smithview. From here, there is only one clear way to get there, and that is through Rooster Pass. My ranch is between Rooster Pass and Smithview. They are going to need fresh horses, and I am afraid a woman, two kids and a crippled old man are not going to be enough to stop them from taking the horses and anything else they want. If Ford does stop at my place, I am praying Jenny and Adam can hold them off long enough for me to get there and maybe they will give up and move on. That's if I can get there in time and waiting on you is not going to improve my chances. So, let go of Smoke and let me go!"

Tomes had never heard this tone of voice from Barton before and had never seen the look of fear on the tall rancher's face either. So, the marshal let go of Smoke's rein, Barton gave the horse a nudge with his heals, and they were both out of sight within minutes.

"Ok, those of you who can, let's go find those horses," ordered the marshal, his mind filled with worry about what his friend may encounter before the sun comes up.

Chapter Three

Any other time, Barton would have loved this late-night ride on the dark, gray horse. The full moon made it seem like daytime, making it easy to see the road, and the paths that Barton needed to take to get to Jenny and the boys as fast as he could. The cool night air would be a plus for Smoke. The mighty horse loved to run. As a matter of fact, it took more effort to get him to stop than to get him going. Barton's father-in-law, Nate, said he thought it wore Smoke out more to trot than to run, that the frustration of going slow was tiring to him. Barton never wore spurs, didn't need them. He just gently nudged his heels against his travel partner and then held on. Smoke didn't have a first step. He would leap forward and hit the ground running. Barton only had to fall backwards from the launching horse once to learn that you had to hold on if you wanted to go with him.

Smoke was unlike any horse Barton had ever had. His stride was like a thoroughbred, his stamina was like a quarter horse, his spirit was unbreakable. There wasn't a horse that could stay with him, within a five-county area. People would remark, when they would come to watch him run that Smoke ran so fast that his legs were just a blur underneath his sleek, powerful body. Barton had quit running him in the county fairs and homecoming events that a lot of the towns would hold because it got to where no one would enter if

Smoke was running. Tonight, there were no trophies or ribbons waiting at the end of this run. What was waiting was far more precious: his family. And, once again, Barton was glad to have the dark, gray horse underneath him.

In addition to making sure that Smoke was doing ok by periodically placing his hand upon Smoke's neck to see how warm, or sweaty, the horse was; Barton's mind kept running over all the things that he would need to do when he got to the ranch. He and Jenny had talked about situations like this. They never really felt like something dark and drastic would ever come to their home, but the biggest mistake would be not being ready if it did touch their lives.

He wondered if she would remember everything he told her... After dark, keep the doors and windows locked if he wasn't home, no matter how hot it may be. Never open the door to anyone, even if you think you know who it is. If anyone tries to force their way in, send the boys to the loft; if they need to escape, they can go out the window and across the roof. His dad's double-barrel shotgun, over the fireplace, wasn't just decoration, but was functional and loaded. Take your father and go into the main bedroom. There is only one way in and one way out. Better to guard against intruders! He kept thinking of everything Jenny would need to do, as if his thoughts would find themselves to her, and let her know he was thinking of her and on his way.

Barton was also thinking of Ford and why he would want to go back to Smithview. He wondered if there was any chance that Ford would change his mind and take his gang in another direction. Barton wasn't worried about following tracks or clues as to where the outlaws were headed. He knew there was only one place that he needed to be this night, and that was at the ranch with his family. The responsibilities of being a volunteer lawman have now been replaced by the responsibilities of being a husband and a father.

The full moon, which was working for Barton, would also work in Ford's favor. If it was a cloudy night and maybe even raining, there would be a chance that the outlaws would be in such a hurry that they would ride across the ranch and never see the house and barn once they got past Rooster's Pass. But Barton knew that with the full moon revealing everything to be seen and the new metal roof he had put on the barn glowing in the moonlight, it was going to be very easy to see a homestead was just off to the left. And that meant that provisions, rested horses and anything else they needed, might be found there. Barton was starting to realize that any hope of them just going on and not stopping at the Anderson ranch was starting to fade the closer he got to home.

There was one fact that was true and could not be changed. No matter how fast Barton and Smoke traveled, in the clear night, Ford would come upon the ranch about an hour before Barton could get there. The sun would not be up yet, which means that his family will be in bed and not know that strangers were on the property until they heard them either around the barn or outside the house.

For one moment, Barton wished that he weren't riding Smoke. The dark, gray horse hadn't done anything wrong, and he was traveling like the champion that he was. But Barton realized that if Smoke was at the ranch, he would have sensed that strangers were in the midst and would have done his best to let Jenny and the boys know. That is just what Smoke always did when things were different from the usual day with the Anderson family. It didn't matter if it was a rattlesnake in the woodpile, a cow getting ready to calve in the field, or the minister dropping by for a visit and piece of Jenny's pecan pie—nothing seemed to get past the attention of the dark, gray horse. Barton imagined that might have given his family another edge they might need. But Smoke wasn't at the ranch. He was under Barton, and that was the second-best place he could be on this night.

About two hours before sunrise, Barton and Smoke made it through Rooster Pass and now they were fifteen minutes from the ranch. As they got closer to the homestead, Barton tried to listen for gunfire, hoping that would mean that any confrontation with the outlaw band was still carrying on, and that would be a sign the family was still putting up a defense. But Smoke was now running so hard, as he sensed the importance of being on home ground, that the sound of his hooves hitting the ground made it impossible to hear anything off in the distance.

Barton looked to see if there were any lights on at the house but did not see anything from the windows of the house that would indicate a lamp or lantern being used. He was too far yet to look for individuals outside, or in the doorways of the buildings. He knew that he would have to be through the main gate which had the family brand on it to know what had happened, if anything.

Maybe his hard ride home was just a wise decision that his instinct caused him to make, and he would find it to be an un-needed one after all.

But Barton knew that something was wrong as soon as he rode through the main gate and up to the front of the house. First, Jenny hated flies, especially when she was cooking or trying to take a nap when the guys were off working the ranch somewhere. She was constantly on him and the boys about leaving doors open when coming in. She had begged him for months to put screens on the kitchen windows, as to let out the heat from cooking and baking, but keeping the flies outside, where they belong. But there was the front door, standing wide open, inviting any living creature to come in and make itself at home. Second, Barton hadn't gotten off Smoke and the dark, gray horse was already making that high-pitched sound when he was concerned for his family; when he sensed that things weren't as they should be. Smoke pranced and dug at the ground with his front feet, as if he was urging Barton to let him help look. Barton didn't even bother to tie Smoke to the hitch ring on the front porch post because he knew the horse would just find a way to unfasten himself. Plus, Barton had this feeling that he was needed inside the house quick.

"Jenny, Jenny!" Barton yelled as he ran through the open door and into the front room, which served as a gathering place for the family. It was a place where Barton would read in front of the fireplace, the boys would do their homework and wrestle each other, and Jenny would work on sewing clothes back together or break beans fresh from the garden. He found the coal-oil lamp by his chair, pulled a match out of his shirt pocket, struck the match on the buckle of his belt, and lit the wick of the lamp. Barton's heart started beating faster as he noticed that all the drawers on his desk, has been pulled out and thrown across the room, as if someone had hurriedly searched for anything valuable. His father's 12 gauge, which hung over the fireplace, was gone. Many of his books, which he kept in the bookcase, were now burning in the fireplace or thrown into a pile in the corner. Barton started to realize that this was not an act of robbery, but was an act of anger.

Barton yelled out again, "Jenny, can you hear me? Are you in here?". As he carried the lamp with him, he gave a quick look in the kitchen, and found it to be a site of more acts of destruction. Jenny's kitchen cabinet, the one that Barton had made for her as a first anniversary present, had been pulled over and all the nicer dishware that she had was shattered underneath it. The wall cabinets had been ransacked, but he didn't have time to see if anything was taken, for he still hadn't gotten a response from Jenny, and that is all that mattered at this time.

There were only two places left to check: their bedroom and the boys' sleeping area in the loft. The loft would have to wait, for Barton was heading into the bedroom when he felt his knees buckle. His breath leave him and his body collapse to the floor, in a kneeling position, still managing to not drop the burning lamp. The pain in his chest was so intense he had to fight to stay conscious. He wanted to scream, but nothing would come out of his mouth. The only sound that he could get to come out was a cross between a sob and a plea. "No, oh God, No!"

He wanted his eyes to stop seeing, but they wouldn't. He wanted his eyelids to close, but they couldn't. He was unable to turn his head away, even though he wanted to. And, even if he could have done any of these, it wouldn't have mattered, because what he was seeing would be burned into his mind for the rest of his life. When he lifted the lamp higher and closer to the bed, he now knew why Jenny did not answer him.

She was laying, face down on their bed. Her petite form didn't make any moves or noises upon Barton's entrance into the room. Her favorite robe and nightgown were laying on the floor beside the bed. It was her routine that, after she would put the boys to bed, she loved to put on her nightgown and robe and sit by the fireplace in Barton's chair, waiting for her husband's return from an important trip. More times than not, if Barton came home late, he would find Jenny asleep in his chair, especially if there was a fire going in the fireplace.

He would just gently pick her up and carry her into the bedroom and let her sleep. This time, though, he had not placed her in the bed, and his heart broke because he knew she was not asleep.

It was plain to see that the robe and the nightgown had been torn off her, both so tattered that if he had not seen her wearing them before, he would not have known what they were. Jenny's hands were tied to the headboard, evidence that she had put up resistance to her assailants. Jenny had never been touched by anyone but her husband. She had been raised to be a lady, and he knew that she fought with all she had to keep her dignity. Anything they took from her would not be gotten because she made it easy. Her fight had been an honorable attempt, but it was plain to see it did not have the results she had tried her best to attain.

Barton raised himself back to his feet with every ounce of courage that he could muster. He walked over, placed the lamp on the end table, and sat on the side of the bed. It kept running through his mind, "What do I do, what do I do?"

He sat there on the bed, his eyes moving back and forth, surveying the scene that was before him. The blood that soaked the back of her hair told him that, at some point, the misery was brought to a quick end. The blood that was upon her body, on the nightgown, and on the pillow told him that it didn't come quick enough to keep her from having to endure the hellish attack. Her last moments on earth should have been in the presence of loved ones and family, not in the hands of godless heathens.

He reached up and untied her small hands and pulled her arms down to her sides. He gently turned her over and wrapped her body in the bedspread that she had made from feed sacks. He pulled her into his trembling arms, her head resting on his shoulder. He kissed her face, ran his fingers through her dark, brown hair, told her "I love you and I am sorry". He repeated it over and over. And then, shock gave way to reality. The anguished scream that he looked for earlier found its way out of his breaking heart and to his awaiting mouth.

"NOOOOOOOOOO!"

The sun was finally up when Marshal Tomes and the remaining posse finally got to the house. They could hear Barton's distraught grief from inside the house. The marshal told the rest to look around the house and property, because he knew that he needed to be the only one going into the house for now. The lawman walked into the house and followed the sounds of Barton's sobbing into the bedroom. Marshal Tomes was a hard man, a man who had been toughened by years of enforcing the law and seeing people who had been hurt by those who didn't respect the law. But he wasn't prepared for the sight of his friend holding his lifeless wife, seeing the blood-soaked bed, the shattered look on the face of a man who had been a rock for everyone else. Tomes' lower lip trembled as he uttered the only thing that would come to his mind.

"Dear Lord, have mercy. Please, have mercy."

Barton didn't hear the marshal; Barton didn't hear anything. There were no thoughts running through his mind, there were no "what next" plans being made in his conscious. The world didn't exist at this time, and he didn't care about anything else. It was just him and Jenny; holding her and talking to her was all that mattered. He knew she couldn't hear him; she couldn't feel his kisses or him stroking her hair. But it was all that he could think to do, and for now, it was all that he seemed to be able to do.

When Marshal Tomes heard footsteps coming across the front porch at a rapid pace, he turned and went to the front door to keep anyone from coming into the house. He could, at least, protect his friend's privacy and the scene in the bedroom. The first one he met was Jason Nash, the young gunsmith.

"Jason, did you find anything else around the place?" asked Tomes. But it only took a second to see the flushed look on Jason's face for the marshal to know that this tragedy would not end in the bedroom.

"Marshal Tomes, you had better come now. You are not going to believe what we found."

The lawman, still moved from what he had seen in the house, followed Jason out toward the barn, which was behind the house. At first, Tomes didn't see anything that caught his attention, except for a few of the posse members gathered around the corral gate next to the barn. But, when the men moved apart to where the marshal could see the gate, that is when Tomes knew what had taken the blood out of Jason's face.

There, strapped to the gate, with his arms tied over the top of the gate, was Jenny's father, Nate. Once the marshal got closer and started examining the old man, he found that Nate has been shot numerous times, possibly as many as thirty hits to the torso, arms, and legs. The old man had been left standing in a pool of his own blood. From the fact that there were only a couple of exit wounds, Marshal Tomes concluded that Jenny's dad had been shot from a distance: the number of wounds was proof that the old man had been hit from more than one gun, and from different locations.

Jason asked, "Marshal, why would they tie him up to the gate like that? Everyone knows that Nate couldn't walk, let alone run, ever since he had that stroke. It just doesn't make any sense."

But it was starting to make sense to Tomes, especially after the evil that was performed in the house. Tomes realized that thinking like a normal lawman would not bring understanding of what had happened here, because these things were not done by normal outlaws. Tomes shook his head as the truth of what happened to Jenny's dad finally hit him. Nate wasn't strapped to the gate because he posed a threat; the old man was on the gate because he made a good target for a sick moonlight game, thought up by some even sicker minds.

It was starting to look like two or more of the

gang had stood across the barn lot and took turns shooting at Nate to kill time, while someone was in the house with Jenny. Not only did the old man die one shot at a time, but he probably had to listen to the attack on his daughter and know the heartache of not being able to help her. Fear, along with anger, was starting to build up inside Tomes as he knows he has never had to go after as soulless a man as Angus Ford and those who admired him and followed him.

The marshal also concluded that this tragedy was probably not over, nor were the gruesome finds, as the whereabouts of the boys were not known. "A couple of you guys take the body off the gate, and Jason, you go in the barn and find something to put over him," ordered Tomes. "Then, starting with the barn and fanning out, we have got to find the boys, or at least find what has happened to them."

No sooner had the lawman finished his instructions, Jason yells from inside the barn, "Marshal, there is a body in here! Come quick!"

Marshal Tomes ran into the barn, and found the body of an unknown adult, probably one of Ford's gang. It looked like he had taken a full blast in the gut from a shotgun. The trail of blood from the barn door to where the body was found means that someone was waiting inside the barn. Tomes felt a slight tinge of hope, as he knew that Barton did not trust Adam with a rifle yet, and had gotten him a 20-gauge shotgun, to go small game hunting or to handle a random rattlesnake getting too close to the livestock. Could the boys have, somehow, made a stand and still be alive somewhere close?

This was not to be the kind of day where hope gives way to good news. When Marshal Tomes stood up from examining the body of the stranger, he thought he saw something move off to his right. He looked closer, finding it hard to see anything because of the contrast between the darkness of the unlit barn and the sunlight that was starting to stream through the cracks between the boards in the wall.

There was the movement again, coming from the back of the barn.

As the marshal walked to the back of the barn, he could see that whatever it was swinging, maybe a bundle of feed sacks or a bag of seed corn for next spring's planting. Tomes, with Jason walking behind him, reached in his pocket and pulled out a match; struck it against the edge of his badge, and held it up to get a better look. The revelation of what was swinging startled the lawman so much that he jumped backwards, dropped the match, and almost tripped over Jason, who was still staring up in shock.

"My Lord, Marshal, it's Adam. They hung a ten-year-old boy!"

Marshal Tomes, upon regaining his balance and senses, struck another match and confirmed Jason's observation that it was Adam that was swinging from a rope wrapped around his neck, tied over one of the barn beams going into a side shed. The boy was wearing a nightshirt, causing the marshal to figure that the family was probably

59

asleep when Ford and his men entered the house. It took a minute or so to comprehend what they were exactly looking at.

Tomes had seen a lot of hardened adults hanging from the gallows, but never an innocent child swinging lifelessly; a sweet voice that would never be heard again. Jason, and a couple of the other men, openly wept as Marshal Tomes pulled out his pocketknife and started to cut the rope that suspended the lifeless youngster off the ground. A couple of the men caught Adam's body as the knife finally worked its way through the hemp line. They gently laid the boy on the ground, upon a pallet of straw that one of them had assembled while the others cut him down. Somehow, giving the boy a place to lay restfully might give them comfort, too. But it didn't. This boy had played with their children, had gone to school with them, had gone to Sunday School with them. With any change in the circumstances, they know that this could have one of their children.

"Jason, you and the rest of the men start looking for Seth. I have to go to the house and tell Barton about what has happened out here". The marshal, reluctantly, knew he had to, but part of him did not want to interrupt a man grieving his dead wife with news that he now had more to grieve about.

"Marshal!"

That was all Jason said when Tomes looked up and there stood Barton, in the doorway of the barn, blood on his shirt and hands from his wife. No one knew what to say, no one knew what to do. So, for a few moments, they just stood and watched as Barton slowly walked to where his oldest son was laying. He stood over him, like somehow, he had caught Adam taking a nap in the straw and he would wake up, and his dad would give him extra chores to do for being lazy on a fall day. Barton stood there and waited, and waited, but Adam never opened his eyes. Barton kneeled and wiped the hair out of Adam's eyes and softly urged, "Son, wake up. We have a lot to do today. Wake up, son!"

Jason wanted to ask why Barton was acting that way, but Marshal Tomes put his hand over Jason's mouth, and kept him from interrupting the moment because the lawman knew that Barton was not capable of rational reasoning. The tall rancher had just spent a few hours holding his dead wife, then walked past the bullet-riddled body of his father-in-law, and now finds his oldest boy lying dead on the ground, with fresh rope marks around his neck. Tomes wasn't ready to deal with whatever came out of Barton when his mind started working again.

So, Tomes and the rest stood watching, as their hearts were breaking for their friend. Barton stood up suddenly, turned around, and walked toward the house. Tomes, again, told Jason and the others to fan out and look for Seth. As the marshal headed toward the house, Barton came out of the house. The look on his face troubled Tomes. Barton's eyes were narrowed, his brow furrowed, his cheeks were drawn, and his lips were tight. The marshal noticed that Barton had a box of rifle cartridges in one hand and what looked like a roll of money in the other. But what he noticed next sent a chill up the lawman's spine. Barton was wearing a holster with a revolver in it.

Tomes had never seen Barton wear a handgun. The tall rancher had always made do with the Henry rifle, while using a 12-gauge shotgun for the occasional community bird hunt or when he had a taste for small game. Tomes didn't even know his friend owned a handgun. But, with this development, the marshal knew that he had to get through to his friend. He had seen this look on men's faces before, and it never ended well. Yes, Barton was very good with the Henry rifle, but whatever he was planning on doing with a Colt sidearm had disaster written all over it.

"Barton, I know you are hurting and what has happened here is not right. I know that if I hadn't asked you to come with me, you would have been here and might have been able to change what happened here. But you have got to get back into your right mind and listen to me. You aren't equal to Angus Ford by himself, let alone with two other cut-throat partners. I am asking you to sit on the porch. Give me time to straighten things out here, and we will go after Angus Ford,. We will go after all of them, together?"

Barton stood there for a moment, like he was considering what the marshal had shared with him. Then, he turned away from the marshal, gave a loud, shrill whistle and, within moments, Smoke came running around the corner of the house. Barton put the cartridges in his saddlebag, slid the roll of money in his coat pocket, and was getting up on Smoke when Marshall Tomes grabbed his friend with his good hand and arm and tried to pull him away from the horse. Barton swung as hard as he could, hitting Tomes across the face with the back of his hand. He hit the marshal so hard that Tomes fell backwards to the ground, stunned by the blow and by the fact this peaceful man, a man he trusted with his life, would strike him with such force without any reservation.

Jason and another volunteer ran and helped Tomes up as Barton rode past them and toward Smithview.

"What about Seth?" yelled the marshal. "What about Jenny, Adam, and Nate? You've got a family to bury!"

Barton just simply coldly replied, "No. I've got men to kill!"

Chapter Four

Any other time had someone come into Smithview and observed so many people in town, they would have thought that it was one of the autumn events that Smithview was known for. Maybe it could be the annual Molasses Festival, which always draws big, festive crowds to smell and taste the sugary concoction as it was cooked, canned, and prepared to be sold as a fundraiser for the school. Or could it be time for the Smithview Homecoming, where people would come from miles around and bring tasty foods, new handmade crafts and their memories of days gone by? Fall was also the time for the last cattle drive of the year, as ranchers brought their livestock to the corrals at the railroad loading dock to be shipped to Topeka. The crowd could be chattering about stock prices, the quality of beef, or what they will do with the money that they hope to bring home from the livestock auction.

No, none of those options would hold true on this day in Smithview. Upon closer examination, even though the skies were sunny and Kansas blue, there was nothing festive about the gathering of these people. If a person were to look closely, they would see those men and women are wearing their Sunday best, but almost all are wearing dark colors. The tone of the conversations, much like the clothes they are wearing, is not in anticipation of joy and frivolity, but just the opposite. It seems like their faces, and their voices, get more somber as the morning moves along.

Smithview is not hosting one of the largest gatherings it would ever see, for a fair or picnic, but it has become the gathering place for people who are hurting. These are people who still don't understand the dark event that has caused them all to come together to seek someone, anyone, who might have an answer for why this day had to be. The only thing they know is they wish it didn't have to be this way.

Smithview is full because they are all here for a funeral.

It has been 3 days since the horrible nightmare that took place at the Anderson ranch. Most of the time, when a person passes away, a funeral will be planned within a day or two of the people leaving this world. But this was far from a normal situation. Not only have dear friends and loved ones horribly died, but there is a precious, little soul that has not been accounted for.

For forty-eight hours after news of the tragedy started to spread out, hundreds of people dropped whatever they were doing. They closed their stores and businesses; they put their lives on hold so they could go looking for the youngest Anderson. On horseback, in wagons, and on foot, people came to do what they could do. They brought dogs, lanterns, shovels, food, anything and everything that might make the operation go better. They searched in shifts, during night or day, on hills or valleys, whether warm or chilly, whether tired or rested. No one complained, no one left. The spirit of community was on full display; Seth Anderson was all that mattered for 48 hours.

U.S. Marshal Lyndon Tomes did his best to keep the search focused and going, while still trying to heal from his wound. He telegraphed area law offices to be on the lookout for the six-year-old and to watch for a child that might be traveling with an unlikely group or individual.

Every spot on God's earth that they could search would be checked, no matter how many they had to search, no matter how tired they might be, no matter how bad the odds were looking. They would not stop, except for one thing, and that one thing had come. Today, they would lay Jenny, Adam, and Nate to rest.

No one knows exactly how many people will be there. Smithview's population had been counted as a little over a thousand citizens, but it seemed like there were more than that gathering for the funeral services. Along with the locals, people had come in on the stagecoach and on the train. There were newspaper people, along with their cameramen, to record the event for those who could not make it. Whether it be for health reasons, distance to travel, or fear that they might not be able to handle such a heart-wrenching event. The story of what happened on the Anderson ranch may have been a local story initially, but it was spreading as more and more newspapers published it.

When Reverend Bill Sutton, Marshal Tomes, and the town council assembled to talk about how this should be handled, they knew that the church was not an option. The church would only hold two hundred, and that was with all the pews full, chairs in the aisles, and the windows open so people could stand outside and listen to the music. And Reverend Sutton preaching as loud as he could. They thought and thought, and no buildings seemed to be sufficient to handle the situation.

Then, they all agreed that they would pray for good weather and that the funeral would be held in the downtown park, which was in the square in the middle of Smithview. The park, with all its oak trees, was always beautiful at this time of year. The preacher, the choir and any family would be located on the raised bandstand, the coffins would be arranged in front of them, each sitting on its own pedestal, and the people could stand, or sit on chairs or blankets, through-out the rest of the park and square. All stores on the square would be closed for the service. There wouldn't need to be any traffic in that area, so the roads into the square would be blocked off. They had a plan, and before they left the church, Reverend Sutton led them in a prayer for God's grace upon the family; upon the weather; and upon the community that had been shaken by this loss.

The funeral service, for Jenny, Adam and Nate, was to begin at 11am, but people started arriving early that morning, as if wanting to make sure they got a place to watch or to spend some time preparing themselves for what was going to take place. Even though the funeral service was hours away, people could be heard sobbing and praying as they held their children or a family member. While their hearts broke for the Anderson family, it was hard to not be thankful that this was not being arranged for their loved ones.

The procession would start at the undertakers, work its way over to Main Street, and then go straight to the square. Arnie Proffitt, the freight line owner, had offered three of his best wagons to carry the coffins to the service location. Some ladies had gone to one of the general stores and bought fabric to dress up each of the wagons, to make them more formal and more adapted to the special purpose they were being used for.

Reverend Sutton would lead the procession. Even though he was older and a little on the heavy side, he would walk all the way to the park. The pallbearers for each coffin would walk behind the wagon that was carrying their responsibility.

The first wagon in the procession would be the one carrying Jenny. Her coffin was draped with a hand-stitched quilt that she had made for Seth when he was a baby. They felt this was right to do, to keep everyone mindful of one who was still out there somewhere. Her pallbearers were six elders of the church. Over the years, she had been so active and supportive of Grace Methodist Church, this was their way to honor her.

The next wagon was carrying Adam. Upon his coffin sat the saddle that his mom and dad had given him for his tenth birthday, which was just a couple of months before the day he would be laid to rest. Eight of his friends from school and

68

church walked behind the wagon that was carrying Adam, a sight that caused many, including some pretty tough men, to wipe their eyes as they thought of how life can be cruel sometimes.

Nate's wagon was last, as he would have wanted it. A humble man, who had battled with being limited physically because of the stroke. Many who watched his wagon go by felt sorrow but also gratefulness that Nate had that "new body" that Reverend Sutton would preach about in some of his sermons. Upon Nate's coffin was an American flag, and following behind were six uniformed cavalry soldiers stepping in time together. Many years ago, Nate had been a corporal in the Army, and the Army always tried to respond when one of theirs was laid to rest.

The crowd parted and made a way for the procession as it entered the square. Reverend Sutton worked his way up to the bandstand, where a temporary pulpit had been placed. Some of Jenny's family were seated up there, a brother and his family, a couple of uncles, a cousin and a friend who always felt like family. Barton had been an only child, and his parents had passed years ago. An empty chair was set in front to cause those in attendance to remember that after the service was over, the search for Seth would start again.

The wagons carrying the coffins pulled off to the side of the bandstand. One by one, the wooden caskets were brought to the area just in front of the bandstand, and arraigned before the large crowd that was assembled. Jenny was placed on the middle stand, Nate to her left, and Adam to her right. Morton Young, the local cabinet builder and coffin maker, had worked for two days nonstop to make these just right. Each coffin had a cross on the top of it, each cross made of black walnut, causing a striking contrast to the pine that the box itself was made of. He carefully and artfully scrawled images of flowers and angels into Jenny's; a depiction of an Army saber and a bugle was cut into Nate's. Morton later said that Adam's was the hardest to construct, not because of different wood or the designs he cut into it. It was harder because he made it slightly smaller than the other two, because he wanted it to look appropriate for Adam to be in. Morton said he would tear up looking at the smaller casket; and having to stop and wipe his eyes made it a challenge to finish. But finish it he did, and many would comment on his workmanship after the service.

Once the coffins were in place, the crowd of people drew closer to the bandstand, closing in and filling ranks like Army columns would do. Reverend Sutton thanked everyone for being there, talking as loud as he could, so that the large gathering would be able to understand what was being said. Reverend Sutton was always easy to hear, especially at church. People had commented that his lungs must be made from leather, as the volume of his sermons never seemed to diminish, as well as the length of them. But, today with the setting in the park, surrounded by the store buildings on the square, his voice seemed to be not only amplified but it also seemed to have an otherworld quality to it, like maybe this day was being helped by a source far greater than could be imagined.

The service started with Reverend Sutton leading everyone in the Lord's Prayer. Then, a group of children gathered at the front of the bandstand, and each one shared a Bible verse that they had memorized for the occasion. This brought a mix of tears and smiles, especially among their family members, who were proud of their presentation and sad that it was such an occasion that they got to do it at. Next came the church choir, standing at the back of the bandstand, with their moving rendition of "Rock of Ages". As a matter of fact, Reverend Sutton noticed that the song had touched the hearts of many in the crowd, and he asked the choir to sing the last verse again, which inspired numerous amens from the crowd.

At this point, in honor of Nate, the Army representatives came forward, folded the flag that was on his coffin, and presented it to Nate's son and Jenny's brother, Jeff. Then, the uniformed soldiers snapped to attention and saluted as the bugle player blew "Day is Done". This presentation brought more tears and sobs from the crowd, as they remembered days that their loved ones, who had served in the military, were laid to rest in a like manner. Veterans, sprinkled throughout the audience, stood and saluted to honor their brother in arms.

The choir sang another song, and then Reverend Sutton stepped to the small pulpit that had been used for political rallies and pie auctions but now would serve as the focal point of the service. The preacher had prayed long and hard about what would be needed this day. He felt that one of his usual stem-winder sermons would not be sufficient for this moment, that hell, fire and brimstone was not what people's hearts were yearning for. So, as loudly and clearly as he could, Reverend Sutton spoke of the promises of God. "We weren't promised lives without challenges and heartaches, but we were promised that we have a Heavenly Father that would never leave us, or forsake us, no matter how heavy the load might get." From time to time, an amen would rise up, or a "That's right, preacher." Not in the spirit of revival, but in the affirmation that his words were helping their hearts. Reverend Sutton, who usually would preach over an hour on Sunday mornings, spoke for a little over twenty minutes this day, bringing his message to a close with a final thought of comfort. "There is no doubt that the Lord is with us here today. And there is no doubt that Jenny, Adam, and Nate are with the Lord today, too!"

Before offering a final prayer, Smithview mayor, Uda Stone, stepped to the front of the bandstand and thanked everyone for coming to this important event. He thanked the Army for their presence and spoke of all the neighboring sheriffs, and other lawmen, that had come to help with managing such a large group. Mayor Stone explained that, because of such a large gathering, the cemetery service would be limited to family. He also announced that there were locations on Main Street where food was available to those who were visiting or local. Mayor Stone ended his portion with the fact that there were two stagecoaches and the train waiting to take as many home as possible. Before he stepped aside, the mayor reminded everyone that the search for Seth Anderson would resume at 2pm, and that he hoped that there would be a good number, well equipped and ready, assembling in front of the livery stable.

Reverend Sutton thanked the mayor for his help and asked everyone to stand for the final prayer. When the last amen was said, the choir sang assorted hymns as the crowd started to disperse. Some headed for the transportation that was waiting for them, some headed to the food that was prepared, for it was almost 12:30pm. Others mingled in the square, not in any hurry to leave as they talked with acquaintances that they hadn't seen in a long time. And a few tried to seek out the family to give their condolences and walk by the coffins, some even reaching out to touch the burial boxes, as if that would be a final gesture or comfort before the day ended.

Eventually, the coffins were placed back in the wagons and taken to the church cemetery, where a final word would be offered and a prayer said.

As the mayor, town council, and Marshal Tomes walked with the procession to the final resting place, someone observed that it had gone as well as anyone could have hoped for, considering how big the crowd was.

"I wouldn't be surprised that everyone in Smithview was here today," responded Mayor Stone.

Marshal Tomes just stayed quiet and looked off into the horizon. For he knew not everyone from Smithview was at the funeral service, and his mind returned to the whereabouts of the tall man on the dark, gray horse.

Where was he? Was he in trouble? Was Barton even alive?

Chapter Five

There were few things that Marshal Tomes knew as to the location of Barton Anderson, what Barton was doing, or if he would ever see him again. Tomes had a fear that, after seeing what state of mind that his friend was in, the marshal may never see the Barton Anderson that he had known for so many years. The man who rode away from the Anderson ranch that morning was someone that the marshal had never seen before or knew could even exist. Tomes found it difficult to try to think like Barton so he could get a feeling about where he would go, what plan of action the rancher would take. He simply didn't know if Barton could have a course of thought other than rage and hatred for the men who brutally destroyed his family. But the marshal was pretty sure of one thing: if he could locate where Angus Ford was, then there was a good chance that Barton would be close by. And, for now, it seemed like Ford would be the easier of the two to find.

This is what Marshal Tomes did know now. First, Angus Ford and his gang did go back to Smithview. It was just after sunrise, so no one was out and about where they could be victims of the bloodthirsty bandits. Ford broke into one of the general stores, stole a few boxes of cartridges for reloading, and enough dry food to last a few days until they could get to another town, or if they had to hold up somewhere and try to let the pursuit of the law slow down.

Second, upon his returning to Smithview, the marshal had been approached by a few townspeople who had reported that they had seen Barton riding wildly into town, that he was asking if anyone had seen Angus Ford, and that he was acting strangely. They reported that he was cold, impatient with people's responses, and had a look about him that was so uncharacteristic for the rancher and family man. They tried to talk with him, get a sense of what was wrong, but he had no time for them. He just blew them off, got on Smoke and rode away, most saying they went out of town on the west road. It would be a couple of hours before word would start to get out of the horror that happened at the Anderson ranch. And then, they would understand why this quiet, gentle man was acting the way he was.

Along with the telegraphs about watching for Seth, the marshal wrote letters, asking any law officers that got the letters to keep an eye out for Angus Ford, Willie Beeler, and a new partner that Ford had rumored to be Coy Newton.

Tomes explained what had happened; about the bank robbery, the murders at the Anderson ranch, and that they may have taken a child with them. Lawmen had been hesitant to tangle with the Ford gang for things like stealing, fights or even shootings, if the victims would survive, because everyone knew of the viciousness of these men. But Tomes knew if a child was at risk, then every man with a badge would be willing to jump into the search. Or at least share the information and help when Tomes got there. Being a federal

76

officer, Tomes was able, and prepared, to go wherever this saga took him, and hopefully the result would be bringing his friend home, sitting on the dark, gray horse, and not laying across it.

The search for Seth commenced after the funeral, and people looked for three more days. No one wanted to stop, but they had searched everywhere a six-year-old could go on foot. The teams of volunteers were tired. Some had to go back to their businesses and ranches. And, while they never gave up praying for Seth's return, they knew that the chances of that happening were getting smaller and smaller. Even when people would travel to visit family, or on business trips, they would talk of always keeping an eye out for Seth just in case someone had found him and taken him to another town, or another home.

Tomes had to get back to covering his area as a U.S. Marshal. But he would check back with the Smithview sheriff's office, or the U.S. Marshall's Topeka office, to see if any telegrams, newspaper stories, or gossip were placing Angus Ford somewhere in Kansas. Ford had not been known to stray out of the state, because he had so many connections and hiding places there. The outlaw might have been violent, but he wasn't known as the smartest criminal out there. Therefore, he was a creature of habit. What Ford lacked in creativity, he made up in fear and intimidation. He simply rode until the money ran out, then he roamed Kansas, looking for opportunities to make quick hits and run. That's why he didn't mind killing any, and all, that got in his way. There is less thinking, and less mess to deal with, when you don't have to figure into the plan how to pull robberies without having casualties. Angus Ford cared about himself, and that was it. Even his own gang members had learned that — some the hard and final way.

Then, about a month after the incident at the Anderson ranch, Marshal Tomes got a telegram from a constable in Prestonburg. The message said that Ford, two other men answering the description of Beeler and Newton, had robbed the bank there, killed four people, and got away with $700 in cash. The constable reported that they had headed north, out of Prestonburg, and might be headed to a little town called Rabbit Flat about twenty-five miles up the road. There wasn't much there. Just a saloon, a general store slash telegraph office, and a building the stagecoach used to use when it ran through there. It was more of a place where the area ranchers and farmers would come to get supplies, meet freighters there for bigger items, and to wet their whistles before they headed back to their home places. There was no law presence there, so it might be a good place for the Ford gang to hold up, at least for a few days.

Marshal Tomes figured that since he hadn't been in that area for a while, he would ride up there. It would take him a day or so to get there, and even if Ford wasn't still there, Tomes figured that this would be a good place to start trailing Ford, in hopes that the marshal's theory that Barton Anderson was hunting him also would be the chance to cross paths with his friend. That is, if he was still his friend. So, Tomes packed up what supplies he would need for the trip and headed northeast, toward Rabbit Flat.

Marshal Tomes figured he would ride until late that evening, find a place to camp, then get up early the next morning and get into Rabbit Flat sometime after lunchtime. The weather was perfect for that time of year, and that would be good for his horse and for him, as he wanted to be at his sharpest when he got to the town. He ran it over in his mind as he rode up the back roads: all the scenarios that he could encounter if Ford and his partners were there.

His first thought was he hoped that anyone who was in town when Ford arrived would get away and not try to confront the short-tempered outlaw. Tomes' wish was that Ford, Beeler and Newton would head straight to the saloon, chase out the owner, and that they would just get drunk and stay that way for a few days. Tomes did not try to fool himself into thinking that he was a match for three outlaws, especially when they were sober. He knew that was not close to being a truth. But, if they were enjoying the peace of a small town, the free alcohol that they always bullied their way into getting, and if no locals did anything stupid; then they might just get over-confident, drop their guards and give the marshal the chance to surprise them and, hopefully, take one or two of them alive. He needed to know what happened to Seth Anderson, and they were the only ones alive that would know what happened that day at the Anderson ranch. All he needed was one, alive, to fill in the blanks of where the youngest Anderson child might be. That, of course, would only be possible if he, along with one of the Ford gang, survived the encounter when Tomes got to Rabbit Flat.

Tomes rode until it was about an hour after sundown. He didn't know these back roads and trails like he did the ones around Smithview or Ellisville, and it would be easy for a horse to step into a rut or hole with the sun being down and not much of a moon tonight. So, he stopped his horse, Hickory, got down off the animal, made a torch out of a stick and some old dry grass, and walked a couple of hundred feet off the road until he found a nice patch of grass for a horse to eat and to make a soft bedding spot once his saddle and blanket were situated right.

"Hickory, does this spot look like a good place to eat and sleep?"

The horse raised his head up and down, as if to understand the question put before him. So, Tomes took all his tack off the horse and arranged it in a way that would make a good place to catch a couple of hours' sleep. Sleep would have to wait until he could have a humble meal of jerky, biscuits, and canteen water. It wasn't the best eating he would have had that day, but you can't be picky when you are out in the middle of nowhere and you aren't staying long.

Hickory found him a spot of tender green grass and the horse would be content for the rest of the evening. The marshal gathered up some limbs and sticks from around some trees nearby and started a fire. He knew that the crackling and popping of the dry wood fire would put him to sleep soon. Seeing that it was a chilly night, he would use the saddle blanket as a pallet, the saddle as a place to lay his head, and the bedroll as a cover. With the fire going, and a few extra limbs to add to the fire if needed, Marshal Tomes would be fine for a few hours.

Before he drifted off to sleep, he laid there and thought of the times that he had been leading a posse and had made camp like this. He thought, especially, of the times his tall rancher friend had ridden with him, the talks that they had shared.

He remembered how Barton loved to talk about his family, how much he loved Jenny, and how he prayed he was being a good father to the boys. Tomes sometimes felt jealous of Barton. Being a marshal never allowed Tomes the luxury of having a home and family, and he envied his friend for the life that he had. Then Tomes realized what he had just thought... the life that Barton *had*. That is exactly what it was now, a life that the Andersons had, and now it was gone, thanks to the senseless violence of a heartless handful.

The sun was coming up when Marshal Tomes got up and started to clear out his camp. Breakfast was pretty much the same as supper: a couple of pieces of jerky and a biscuit that was starting to get some age on it. He took a swig of water out of the canteen, and poured some in his hand for Hickory to have.

Then he started to tie down the bedroll and

tighten the cinch straps on his saddle. As he tied and tightened his gear to his horse, Tomes noticed that Hickory was antsy, and Tomes thought it was just the rest and fresh grass that had him jittery. But soon the marshal saw what had Hickory stirred up. It was a rider and horse, and they were coming toward them as fast and hard as two could go.

Marshal Tomes stepped out into the road, waved one hand, and pulled his coat back with the other hand, so the rider could see his U.S. Marshal badge.

"Hey, rider, what's the problem? Why are you in such a hurry?"

The stranger, on a horse that looked like it couldn't travel another step, pulled up by Tomes and answered, "I have got to get to Prestonburg and find a lawman. Angus Ford is in Rabbit Flat with a couple of other men. They got there yesterday and have been shooting up the town, and now they are holding up in the saloon. Have been there since last evening, and they are drunker than skunks and threatening to burn the whole town down; what town there is!"

Figuring the rider was too excited to see his badge, Tomes introduced himself.

"I am United States Marshal Lyndon Tomes, and I am on my way to Rabbit Flat. Has Ford killed or hurt anyone?"

"No, sir!" the emotional rider shared. "Once those outlaws started shooting, most people went and hid in their fruit cellars, attics, or out on the edge of town. Ford and the other two pretty much helped themselves to the general store, shot out all the windows in the store, walked outside and started yelling, cussing and shooting up anything that they felt needed a bullet hole in it. The first night when they arrived, they stayed in the old stagecoach building. I guess they were anticipating a posse to show up, and that is where they were going to make a stand. When the law never showed up, then last night they decided to settle into the saloon. The owner is out of town, left his son to run things. Don't know if he was in there when Ford went in. He is a young boy, big for his age, kind of touched in the head, no threat to anyone, but I don't know if Ford knows that."

Tomes listened intently, as to know what his plan of attack would be. At least one of his wishes had been answered. The outlaws had been drinking all night, and maybe they will still be drunk, or better, passed out when he gets there and makes his play.

"What's your name, stranger?"

"My name is Jim Fish; I was visiting family and was going to the general store to get some flour and apples for a pie my aunt wanted to make when all the ruckuses broke out. I hid behind anything I could find until I got back to the house, saddled my horse, and got out of there. Marshal, you have got to go there. If Ford keeps his word and burns the town down, there are a couple of houses where people are hiding, and they will be burned alive!"

Tomes got up on Hickory. As he slapped the reins against Hickory's behind, he said, "Jim, you let that horse rest for a while, then you get to Prestonburg and find a sheriff, a constable, someone, and tell them to come to Rabbit Flat as quick as they can. I am going to go on and, maybe, I can distract Ford and the other two long enough to keep them from setting the town on fire and for help to come. After you have found a lawman, go to the telegraph office, and get in touch with the U.S. Marshal's office in Topeka. Tell them Tomes needs help with the Ford gang in Rabbit Flat. That is all you will need to say. Do you understand me?"

"Yes, sir."

Within minutes, Tomes was out of sight. He figured that he was at least five hours away from Rabbit Flat. Hickory was a good horse, had always done what he was asked to do. But Hickory wasn't Smoke. Tomes would have to alternate between a slow run and a trot to keep the horse going. Stopping to rest along the way wasn't an option because the marshal needed to get to Rabbit Flat as quickly as possible— the only advantage he would have against Angus Ford, and whomever was with him, was to get there while they were still drunk, or maybe still passed out. Tomes caught himself wishing that Barton Anderson would show up, no matter what shape the rancher's mind was in, because any help with the outlaws was better than none at all.

It was 11:55 a.m. when Tomes got his first look at Rabbit Flat. Three large buildings and five or six small homes scattered around were the extent of this spot on the road. The marshal didn't see any smoke or other signs that would indicate the outlaws had started keeping their promise to burn the town down. Again, he hoped that they were passed out in the saloon, or severely hung over.

Tomes figured that if Ford was still in the saloon, then he would swing Hickory around the north side of town, tie his horse behind the old stagecoach building and try to find someone that might know where the gang was holding up. If he didn't find a citizen to ask, then the marshal would need to work his way to the front of the saloon, where it would be easier to see into the building through one of the big glass windows. Trying to get in through a back door would only work if he knew where the outlaws were located inside. But, for now, he didn't, and that means he would have to go in the front, and then pray that he sees them before they see him.

Tomes slowly walked Hickory up to an old post that had been part of the stagecoach corral behind the old building and tied the horse off there. If nothing else, Hickory would be out of the line of fire if trouble did break out. Tomes looked around, didn't see anyone moving about, so he walked over to the back of the aging stagecoach building and peered through a couple of places where boards were missing from the back wall. There were horses in there, probably the outlaws' mounts. Jim Fish had said the robbers had spent the first night there. The horses were standing with their heads lowered, as if they were asleep. That meant that neither Ford, nor anyone else, was in this building, for the horses would have awakened if anyone was in there.

Just as Tomes started to turn to head toward the saloon, he was startled by a voice.

"Hey mister, who are you?"

The marshal, shaking from the scare, managed to turn and whip his pistol out and discovered the voice was coming from an elderly, white-haired man who was walking with a cane. Although the old man didn't look like he was sinister, Tomes wasn't going to lower his gun until he knew, for sure, that this man was a citizen and not a sympathizer with Ford and his crew.

"What in the devil are you doing sneaking up on me, old man?" Tomes asked, still too shaken to be mannerly about his approach. "Don't you know you could get killed doing something like that?"

"When you get my age, sneaking is not a talent you have anymore. Shuffling along is about all I can muster these days," explained the old man, not seeming to know, or care, how close he may have come to meeting his Maker. "I was hiding around the corner there, waiting to see if you were coming to meet with those ruffians or whether you were just some poor fool who picked the wrong day to ride into this town."

"Well, don't do that again, especially today," Tomes stated, as he put his sidearm back in its holster. "My name is Lyndon Tomes. I am a U.S. Marshal, and I was told that Angus Ford, and a couple of other men, was in this town."

"Yep, they've been raising sand around here for the last 30 hours. Whatever they haven't been drinking up or eating up, they've been shooting up. The few people that live here have been praying they would get tired, or bored, and leave. We don't have any banks or anything for them to rob."

Tomes looked down the street toward the saloon and shared with the old man that he had run into a young man named Jim Fish, who had filled the marshal in on what had been happening. That, as of last night, the outlaws had settled into the saloon, and other than an occasional gunshot, cuss word, or loud laugh, the three of them hadn't been seen or heard from.

"Jim's my nephew," the old man said proudly, and relieved to know the boy was safe and headed for help. "My name is Otis Fish. I farmed a place east of here until I got too old for farm work. Jim was visiting and the only one at the time that was young enough and had a horse good enough to ride to Prestonburg for help. I am glad you two crossed paths."

"I don't think he would have made it much further, if I hadn't run into him," Tomes said. "He had pretty much run that horse of his into the ground. I think he was too scared to think straight. I just hope he will remember everything I told him, or there may not be much I can do about this situation."

"Jim's a good boy. He will do whatever you told him to do. I would depend on him if I were in your place."

Tomes continued to look at the saloon, trying to figure out the best way to get in and not get shot. He remembered something Jim had said and decided to follow up on it with the old man.

"Are Ford and the other two still in there? Your nephew said that there was another person in there last night. I believe he said it was the saloon owner's son, a slow-thinking kind of guy," inquired Tomes.

"Yeah, they are all still in there, haven't heard a peep out of them, since about 6 a.m. I figured they fell out of the drinking tree and knocked themselves out about that time. They were hitting it pretty hard until then," Otis shared. "As for the boy, his name is Curt, and he's not the brightest spoon on the table. He's big for his age, big as an ox and about as smart. He came out on the front porch of the saloon last night. That fool Ford must have given him a handgun, because Curt had one, shooting it up in the air, telling everyone that "No one was going to make fun of him anymore, because he was a member of the Angus Ford gang, now." They must have really been teasing him and riding him pretty good. I haven't heard or seen him, either."

Tomes figured that was all he needed: three hardened outlaws to worry about, and a slow-brained kid to keep out of harm's way. This just got better by the minute.

Otis, getting curious by now, asked, "Got any idea how you are going to get in, with five people to deal with, and live to talk about it?"

Marshall Tomes turned to the old man and asked, "What did you say? What do you mean about five people being in there? Ford, his two partners, and the boy makes four."

"There is that other guy that went in there this morning," the old man started explaining. "He rode into town this morning, right about sunrise. Tall, scruffy looking guy, riding on a dark, gray horse. He rode up to the saloon, got off the horse and his horse ran up the street. Then, the tall fellow walked right into the saloon, like he knew who was in there. Then, about thirty minutes later, five shots rang out, and it had been quiet ever since. Nobody has had the nerve to go up there and check things out. We've been waiting for my nephew to get back with the law from Prestonburg."

"Old man," Tomes spoke while shaking his head. "At what point were you going to tell me about the fifth man? Don't you think that would be important for me to know?"

"I guess my memory is about as good as my sneaking, especially at my age," Otis explained.

Tomes was pretty sure that the last man to go in was Barton, and the dark, gray horse running away was Smoke. But Tomes was worried that Ford, or one of the others, had shot Barton down. But five shots are a lot of shots, especially at close range. Could Barton have gotten one, or more, of them before he was hit? Are the outlaws in there, waiting for someone to come in and check on the strange rider, and then they will kill whoever goes in next? There was only one way to find out, and Tomes wasn't looking forward to it.

The marshal started walking down the street that runs in front of the general store, and then the saloon. He could see that the general store had been ransacked and shot up in a way that would lend itself to vandalism more than robbery. When Ford and his guys were bored, they were known to find entertainment by destroying other people's property. Ford's mindset had always been, "if I can't have it, then you can't have it either." Then, at some point last night, they turned their attention to liquid entertainment and moved to the saloon. There, they would keep themselves occupied with straight poker, tall tales, vivid lies, and the challenge of performing these feats while being in varying stages of drunkenness. At some point, the boy Curt must have been enchanted with their act and they played with his simple mind, making him think that he was just as bad as they were, the whole time using him as a human toy to play with.

When Tomes got to the front corner of the saloon, he slowly worked himself to a place where he could investigate one of the big windows on the front of the building. He had difficulty getting a clear view, as they had put a few bullet holes in the window, and the cracks in the glass distorted the view inside. He couldn't make out much other than the bar itself and a big mirror behind it.

At this point, Marshal Tomes figured he was going to have to go in if he was going to pursue this encounter any further. Announcing who he was wouldn't have any positives as Angus Ford had never been intimidated by a badge before. So, Tomes set his mind on running through the front doors as hard as he could, heading to the bar, jumping over it, and getting behind it. Once he was there, he would draw his gun, quickly scope out the area behind the bar, and then wait to catch his breath before he made his next tact. Of course, he would have to figure out a next move then, because he didn't have one now.

Tomes was running hard when he made it through the doors. He didn't look around as he ran, because it didn't matter if he saw the bullet coming, in case someone had him in their sights. He just wanted to get to cover and regroup there. He had jumped over a bar a couple of times before, but usually with some sort of back-up deputy covering him. But this time, he was on his own. And this time, he was trying to apprehend the worst outlaw he had come across in his lengthy career as a lawman.

Tomes made it over the bar, landed against the wall behind the counter, and quickly drew his pistol and searched up and down each end of the standard saloon bar, and found no one else behind it. It was a little dark in the room, but it didn't take long for his eyes to adjust. He hunkered down quietly, trying to catch his breath and to listen for any sound that would tell him what direction anyone was located in.

At first, he didn't hear anything but his own breathing. But then he thought he heard something, like someone else breathing. He strained to hold down his breath so he could better hear. And there it was, the sound of labored breathing coming from his left, maybe about twenty feet away. He now knew that there was

91

someone else in the bar besides him. He hoped that it might be Barton, but he had to approach this situation as if it were Angus Ford. Even though he wanted information about Seth, Tomes made the decision that, being by himself, he would not spend much effort trying to take anyone alive today. The only thing on his mind was bringing an end to this episode and living to write a report about it.

He squatted there for what seemed like hours, although it was really a minute or so, listening to the loud breathing. It hadn't changed direction nor sounded like it was getting closer. Whoever it was, they were stationary, and they were probably wounded. Was it Barton? Was it Ford? Was it the boy?

Marshall Tomes was getting ready to work his way to the end of the bar, in the opposite direction from where the breathing was coming from, when he heard a cough.

"HAAAAARRRGGGHHH! Oh, Momma!"

Tomes' heartbeat sped up when he heard it. He knew who it was, for every time he had heard Barton cough, from riding on a dusty trail or working in hay, Barton would always cough and then end it with "Oh, Momma." A habit he had from being sick as a young kid.

"Barton, is that you? This is Marshal Tomes!"

The marshal waited for a response, and when he was about to give up, heard, "It's me, Tomes!"

The momentary joy of hearing his friend quickly gave way to the reality that his friend was hurt. But Tomes didn't know where the others were, what shape they were in, and if jumping up to help, his friend might lead to getting gunned down himself.

"Barton, where are Ford and the rest of them?"

Tomes heard Barton take a long, painful breath and then the reply came, "They are across the room, sitting at a card table."

Tomes, not wanting to stress Barton any more than he had to, or cause him to use up any more energy than needed, gently dug a little deeper. "What are they doing at the table, Barton?"

"They are not doing anything. They are dead."

The marshal was relieved to hear this news. But what if, due to his apparent injury, Barton was not seeing things for what they really were? Tomes wondered if Ford, and anyone else that was alive, could be sitting there, guns drawn, waiting for him to stand up and ready to plug Tomes full of death.

"Barton, are you sure they are dead? How do you know they are dead?"

Barton struggled to respond. "Because I shot them all, then sat here and watched them die. Do you think I would be sitting here, talking to you, if they weren't dead? Get up and see for yourself, or do you want me to drag them over there behind the bar so you can see each one for yourself? You are the one with the badge. Do your job."

Tomes realized that he was going to have to make a move, because if they weren't dead, he would have to control the situation and force them to react to him. Plus, it didn't sound like Barton had too much time left, and the marshal needed to get him to a doctor. Tomes, knowing that Barton was to his left, pulled the hammer back on his Colt pistol, crawled to the right end of the bar, slowly looking around the corner. Sure enough, in the dimly lit room, there were three people sitting at a table. It looked like they may have had a card game going before they were, hopefully, terminally interrupted.

Before he would totally expose himself, Tomes pulled a bullet cartridge out of his holster belt and threw it onto the table. No one moved. He then reached into the bar and pulled out a beer mug, and threw it onto the table. No one moved. Tomes, slowly, worked his way to his feet, his pistol pointed toward the table, and walked toward the three bodies, or at least, that was what he was hoping they were. The marshal found a lamp nearby and lit it so that he could examine the scene more clearly.

The marshal recognized the one in the middle as Angus Ford. Tomes had seen enough wanted posters on Ford to know that it was the outlaw that so many had feared.

Ford was sitting in the chair, his head laying back and chin sticking up in the air. Tomes looked closer and noticed that Ford had two wounds, one in the left chest area and one between the eyes. Ford's right arm was hanging limp and down by the chair, his gun was still in his hand, like he had cleared leather to return fire. Tomes removed the pistol from Ford's hand, sniffed the barrel and realized that it had been fired. This may be how Barton was wounded.

Tomes moved to the body to the right of Ford. It was face down upon the table, and when Tomes lifted it back in the chair, he immediately identified it as Willie Beeler. Again, the marshal had papers on Beeler, and Beeler was known to like bright colored bandanas. This body had a fire-red colored one tied around its neck. Beeler's gun was still snug in its holster, so he never had a chance to pull it. Tomes decided a large wound, one inch to the left of his heart, was what brought Beeler's dirty deeds to an end.

The third body was slumped down in the chair to the left of Angus Ford. The head was pitched forward, and the chin was pressing against his chest. Tomes had never gotten any papers on Newton, had never seen him. So, if this was Coy Newton, the marshal would have to send away for a description or a wanted poster from another marshal's office to make a positive identification. A gun was lying on the table in front of the body. Tomes didn't know if it had been dropped there or been thrown there. After smelling the barrel of what looked like a .38, it was clear that it had been fired as well. Cause of death: a large wound to the middle of the chest. The marshal concluded that death was instant and painless for the third person at the table.

After checking over the scene at the table, Tomes went back to check on

Barton. He was sitting in a chair, his right arm resting on a table beside him, his Colt .45 still in his hand. Barton's eyes were closed, his head was tilted forward and to the right. The marshal gently put his hand on Barton's shoulder and asked, "How are you doing?"

Barton slowly opened one eye and roughly replied, "It's about time you checked on me. Did you have a nice visit with your friends over there?"

Marshal Tomes removed his hand, slightly put out by Barton's response, and proceeded to remind the tall man that "The last time they saw each other, Barton had backhanded the marshal to the ground, and Tomes didn't owe him nothing."

"I never took you as one to hold a grudge," was Barton's sharp reply as Tomes tried to make him more comfortable in the wooden chair. Tomes was going to need a wagon, because he was pretty sure there was not a doctor in Rabbit Flat, and the nearest one was to be found in Prestonburg. Barton would never be able to sit a horse for the five or more hours it would take to get there. Plus, Barton had a wound in his left side, and if Tomes could get the bleeding stopped, riding in a wagon padded with hay or blankets would be easier on the wound than sitting in a saddle.

While Tomes was trying to figure out how to stop the bleeding and look for a wagon, the marshal heard a familiar voice coming from the front doors.

"Hey Marshal, do you need any help? I am not swift, but I am steady."

It was Otis, the old man Tomes had met at the old stagecoach building. It had been an hour or so since Tomes had left Otis and gone to the saloon. Not hearing any gunfire, Otis figured someone had better check on the marshal, and Otis was the only one curious enough to take the chance of going to the saloon. "You are exactly what I need, old man," a relieved Tomes answered. "The three outlaws are dead, and the tall man that you saw this morning is bleeding bad from a gunshot wound. I am going to need a wagon with hay or something soft in it to get him to Prestonburg. Do you or anybody else have a team and a wagon?"

Otis didn't answer. Marshal Tomes stopped packing Barton's wound and looked up to see Otis staring at the table where the bodies were still located. Pressured by needing to get Barton's wound cared for and locating transportation to get him to a doctor, Tomes yelled at Otis, "Hey old man! Did you hear what I ask you? What's the matter with you?"

Otis turned to Tomes with a puzzled look on his face, rubbed his chin, and he asked a question that would change everything. "Sorry, but where is the third outlaw at? You said there were three dead ones here."

Tomes, really feeling perplexed at the old man, angrily bellowed, "Can't you count? Can't you see? There are three bodies right there in front of you. Are you too old and blind to see that?"

Otis, getting a little peeved himself at having his intelligence questioned, snapped back, "I know you have a lot on your mind, but that doesn't give you a right to talk to me like that. The fact is that there may be three bodies at that table, but only two of them are the knot-heads who were shooting up the town. That other one sitting there is the saloon owner's son, Curt!"

Suddenly, Tomes' attention left the wound on Barton's side, and was directed back toward the card table, where the bodies still sat. In the dimness of the morning and the saloon, the marshal had not noticed the age of the third body.

But, as he squinted to get a better look, Otis grabbed the hair of the decedent and pulled back to expose that, indeed, the one sitting to the left of Angus Ford was but a young man, not a trail-hardened outlaw.

And with that observation, Marshal Tomes realized that he still had a murderer on the loose somewhere. And, just as important, he realized that his friend had more than a serious wound to worry about. In his rage and grief over losing his family, Barton Anderson may have killed an innocent man.

Chapter Six

Barton had lost consciousness long before they got the wagon ready to take him to a doctor. Tomes was glad Barton wasn't aware of how bad the wound was, or how painful it was. Without having to worry about keeping the tall man still, during the trip, Tomes could keep his thoughts on getting the wounded rancher to Prestonburg, before it was too late. It would be after dark when they got there, and the marshal hoped a doctor would be available, and would have the skills needed to keep Barton alive.

Otis had rounded up the perfect wagon to haul Barton to Prestonburg. A ride in a buckboard would be too rough and would surely have the wound re-opened and bleeding before too long. But Otis remembered that there was a delivery wagon, stored in the old stagecoach building that would be much better for the trip. No one knew who owned it or how it got there, but Otis knew it was in good enough shape to get to Prestonburg. Because it was used for hauling eggs, milk, glassware, and other delicate items; it was a lighter wagon with leaf springs on it, capable of absorbing a lot of the bumps along the way. And, by being smaller and lighter, it would only need to be pulled by one stout horse, and Otis secured one from a local farmer. Tomes offered to leave Hickory behind, if the farmer needed assurance that he would get his Morgan horse back. Otis said there was no need for that, because everyone in town was glad the ruckus was over, and the word of a U.S. Marshal was good enough, especially the one that killed Angus Ford. Tomes figured that now wasn't the time to straighten out the facts about what happened in the saloon. Plus, if that version got him out of town faster, and got Barton the help he needed, then that is the version they would go with.

Otis, the farmer, and Tomes, gently carried Barton out of the saloon and into the wagon, settling him into a bed of straw covered with a quilt. A few other people of the town stood watching them load the tall man, and they would, from time to time, try to look into the saloon to see the bodies of the famous bandits. Otis' wife brought a small basket of food, consisting of fried chicken, corn on the cob, a couple of rolls, and a mason jar of fresh, black coffee. This would be a meal that would be easy to eat while driving the wagon.

Tomes was making last preparations on situating Barton in the best possible position and hitching the Morgan horse to the wagon, when he heard a familiar high-pitched whinny, and the sound of rapid hoofbeats coming down the street behind him. He didn't need to turn around to see what it was, because he knew that Smoke would never let Barton leave town without him. The horse had a bond with his owner unlike any that the marshal had ever seen. It was as if they were joined in some way. Tomes watched as Smoke ran up to the wagon and stopped. The dark, gray horse took a couple of steps toward the back of the wagon, looked at Barton for a moment, then Smoke lowered his head and touched his muzzle against Barton's boot, as if letting Barton know that he was there.

"Marshal, what do you want me to do with this one?"

When Tomes turned and looked, it was the farmer, standing there with Hickory. The marshal realized that he had been so wrapped up in getting Barton ready; he had forgotten about his own horse.

"Just tie him to the back of the wagon. He will be fine there. And thanks for going and getting him."

The farmer, after tying Hickory to the back of the wagon, offered to get Smoke and tie him, too.

Tomes chuckled a little, and replied, "Sir, if I wasn't in such a hurry, that might be worth staying and watching you trying to catch the big gray and tie him to the wagon. No one catches that horse, no one ties that horse, no one rides that horse, except for the man lying in the wagon. Smoke will walk behind the wagon where he can keep an eye on Barton, and he will walk there all the way to Prestonburg."

As he was getting up on the wagon, Tomes told Otis that if Jim Fish came back with the law, explain what had happened, where Tomes had gone, and to bring the bodies of Ford and Beeler back to Prestonburg. Also, when the saloon owner returns, explain to him that Tomes was sorry for what happened, and until the marshal could come back and explain what went on in the saloon, he would just have to bury Curt and wait to sort it all out later.

Otis reached up and shook Tomes' hand, said he hoped the lawman would make it in time to save his friend, and if the marshal was ever back in Rabbit Flat to be sure to look him up and plan on a dinner-table meal the next time. Tomes grabbed the front brim of his hat, gave it a tug, and thanked Otis for the invitation. The marshal made sure to thank Mrs. Fish for the food, and the farmer for the use of the horse and for his help. If everything worked out well, maybe the Marshal's Office would let him return the wagon and the Morgan horse himself, and he could enjoy their hospitality then.

With that, Tomes slapped the reins across the broad

rear-end of the farm horse, and Tomes started his journey to Prestonburg. Hickory followed behind the wagon; his lead rein firmly tied to the back. Smoke stayed close to the rear of the wagon, hardly ever taking his eyes off Barton, who was still unconscious.

The plan was to go at a steady pace, stay on the main road, and try to keep an eye on his passenger, lying behind him in the delivery wagon. Every thirty minutes or so, Tomes would stop to check on Barton's wound, making sure it hadn't opened again. The marshal would also use the time to make sure the lack of movement, on Barton's part, was because he was still unconscious, and not because of a more terminal reason. The brief breaks would allow the horses to catch a breather, get a few laps of water from Tomes' hands, and for Smoke to get a closer look at his friend. The dark, gray horse had never seen Barton like this. So still, so quiet. The marshal, when stopping to get into the back of the wagon so he could check and freshen the bandages, would leave enough room for Smoke to get his head into the rear opening. There, the rancher's horse would take his nose and rub it against Barton's leg, as if that would be the thing that would bring the tall man around. Tomes had remembered Barton talking of how this horse had a gift of sensing whether the Anderson clan was alright, and the marshal was seeing it was true.

In the period of five hours, riding alone in a wagon, a person can do a lot of thinking. And that is exactly what Marshal Tomes did when not checking on Barton. His mind never rested for a minute, all the way to Prestonburg. There were so many things to take care of if Barton survived his wound; so many things that had to be accounted for, so many things to be carefully planned and

101

acted on, like a lawman and a friend. If Barton doesn't live, then it all may be water under the bridge.

Among all the things the marshal tried to work out in his mind, the one thing that kept coming back was the death of Curt, the saloon owner's son. Did Barton shoot him, or did Angus Ford? The wound that killed Curt was in the middle of his chest, not a convenient angle from where Ford was sitting. So, there is a good chance that, during the confrontation, Barton shot Curt. Why? Did Barton, like the marshal, mistake Curt for Coy Newton? Barton wasn't familiar with the town, or the town's people, so he wouldn't know. He would just know that it was Angus Ford, and two other males, together in a saloon. That was the description of the outlaws that left Smithview, the description of the robbers in Prestonburg, so it would be easy to see where someone would make that assumption.

Did Curt, in trying to impress Angus Ford, pull his gun and point it at Barton when the shooting started? Was the young man scared and just acting out of self-defense? Did Curt even pull his gun, for it was lying on the table when Tomes discovered the scene of the shooting? Did Barton, out of rage and hatred, just start shooting and not even care who was sitting at the table with Ford? Guilty by association?

Tomes had another thought, which was birthed by the reaction of the people of Rabbit Flat... Should the marshal take the credit for the shootings and let Barton stay clear of any legal ramifications that are sure to follow any report the marshal files? The legal system might look more favorably upon a U.S. Marshal trying to perform his duties to clear out a violent outlaw from a secured position, and in the process, an innocent bystander getting hit in the crossfire. Tomes kept figuring that the story would probably play better in the minds of a jury than a report of a man, out of his mind with rage and grief, walking in and opening fire on any and all who happen to be in the site of his gun. Would Barton be vindicated because of the tragedy suffered? Tomes was willing to risk the chance of taking the credit, or the blame, if vindication for Barton was not available.

But would Barton let him take the blame? Would Barton stay quiet and grab the opportunity of walking away from all the bloodshed that he had experienced at the Anderson ranch and at Rabbit Flat, and start his life over? Tomes knew, in his heart, that the Barton Anderson that he had known for so many years would never let someone take the blame for something the tall rancher was responsible for. Barton would never take advantage of someone else's generosity to escape the justice that he had to account for and pay. But is the man that is laying in the back of this wagon, that Barton Anderson? Or is he the one that hit Tomes that day and declared he was going to kill men? Is Barton Anderson the man that didn't show up for his own family's funeral? So many questions. Tomes knew there would be no answers until the tall man in the back of the wagon could tell what happened this morning in Rabbit Flat. And that wouldn't happen until the marshal could get Barton to a doctor, get him treated and healed, and then sit down for an in-depth conversation. No plans, no options, no offers could be made until Barton was physically okay, and hopefully, mentally restored.

One other question that would work its way into Tomes' conversations with himself was "Where was Coy Newton?" Was he in the saloon when the shooting started? If he was hit, where did he make off to? Was he passed out in another room, heard the shooting, and ran off? Was he still in the saloon, unobserved, and was he waiting for his chance to sneak away while everyone was involved with the scene of the shooting? Newton was observed being in town, with Ford and Beeler, and he was observed going into the saloon the night the three decided to drink and hold up there. Any other day, Newton would be a priority of the marshal's. But getting Barton to a doctor was what was needed the most, and that is where the marshal was headed.

About seven miles from Prestonburg, Tomes noticed three riders headed his way. Upon coming together, the marshal discovered that it was Jim Fish, the young man Tomes had met earlier that morning and had sent to get help with apprehending Ford and his gang. Jim was accompanied by the constable of Prestonburg, and a local deputy sheriff.

Tomes introduced himself to the constable and deputy, and congratulated Jim for getting help, even though the threat had been neutralized.

"Marshal, I liked to never found anyone to come with me," Jim started explaining. "Seems like everyone was busy or going to be busy. I think they were mostly cowards and didn't want to get involved with going up against Angus Ford."

Tomes, feeling a little awkward that the two lawmen had been called cowards in front of him, tried to add a little salve to what might have been the blistering truth.

"Jim, I appreciate your sincerity and the fact you stuck with it, but I can understand anyone being a little apprehensive about going up against Angus Ford, especially when there is only one lawman there to help."

The constable cleared his throat and chimed in. "Marshal, it wasn't that I didn't want to help, but I needed to stay and protect my town, in case you weren't successful and those outlaws decided to come back to Prestonburg. You understand, don't you?"

Tomes shook his head, realizing that Jim Fish had hit the nail on the head about why the young man had had a hard time getting any help. Tomes looked at the deputy sheriff, and the deputy just lowered his head and offered no words at all.

"Well, it doesn't matter now, for Angus Ford and Willie Beeler are dead. The threat to Rabbit Flat, and to anyone else, is over. I have a man in the back of this wagon who got shot, and he needs a doctor as soon as possible. So, here is what we are going to do. Constable, you ride back to Prestonburg, find the doctor and tell him a U.S. Marshal is bringing a wounded man to town. This man is an important witness for the government, and I expect the doctor to be ready to do whatever it takes to keep this man alive. Do you understand?"

"Yes sir! I will ride back and tell Doc Tilley to get his operation room ready," the constable said, relieved he would not have to face any dangerous outlaws, at least not on this day.

Tomes turned to the deputy and ordered him to ride to Rabbit Flatt with Jim and get the bodies of Angus Ford and Willie Beeler. The marshal shared that their horses were in the old stagecoach building. As soon as they got the bodies loaded on their horses, the deputy was to bring them to the constable's office in Prestonburg. Ford and Beeler would have to be officially identified, and autopsies done, so that the U.S. Marshal's office could close the case, and all cases that pertained to the crimes of the two deceased outlaws.

"Marshal, is my family, okay?" Jim asked Tomes, afraid of what the answer might be.

"Jim, not only is your family okay, but they played a big part in helping me do my job," Tomes answered, trying not to give away the fact he might have embellished his answer, a little.

Jim smiled big, and proclaimed, "It's a great day to be a member of the Fish Family!"

Tomes chuckled and agreed as he jumped off the wagon to check on Barton again. The tall man had not regained consciousness, but the wound had not opened back up. That could be good news, or that could mean that Barton was so low on blood that he didn't have enough to cause new bleeding. Tomes let Smoke have one more look before he got back up on the wagon.

"Do you think that man will make it?" inquired the constable.

"Well, I know one thing. His chances aren't going to get any better with you sitting there gawking at him," Tomes barked, trying to get everyone to get to what they were supposed to be doing.

"I think you need to get back to Prestonburg and find that doctor and help him get ready for my patient, don't you agree?"

"Yes, sir! I am leaving right now, I will get back to Prestonburg as fast as I can," The constable realized that he should have left before now, as he spurred his horse and turned toward Prestonburg.

Tomes waves to Jim Fish and the deputy and pops the reigns against the hindquarters of the Morgan horse, and the wagon continues its journey toward Prestonburg. Tomes figures he will have to find where the doctor is, get

Barton unloaded and situated, and the doctor will have to get Barton prepared for whatever surgery he will have to perform to try to save the marshal's friend.

Tomes had seen all kinds of wounds during his years as a U.S. Marshal, and he had seen wounds like the one Barton had. Doctors had told him that if you are going to get shot in the torso, the lower left side was the preferred location, for there were fewer organs and major arteries in that area. Tomes wasn't worried so much about the wound as much as how long it had been since Barton was wounded, and how long it would be until he got medical treatment for it. What the marshal had done up to this point was just trying to keep the wound clean and the bleeding stopped. Tomes knew there was still a lot of repair surgery to be done and his friend may not have enough blood left to survive whatever surgery was needed this night. As important as the doctor was to Barton's survival, Tomes got a feeling that the tall man's life was in the hands of someone a lot bigger.

It was after 7 p.m. when Tomes drove the wagon into the city limits of Prestonburg. Luckily for him, the constable was waiting on a horse, ready to escort the wagon straight to the doctor's office. Tomes was relieved that he wouldn't have to haul Barton around while he looked for Dr. Tilley's medical office.

Unfortunately, Tomes would later find out that the constable, after finding the doctor and advising him of what was needed, would tell anyone who would listen that Angus Ford and his gang were dead. The U.S. Marshal that killed them, single-handed, was coming to Prestonburg and was trying to save his dearest friend, whom the marshal had saved from the Ford gang, before the marshal had killed them all. Tomes was not too happy when he saw the crowd of people waiting to congratulate the marshal and catch a peek at the wounded stranger.

When Tomes pulled the wagon up in front of the infirmary, Dr. Tilley, along with his nurse, were waiting.

"Hi, you must be Marshal Tomes," the doctor started, offering his hand to the lawman. "I am Dr. Lance Tilley, and this is my nurse, Wanda Baird. How is the patient doing?"

Tomes extended his hand to meet the doctor's grip. "Nice to meet you, Dr. Tilley. You too, Nurse Baird. The patient has seen better days and, unfortunately, today is not one of them. I have done the best I can trying to keep the bleeding stopped and the wound clean. Doc, he has lost a lot of blood, and it's been a long time since the injury happened. Plus, he hasn't regained consciousness since before we started here."

"I am not surprised that he has been out of it, if he has lost as much blood as you say he has," Dr. Tilley observed, as he poured alcohol on his hands to try to sterilize them. "Let me get up in the wagon and look at him. Then I will have a better idea of what I am going to need and whether your friend has a good chance of recovering."

The doctor instructed Nurse Baird to stand at the back of the wagon, with a lamp in hand, and be prepared to hand him fresh bandages if the wound opened again. As she prepared to take her place, and Dr. Tilley got ready to climb into the wagon where Barton was still laying, an unforeseen problem presented itself: Smoke.

As soon as the doctor started to go into the back of the wagon, Smoke started making that high-pitched whinny and slapping his front hooves against the ground. Smoke

108

was in a new town, surrounded by a lot of new people, and the dark, gray horse was concerned for the Anderson that was in the back of the wagon. The doctor asked if it would be safe to be around that horse? Dr. Tilley explained that he would have to get into the wagon, try to position Barton on the stretcher, and then he would have to be carried into the infirmary. The doctor said he didn't have time to treat himself, or anyone else, for horse bites and kicks.

Tomes wished Barton was conscious, for then he could explain to Smoke that it was okay, and that the horse didn't have to be concerned or protect him. But Barton was still out, and Smoke was getting more agitated. Tomes had watched when Barton would talk to Smoke. Barton always talked to his horse in a regular voice, never yelled or admonished. And Barton always put his hand under the horse's chin and looked Smoke right in the eyes, never turned his head away or down. Barton would say that it was a way of showing respect and keeping a trust when you kept your eyes in line with a horse's eyes. It was almost like you were reaching into their very soul when you kept eye contact and spoke like a friend.

The first couple of attempts, Smoke didn't want to hear anything from anyone, even though Smoke had been around Tomes from time to time. Tomes would step toward Smoke, speaking in a regular voice and trying to place his hand out where he could place it under the horse's chin.

"Okay, Smoke, It's okay. Be easy, be easy and let them help Barton," Tomes kept repeating.

But Smoke would jump back, throw his head up in the air, and make a low noise that sounded almost like a growl. Tomes knew he could not show frustration for fear that Smoke would mistake it as aggression. So, Tomes continued to try to calm the dark, gray horse down, knowing that time was of the essence and Dr. Tilley needed to get Barton into the infirmary so he could start working on the wound as quick as possible.

On the third attempt, something connected between Tomes and Smoke.

Maybe the horse sensed the urgency of getting Barton out of the wagon. Maybe Smoke was tired of not being able to get to Barton, and this man, with the shiny metal on his chest, was going to help Smoke take this Anderson home. Whatever the reason, Smoke stood still and let Tomes put his hand under the mighty horse's chin.

"That's right, Smoke, good boy. Barton is going to be okay. Stay easy, and it will be alright."

Tomes stood there, rubbing the horse and reassuring Smoke that the doctor was trying to help Barton and needed to be allowed to do so. Tomes, for a second, wondered how silly it looked to be holding a conversation with a horse. But it seemed to be working, and that was all that mattered. The marshal promised to remember this moment and share it with Barton someday if the tall man survived.

Dr. Tilley asked a couple of men who were standing there watching to grab the stretcher and slide it into the back of the wagon. It would have been easier to get Barton on the stretcher if he was conscious, but that was not the case and the doctor would have to ease him upon the carrying device by himself, as there was not enough room in the wagon for another person.

Slowly and with great care, Dr. Tilley tried to move Barton onto the stretcher, but he just couldn't get the stretcher underneath Barton, as the straw was loose, and the stretcher wouldn't slide across it. The doctor thought of rolling Barton on his side and then placing the stretcher underneath him, but he was afraid of opening the wound and losing what blood Barton had left.

Then, the doctor noticed the quilt that Mrs. Fish had placed in the wagon for Barton to lay on and to help keep the straw dust at a minimum. Dr. Tilley asked the two men who had placed the stretcher in the wagon to remove it and place one end on the tailgate of the wagon, and the other end would be held by one man away from the wagon. Once the stretcher was where the doctor wanted it, he jumped out of the wagon, and explained to the other man how they were going to grab the closest end of the quilt and pull it toward the stretcher with Barton on it. With any luck, the quilt would slide upon the medical device and Barton would slide with it, without having to lift, twist, or turn him.

"Doc, can I help you in any way?" Tomes asked as he continued to keep Smoke calm.

"Marshal, right at this moment, you are doing exactly what you need to be doing, and that's keeping that horse from coming after all of us," the doctor answered as they slid Barton out of the wagon and onto the stretcher.

Once the doctor was satisfied that Barton was secure for the move inside, the doctor turned to Tomes, and said, "Marshal, if I was you, I would go find me a place to get some rest. You have had a long day, and I have a feeling I am going to have a long night. I can't make any promises, but I am going to do the best I can to keep your friend on this side of eternity. I will send somebody for you as soon as I get a fix on whether we have made a difference or not."

"Thanks, Doctor. I will do just that. I've got to get this

111

wagon off the street, the horses tended to, and then find a place at the jailhouse to bunk down for a few hours. If I don't hear from anyone, I will check back at sunup," Tomes replied.

"Hopefully, I will have good news for you when tomorrow comes," the doctor said as he turned to go inside the infirmary.

Tomes turned to Smoke, rubbed the horse's chin, and then softly said, "That would be nice, wouldn't it, big gray?"

Chapter Seven

Tomes never made it to the jailhouse to look for a place to bunk down. After leaving the doctor's infirmary, Tomes found the local livery stable. No one was around the livery, so Tomes thought he would pull the delivery wagon out of the street, unhitch the Morgan horse, take the saddles off Hickory and Smoke, and fix himself a semi-comfortable place to bed down in the back of the delivery wagon. Tomes figured, at sunrise, he would check on the horses, find the blacksmith to explain who he was, what all he had left there, and to make plans for the next few days of livery care.

It all pretty much went as planned until he got to the part of taking the saddle off Smoke. Tomes had Hickory and the Morgan horse fed and placed in a stall for the night. When he turned to take care of Smoke, the dark, gray horse wasn't there. Tomes wondered if Smoke had tried to find his way back to the infirmary. But when the marshal stepped outside the stable, what he saw made him shake his head and walk slowly toward the delivery wagon. Smoke was standing behind the wagon, not moving a muscle, just diligently looking into the back of the wagon, as if Barton was going to show up at any minute and they would go home.

With a bucket of oats in one hand, Tomes slowly approached Smoke. He gently stuck his other hand out to find Smoke's chin, and the marshal started speaking in that soft voice that had worked earlier in the evening.

"Smoke, I don't think Barton is going to be showing up tonight. Why don't you and I stay here with the wagon, and I will put this bucket of oats right here? If you get hungry, you can help yourself. You know where the water trough is, so you can get a drink, too. I promise we will go check on Barton in the morning?"

Smoke turned to look at Tomes, as if to agree with the plan, and then the dark, gray horse lowered his head into the bucket, and munched on some oats as Tomes took Smoke's saddle off and threw it, along with Barton's Henry rifle, into the back of the wagon. Then, Tomes crawled into the back of the delivery wagon, untied Barton's bed roll from the saddle, and made himself comfortable in the straw still there from hauling Barton from Rabbit Flat. It had been a long, eventful day, and within minutes, Tomes was asleep.

It was around 5:30 a.m. when the marshal awoke to the sound of someone saying, "Marshal? Marshal Tomes, are you awake?"

Maybe due to being groggy and still wore out from the previous day, Tomes had the strangest thought come to himself. *If that is Smoke talking, I haven't given that horse enough credit.*

But, upon wiping his eyes and sitting up in the back of the wagon, Tomes found the Prestonburg constable staring into the back of the wagon, his hands hanging over the tailgate.

"Marshal, I thought you were going to bed down at the jail last night. We waited for you, never figuring you were down here. Did you get chilly last night, sleeping in the wagon?"

Tomes started working his way out of the back of the wagon, and replied, "I was too tired to get chilly. I was out like a light when my head hit that saddle in there. I figured the big, gray horse needed some company, too."

"Well, sir. You must have snored too loud or something, because that horse was standing outside Dr. Tilley's infirmary the last time I looked. Nurse Baird said he has been up there, whinnying and doing that stomping thing with his front feet, for the last hour or so. She said they were afraid he was going to try to come to the infirmary."

Tomes wasn't surprised that Smoke had made his way back to where Barton was, and that it was just wishful thinking that the marshal sleeping in the wagon would calm the horse down and keep him away.

"Constable, have you had a chance to talk with the doctor, or nurse, as to how Barton is doing and how the procedure went?" Tomes asked as he put on his gun and his hat.

"I just stuck my head in the front door and Nurse Baird said I needed to find you as soon as possible; that the doctor would fill you in," replied the

Prestonburg lawman. "From the looks of her, it must have been a long night."

"I would have been surprised if it had not been," Tomes responded. "Not wishing any hardship on them, but I would probably be sad if it had been a quick night for them. "

The marshal followed the constable back to the infirmary. There, he found the dark, gray horse pacing in front of the medical facility. Tomes wondered how he would explain it to Smoke if Barton did not make it out of surgery or did not recover after the surgery. But that would have to be a bridge to cross later, as the first thing he needed to do was to talk with the doctor and see if explanations would be needed.

Tomes walked into the waiting room, followed by the constable. There sat Nurse Baird, behind the desk where patients were to sign in, upon arrival at the infirmary. She was working on some paperwork, and Tomes figured that was Barton's file, and she was updating the latest status, and actions, of the doctor since the marshal was last there.

"Good morning, marshal. I hope you found a place to bed down, and you got a little rest last night. Would you like some fresh coffee?"

Tomes took his hat off, and carefully searched for his words. "Nurse Baird, I appreciate your kind thoughts. I would say the same to you, but if you got a good night's sleep, I am afraid that would mean that my friend did not have a good night and I have a lot of explaining to do to that horse outside. And, yes, I would love a cup of coffee."

Nurse Baird walked over to the coffee pot, poured Tomes a cup of coffee and handed it to him. Then, she looked out the window, shook her head and chuckled. "I have seen a lot of things in my life, both human and animal, but I swear I have never seen such loyalty and concern of one for the other as I have that horse out there. He has been out there for over an hour. I tried to talk to him, but I don't think anything is going to settle him down except to see your friend walk out the front door. Then, that horse will be happy."

Tomes found a chair, sat down, and took a slow sip from his coffee cup. "I think you are very wise, ma'am. I thought sleeping at the livery stable would comfort him and keep him away from here. But I think Smoke was just putting up with me until I finally went to sleep. He planned on coming down here all along."

At that moment, Dr. Tilley stepped through the door that was right behind where the nurse had been sitting. He looked like he hadn't seen the cool side of a bed pillow in a long time. He was unshaven, slow afoot, and his eyes appeared as if they didn't know whether to open or close.

Marshal Tomes reached over to pull a chair up beside him, but the doctor waved it off. "Thanks, but no thanks, Marshal. If I sit down, it will be even harder for me to stay awake. And I am pretty sure you are not up here this early in the morning to watch me get my beauty sleep."

"No, Doc. My mind has been on one thing this morning, and that is being informed of the latest on that man you have in there. I take it you kept the coffee pot going all night?"

Dr. Tilley crossed his arms, took a long breath, and then started filling in Marshal Tomes on Barton's status. "There wasn't anything out of the ordinary as far as the wound itself. I have seen a lot of left side abdominal gunshot wounds, this one didn't cause any special alarm at first. Bullet went in the front, came out the back, missed his kidney by a few inches. Unfortunately, the bullet clipped the renal artery going to the left kidney, and that is where all the blood was coming from.

It took me a little while to try to repair the renal artery, clean out the pooled blood and clots that were inside him, and then sew him back together and close the entry and exit wounds. As I said, it should have taken me a couple of hours of medical procedures, and then I could tell you that he will be awake, and aware, in a day or two."

Tomes leaned forward in his chair, knowing the next part of the doctor's explanation was going to be the part that he needed to pay the closest attention to, and will be the part that decides whether Barton ever goes home to Smithview.

"Doc, I get the feeling that you aren't going to tell me I can talk to my friend in a day or two. Is that right?"

Dr. Tilley leans back on the desk, puts his hands behind him to support himself, and continues, "I can't even tell you that you can have a normal conversation in a week or two, let alone a day or two. It is unexplainable how he has even lived this long, considering how much blood he lost and how long it took to get him medical help. You did everything you could, and that has played a part in whatever shape he is in. He just needed to get medical help sooner. To be honest, for all medical reasoning any doctor could muster up: the man should be dead. He practically didn't have any blood in him when I started working on him. His vital organs didn't have enough supply to keep him alive and he should have gone into organ failure. And Nurse Baird and I sat up all night, just waiting for something to shut down,

118

and therefore, causing every other organ to follow. But, by the grace of someone a lot more powerful than me, your friend is still breathing, and his heart is still beating. Just barely, but at this point, we will take what we can get."

Tomes slid back in his chair, ran his fingers through his hair, and tried to process what the doctor had just shared and what it all meant.

"Doc, be straight with me. What are the chances that the man in the other room pulls out of this and sits on that horse out there, someday?"

Dr. Tilley uncrossed his arms, walked over to the window, and stood there looking at Smoke, who was looking back at the man in the window like he was waiting for the doctor's response, too.

"Marshal, I want to say your friend doesn't have a prayer's chance of pulling out of this. Every medical book that I have would tell me that anyone who has been through what your friend has been through, could not make it. But there is one truth that I just can't deny. He has made it this far beyond explanation. He was a healthy, strong man when he was wounded. I won't be surprised if he is at the undertakers before the sun goes back down. Then again, I wouldn't be totally shocked if he lives long enough to shake my hand and pay his bill."

Tomes rose out of his chair, extended his arm, and grabbed the doctor's hand, and said, "Dr. Tilley, if he pulls out of this, I may just come and pay his bill for him, and take you out for the biggest steak that the city of Prestonburg has to offer."

Dr. Tilley laughed and told Tomes that he would love to take him up on that, but that would be another day, and the doctor was sure that Tomes could use a good meal. Tomes had forgotten all about himself and the fact that he had not eaten since Mrs. Fish's fried chicken yesterday afternoon. The marshal informed the doctor that he would check back with him, or Nurse Baird, in a couple of hours. For now, he needed to go back to the livery, locate the owner, and make sure the other horses and tack would be ok where they were. Then, he would find a place for a good warm meal.

As Tomes and the constable walked through the front door of the infirmary and stepped off the front porch, Smoke came trotting over, anticipating a report on the status of the Anderson who did not come out with them.

"Smoke, I don't have a clue whether you understand what is going on, what I am going to say, or whether you are going to be eased by what all I am going to tell you. I just know one thing; I can't expect anything different from you if I don't try."

If anyone had closed their eyes and just listened, they would have thought that Tomes was informing a family member or one of his deputies of the status of Barton Anderson and what the plan would be for the next few days. Smoke walked right beside the marshal, seeming to take in each word, and the big, gray horse didn't offer any dissenting opinion or action to the contrary. There was no doubt who Smoke's main rider and companion was. That had been and always would be, Barton Anderson. But it seemed like Marshal Tomes had established himself as someone that Smoke could trust, and he may be on his way to the rank of "friend".

As Tomes, Smoke and the constable got closer to the livery stable, they could hear hammering on an anvil. That meant someone was there and Tomes could explain his situation.

"That is probably Big Mike," the constable offered. "he owns the livery stable, the feed store and rents out carriages and wagons. He will be the one you will want to talk to about your belongings."

Tomes nodded his acknowledgement of this new information, and as soon as the marshal stepped through the double barn doors, it was plain to see how Big Mike got his name. Tomes wasn't a small man, by any stretch of the imagination. He often told Barton that the tall rancher was the one person that he had to look up to. But the blacksmith had Barton beat. Not only in height, but in every department of physical stature. The blacksmith's neck was as big as a normal man's thigh. His hands were huge from years of grasping a hammer and beating out horseshoes, nails, and anything else that needed to be reshaped. The big man's arms were like oak logs and his shoulders looked like they could carry a side of beef across town.

"Hello, marshal! I think you are probably looking for me. Everybody around here calls me Big Mike!"

Marshall Tomes reached out to greet the huge man, and his hand disappeared in the grip of the blacksmith's hand.

"If you don't mind," Tomes smiled, "I think I will call you 'Sir', if that's okay."

Big Mike laughed out loud and responded, "That's funny, that seems to be what everyone says when they meet me!"

Big Mike explained that he found Hickory and the Morgan when he got to the livery. He had heard about the marshal's story from people in town, and figured that the horses, the delivery wagon, and the tack were each a part of Tomes' story. The huge blacksmith said he had already taken it upon himself to water and feed the horses, pull the wagon around behind the livery stable, and that he had cleaned out the straw in the back of the wagon, and had put Barton's saddle and Henry rifle in the barn where it would be safer.

"Sir, I don't know how to thank you for all your help. I don't know how long I will need to use your facilities. But if you will keep a tab going, I will make sure the U.S. Marshal's office in Topeka returns to you every cent you are owed," Tomes shared as he checked out Hickory and the Morgan horse.

"Marshal, don't you worry one thing about keeping your things here. Stay as long as you need. As far as the bill; won't be one. I consider it an honor to help the lawman that killed Angus Ford and Willie Beeler," the blacksmith said with a big smile.

Tomes turned and looked at the constable,

who just shrugged like he didn't know where the blacksmith had heard that. Tomes is now wondering what he is going to run into when he goes to find a place to eat breakfast.

"Constable, I need to find the telegraph office. I want to send word to the Topeka Marshal's office of the status of Ford and Beeler. I would think the deputy sheriff who rode to Rabbit Flat to get their bodies will be coming back today, or tomorrow. I will need someone to do an autopsy so I can get an official report started. Then, I need to find a place to get something to eat. And by the time I have done all of that, it will be time to swing by Dr. Tilley's and see what the latest is on Barton."

The constable, feeling important again, told Tomes that the telegraph office was three blocks west of the livery. Right across from the telegraph office was the best breakfast in Prestonburg, called Granny Ryan's. Anyone with a badge got a discount, as Granny's late husband was the sheriff of the county. And, of course, the constable made sure to remind Tomes to tell Granny that the constable sent him, because Granny gave him a free meal if he sent enough people her way.

Tomes gave the constable a look that said that lawmen and free stuff usually is not a good idea. But Tomes has too much to do to take the time to explain the particulars of the law and taking advantage of your profession.

Big Mike pointed at Smoke and asked, "Marshal, do you want me to feed this
horse and put him in the corral while you are

running your errands?"

Tomes looked at Smoke, pushed his hat back on his head, and explained to Big Mike that there wasn't a corral that could hold the dark, gray horse if Smoke didn't want to be corralled. Tomes suggested that a bucket of oats be put out for Smoke, maybe close to the delivery wagon because it seemed that the wagon was a place that Smoke could relate to, as that was the last place the horse had seen Barton.

"I have a feeling this horse will probably make his way back to the doctor's place before too long. He won't cause any problems, or anything, if we just give him some freedom to follow his instincts. Especially when it comes to him worrying about Barton," Tomes said as he turned to go to the telegraph office.

As Tomes walked up the street to the telegraph office, he noticed that some people were watching him and engaged in conversation with each other. Tomes figured that the constable's version of what happened in Rabbit Flat was causing quite a stir in town. Some would just stare at him, some would wave and tip their hats, some walked on past, either not concerned about what happened at Rabbit Flat or had not heard any version yet. And, for now, that was okay with the marshal.

Tomes walked into the telegraph office, introduced himself, and asked if it would be possible to send a telegraph to the U.S. Marshal's office in Topeka. The on-duty clerk said it would be fine, handed Tomes a pencil and a piece of paper, and asked him to write down what he wanted in the telegram. Tomes was advised that the shorter the message, the better, but to include all pertinent information. The clerk said he would send it as soon as possible and would hopefully hear back that morning.

Tomes took the pencil and paper and sat at a small table across the room. He realized that he had never really thought about what his first words to his superiors would be. As he brought Barton to Prestonburg, he had contemplated what version he would report as far as Barton's part in the shootings in Rabbit Flat. Would his report say that Barton had killed all three, including the boy? Would he tell them that he had had an encounter with Ford, Beeler and Newton and the boy, and Barton, got shot in the shootout?

For now, Tomes felt what the telegraph clerk had suggested was the way to approach this initial contact, keep it short and simple. So, he wrote:

```
Ford,    Beeler,    another
unidentified male dead.
STOP.    Newton   escaped.
STOP.    Another    male
citizen critical. STOP.
More   to   come.   STOP.
Tomes.
```

Tomes figured that was enough, for now. He would just have to delay sending, or sharing, any other particulars until he could talk with Barton and get a better idea of what happened, as far as who shot who, and if Barton knew about the boy. As the marshal had pondered before, this could play out two different ways, and Tomes would decide which direction to take after getting a better idea of what happened that morning in the saloon.

After handing the script to the clerk and asking to be informed when a reply was received, Tomes walked across the street to get something to eat. A sign proclaiming that the place was Granny Ryan's hung over the door. Once Tomes opened the front door, the aroma that met him left no doubt that he was about to have the best meal he has had in a long time. Other than Mrs. Fish's fried chicken and corn-on-the-cob, Tomes had been surviving on old biscuits and beef jerky, and sometimes not even taking the time to eat that. Tomes had some time before he was going back to Dr. Tilley's, so he was going to enjoy the culinary treat of a home-cooked meal.

"So, you must be the one we all owe a good night's sleep to!"

Tomes, looking through a crowd of people waiting to get a seat, noticed the voice had come from a short, elderly, white-haired lady who was fighting her way through the crowd and heading his way.

"Marshal, you come on around these people and I will find you a table close to the kitchen!"

Tomes, not wanting to offend anyone who might have been waiting awhile, thanked her for the offer and assured her that he would wait, like everyone else.

"I won't hear of it, you follow me, and if anyone gives you a hard time, you just tell them that Granny said it was okay, and if they don't like it and keep on griping, they might find their biscuits a little done on the bottoms." The little old woman is now laughing as she grabs Tomes' arm and leads him to a table in the back.

At this point, Tomes realizes that protesting any further would be futile. So, he follows the tugging of the small, elderly hand that has a death grip on his arm. She pulls a chair away from the table, in the very back of the eatery, and makes a grand gesture with her arm, inviting him to sit down. Tomes takes his hat off, lays it in the nearby chair, sits down and prepares to enjoy the moment and the food.

The little, feisty lady pulls a chair out, next to Tomes, and before taking a seat, asks the marshal if it would be alright if she joins him.

"Ma'am, if you are who I think you are, I think there is a pretty good chance you do whatever you feel like doing in this place," Tomes shared with a slight smirk on his face.

"Ha, Ha, Ha! You have done got me figured out, don't you, lawman? Well, for the record, I am Granny Ryan and it's an honor to have you in here today, or any day you happen to be in Prestonburg," she roared in a loud, commanding voice.

"Thank you, Granny." As Tomes reaches out to shake the elderly lady's hand, he says, "I am U.S. Marshal Lyndon Tomes and it's a pleasure to share a table with you."

"Oh, I know who you are. I was hoping you would come see me. As a matter of fact, everybody in town knows about you—about your friend up at the doctor's office. You are the talk of the town this morning."

Tomes smiled and said, "Your local constable did a pretty good job of talking you, and this place, up. He made it sound like I just couldn't pass on having a sit down and digging into a plateful of homemade heaven. Plus, I guess he gets a little something if I mention him."

Granny frowns and proclaims, in a gruff voice, "He is an idiot! Good thing the county sheriff keeps an eye on things around here, or we would be hurting for any kind of law in Prestonburg. Just the sight of a badge will cause most people to act right, and our constable has wearing a badge down to an art. He is the prime example of the old saying 'better to be seen, and not heard', as you have probably figured out. I give him free eats just to keep something in his mouth, so he can't talk. Yep, the man is an idiot."

Tomes doesn't know how to respond to this oratory, so he decides to move the conversation on to another subject, and hopefully get Granny in a jovial mood again.

"Ma'am, the smell that I was greeted with when I came in the door was good enough to pay for. I bet it tastes better than it smells. You think I could get a cup of hot coffee and something to eat?"

Now, the smile comes back to Granny's face, and she turns to one of the waitresses and bellows out, "Sissy, get our guest the breakfast special. That ought to get him off to a good start."

Tomes takes a big breath, like he has been

handed a daunting responsibility, and says, "Get me started? Ma'am, sounds like you are expecting a whole passel of marshals to join me. And, for my sake, I hope they do, to help me eat all that food you are sending out."

Granny, smiling even broader now, responds to Tomes' worry, "Hey, marshal. I was married to a lawman for 40 years, and I know that eating can be something that takes a back pew to other things that need to be done. You eat what you can, and I will have them cover the rest. It will be here, waiting for you, when you get a chance to come back later."

The marshal smiled and said, "I appreciate it, ma'am. I don't know if I will make it back this way any time today. But, if I don't, it won't be because of the company or the hospitality. You say your husband was a lawman. The constable said he used to be the sheriff of this county. I am sorry I will not have the honor to meet him. I would have loved to have shaken his hand and told him he was a lucky man to have married such a fine woman."

At this point in the conversation, Granny's smile fades away into a look of longing for a day gone by, a day that will never be again.

"I think you would have liked him, marshal. Jess Ryan was a good man, an honest man. Believed everyone had a right to be protected by the law, and to have a good life under the law. He didn't play favorites, respected the down-and-out, just as much as the high-and-mighty. The county kept voting him in, so he kept putting the badge on until the day he died."

Tomes, hesitant to ask, but wondering if she got to talk about her husband very often, leaned forward in his chair and inquired, "Did old age or sickness catch up with him?"

Granny shook her head in a side-to-side motion, and her eyes teared up. "No, old age or sickness didn't catch up with Jess. A bullet from a carbine rifle did. Took one in the back. He was coming home from breaking up a dispute over ownership of a horse. Never did find out who shot him. The general thought was some coward, whom Jess had sent to prison, or something like that. Probably someone decided to have their vengeance and just happened to see their chance that day. They say he was dead, in the saddle, when his horse came walking into town. I knew I had lost him when Dr. Tilley and a couple of deputies came riding up to the house. A lawman's wife just knows when the bad news is coming."

Tomes reaches over and takes her small, wrinkled hand, gives it a squeeze, and offers words of comfort. "I am so sorry for your loss, and I am sorry that it had to happen that way. Every lawman's hope, and even his dream, is to serve well while he wears a badge, and then retire in the peace of knowing you gave it your best."

"That's the saddest part, marshal. Just that morning, Jess had told the county board of election that he would not be running for sheriff again. He said that it was time for someone younger to watch over a growing county, and that he'd back whoever took his place. He was just a few weeks from handing in the badge, taking off his gun and taking a place on our front porch, where he could watch sunrises, drink coffee, and tell stories to our grandkids."

Tomes and Granny had been so involved in their conversation that neither noticed when the food and coffee arrived at their table. Granny apologized and told Sissy to freshen the marshal's coffee. As she encouraged him to dig into the plateful of breakfast goodies, she also asked him a question that took him by surprise.

"Marshal, if it's none of my business, just tell me. But I get the feeling your friend up at Dr. Tilley's is that Smithview rancher whose family was butchered by Angus Ford and his gang. Am I right?"

Tomes is caught off guard by her question. So, he chews the food in his mouth, swallows to clear it, takes a sip of coffee, and then measures his next words.

"Granny, what in the world would cause you to think about that? There are a lot of people that Angus Ford brought unwanted heartache to. The man at the infirmary might have been an unlucky stranger who was in the wrong place at the wrong time. Don't you think that is possible?"

The elderly lady leans forward in her chair, looks Tomes in the eyes, and replies, "Here is a truth, marshal. You can't be married to a lawman for forty years, and not learn a few things, develop a feeling about things. Just get that chill when you realize things could be and probably are. You don't have to tell me, and it won't change anything if you don't. I just have a feeling there is more to the story than what that idiot constable is blabbering around town about. Again, there is nothing that must be said or needs to be known, if that is your way of handling a curious old woman."

"I won't say you are right, and I won't say that you are wrong. I admire your intuition and I respect your life as a lawman's wife. But, for now, the story that is being told is the one that people will have to chew on, until another version presents itself," Tomes answered as he turns back to the food on his plate, while it's still warm.

Granny gets a slight smile on her face and nods her head affirmatively. "Yes, my husband would have liked you, marshal. If you had said anything else, or shared any more, I would have lost some respect for you. It doesn't matter what I think, or anyone else thinks, the only thing that matters is letting the truth work its way toward the final goal, which should be justice. That's what my husband always said, and that is how he handled everything that came before him. The court of public opinion can never be allowed to derail the process of justice. And the best way to kill public opinion is to starve it by denying it any information that the public can chew on. You agree with that, lawman?"

Tomes takes one last bite of breakfast before pushing the plate away. He wipes his mouth with a cloth napkin, leans over toward his new friend, and softly makes an observation. "Granny, I think you may have missed your calling. If this eatery ever runs its course, you should seriously consider running for the constable's job."

Granny lets out a big belly laugh, slaps Tomes on the hand, and declares, "Just because I am good at shooting off my mouth doesn't mean I could shoot off a gun. I think I am better at putting food in people's bellies than putting people in the city's jail. Yeah, marshal, my husband would have liked you. If for no other reason, I like you."

Tomes stands up from the table, picks his hat up from the chair, reaches into his pocket to pull out money for the meal. But, when Tomes lays an amount on the table that he hopes will cover his meal, Granny picks it up and puts it in his shirt pocket.

"Marshal, you don't ever have to worry about that here. You are always welcome. I know lawmen aren't paid near what they are worth, so this is my way of saying thank you. And you don't have to worry about what we talked about earlier. Lawmen's wives are a lot like preacher's wives. They both hear a lot of stuff and can't repeat any of it, or someone will get hurt, usually their loved ones. You may not believe it, but I am a praying woman, and I will say a few for you and your friend."

"I am indebted for your mentions," Tomes replied, as he headed for the door.

Chapter Eight

As the telegraph clerk said it would be later in the morning before he would get anything back from the Topeka U.S. Marshal's office, Tomes figured he would stop in Dr. Tilley's office and see what the latest was on Barton. Then, he would go to the jailhouse and find out if the bodies of Ford and Beeler had made it back to Prestonburg. Before heading to check on the telegram, he had better go to the livery and check in with Big Mike, in case there were any issues with Hickory, the Morgan horse or Smoke, although Tomes figured he would find the dark, gray horse at the doctor's office.

Sure enough, as the marshal got within eyesight of the infirmary, he saw Smoke standing out front, but Smoke wasn't pacing and digging at the ground with his front feet. Maybe the big horse was settling into the situation. Still, Tomes didn't know what to do with Smoke, as the marshal knew he couldn't just wait for Barton to get better. Tomes had responsibilities to other towns and people, as a U.S. Marshal, and he couldn't just neglect all of those to stay in

Prestonburg, in hopes of Barton waking up. There was also the issue of Coy Newton and bringing him to justice. Tomes knew Smoke would never leave Barton, that was one thing for sure. So, a plan would have to present itself before the end of this day.

As Tomes walked up the sidewalk that ran in

front of the infirmary, he noticed Nurse Baird sitting on the porch. She was holding a knife in one hand, and an apple in the other, and would cut off a slice and throw it on the front steps of the porch, where Smoke could get to it. It was starting to make sense why Smoke was more at peace, and not so agitated, as he was yesterday.

"You figure you have enough apples to keep him occupied?" asked Tomes.

Nurse Baird smiled. "I think all I am doing is just keeping myself busy. I don't think I am distracting that horse one bit. He isn't hungry. He is just doing it to keep me happy."

Tomes stuck his hand out and took Smoke's chin in his palm. "Big gray, you have us all figured out, don't you? There isn't anyone going to pull anything on you. You just want to be where Barton is, apples or no apples, isn't that right?"

Smoke made a little whinny noise and looked up at the door of the infirmary.

"Is Doc Tilley in with Barton?"

Nurse Baird shook her head no and replied, "Actually, he is down at the undertaker's place. Those bodies you were waiting for showed up a little while ago, and the undertaker asked the doctor to come and examine them for your official report."

Tomes thanked her for the information, tipped his hat and headed toward the undertaker's office, which was next door to the jailhouse. As Tomes was stepping up onto the entrance of the funeral parlor, he met Dr. Tilley coming out.

"Well, Doc, did you come to any conclusions

about Ford and Beeler?"

Dr. Tilley closed his eyes, ran his fingers through his hair, took a big breath, and responded, "Well, I am pretty convinced they are dead, and the holes in their bodies played a big part in it. I am glad I can report all the holes were in the front and that you haven't resorted to backshooting your prisoners yet."

The marshal frowned, tilted his head, and said, "Doc, they were pretty dead the last time I saw them yesterday morning. I don't think your prognosis is any more than what I have already told my bosses in Topeka."

The doctor opened his eyes, lifted his eyebrows in emphasis, and proclaimed, "But it sounds more official when a medical man says it. It just becomes a final fact when I look them over, give it an educated opinion, and then sign the paper to make it official. You can shoot them all day long, marshal, but they aren't officially dead until I sign the paper that says so!"

Tomes nodded in agreement, and then asked, "How about my friend up at the infirmary?"

Dr. Tilley leaned against a porch post, turned to Tomes, and sighed. "I am glad to say Mr. Anderson is still alive. But I would hate to have to make a bet on how solid he is in that state of living. Nothing has changed, as far as his condition. He is breathing, his heart is beating, he is not bleeding, and for those three things, we can be grateful. For now, it's not a case of watching him day-by-day, but it's more a case of monitoring him hour-by-hour. He is still going to need a lot of watching, a lot of waiting and even more prayers, to get him back on his feet and back on that horse."

Tomes shared with the doctor that he was going to leave Barton in his care, that he needed to get back to his law duties. Tomes asked Dr. Tilley that if anything changed one way or another, if he would send word to the telegraph office in Smithview that Tomes could check with them. It would be easier than trying to run him down, out on the trail somewhere. In the back of his mind, the marshal did not want any telegrams going to Topeka, at this time, because Tomes still didn't know how he was going to play what happened in Rabbit Flat, and he wanted to be able to control the flow of information, especially how the official version would be written.

Tomes said his goodbyes to Dr. Tilley and headed toward the livery stable.

Upon finding Big Mike, Tomes was informed that a young gentleman named Jim Fish had ridden in with the deputy that brought the outlaw's bodies back. To save the marshal the trouble and time, Jim Fish offered to take the Morgan horse and delivery wagon back to Rabbit Flat.

"I didn't see any problem with letting him go back with them. Did I do the right thing, marshal?"

Tomes put his hand on the big man's shoulder and said, "You did just fine. I don't have the time to do it, and I am sure that the farmer would love to have his

137

Morgan horse back. I just wish I could have thanked Jim myself."

"Oh, I told him that, marshal," Big Mike replied, "but the young man seemed to be in a hurry to get back. Probably wanted to get back before it started getting dark. I told him you would be grateful that he went to all that trouble to help you out."

Tomes shook Big Mike's hand, thanked him for his kindness, and asked him to keep an eye out for Smoke until the marshal could get back to Prestonburg. The blacksmith smiled really big and said he would try to keep watch on the horse, but he figured that Smoke would be just fine, between going back and forth between the livery and the infirmary.

Tomes took Hickory out of the stall, threw his saddle and bags upon the horse's back, got up on him and headed toward the telegraph office before leaving town. When Tomes rode up in front of the office, the telegraph clerk came running out and said, "I was just coming to find you. This came in a couple of minutes ago. I figured you would want it as soon as possible."

Tomes, still sitting on Hickory, reached down and took the piece of paper from the clerk. When he read it, it simply said:

```
More    details    will    be
needed. STOP.
```

Tomes knew that would be the response from the home office. He also knew he was not ready to share anything official and on the record until he had a conversation with Barton. And, for now, that wasn't possible. Until he had that conversation with the tall rancher, his current priority would be trying to find where Coy Newton was. If Newton was in the saloon when Barton came in and the shooting started, then he represented someone who could either substantiate the marshal's report or Newton could cause a lot of trouble with a different version. More and more, Tomes realized that he may not be able to protect his friend, especially in the death of an innocent person. Tomes had always tried to be honest and above board, in the performance of his duties as a U.S. marshal. And that may be the road he takes on this journey; friend, or no friend.

It was a cool November afternoon, a little more than a week after Tomes left Prestonburg, when the marshal rode into Smithview. Tomes had spent most of this time riding his circuit, visiting with area lawmen, and trying to put together some kind of map of where Coy Newton might have gone. It wasn't the information that he had gathered that made him think that Newton was still in that part of the state. But it was the fact that there hadn't been very many sightings, or reports of Newton's activities, that made Tomes think that the outlaw had settled in somewhere and wasn't taking a chance of drawing attention to himself. In the many years of him being a lawman, Tomes had found that it wasn't uncommon for a fugitive to stop running and try to keep a low profile wherever he was. One of the more popular actions was to look for a simple job on a ranch or farm, something that would provide room and board, let the wanted man stay away from communities of people, and give him time to think of a plan. As the marshal rode up the main street in Smithview, Jason Nash came running out of his gun shop, waving a piece of paper in his hand and, loudly, proclaiming, "He is awake, Marshal, he is awake!"

Chapter Nine

It was the next evening, after hearing that Barton Anderson had awakened from his coma, that Marshal Tomes arrived back in Prestonburg. The marshal headed for Dr. Tilley's infirmary first, even though the sun was just about down. Tomes figured that someone would be there, if for no other reason than to watch over Barton.

The marshal's thoughts on Barton's whereabouts were confirmed as he rode up to the infirmary. Standing out front was the dark gray horse that Tomes knew would be where the tall rancher was still staying.

"Hi there, big gray!" were the opening remarks of this reunion with Tomes' equine friend. "You still keeping an eye on our tall friend, aren't you?"

Smoke shook his head up and down. Or at least you would think he did if you were there. The marshal tied Hickory to the hitching post and made his way into the infirmary, where he found Nurse Baird sitting at her desk, eating what looked like a meal that could have been prepared at Granny Ryan's.

"They always send too much for me to eat. In one sitting, would you like to have some supper, Marshal?" asked Nurse Baird.

"Thanks, but no thanks. I will try to find something later once I get caught up on the situation around here. I got a telegraph in Smithview that your tall patient had finally decided to wake up."

Nurse Baird, taking a sip of coffee, started her report. "It all started a couple of days ago. We first noticed him making a moaning sound, then he would try to speak, but it just came out as weak mumblings. He did that for a couple of hours, and he finally opened his eyes a little. He is still weak, and any activity or effort seems to wear him out for an hour or two, and then it all starts over again. That is how it has been until yesterday, when we had our first sign of improvement."

Marshal Tomes is now sitting on the front of the chair. "And what was this great moment of recovery from my friend?"

"He spoke for the first time. Just a few words, but clear enough to understand," responded Nurse Baird.

"What did he say? What did he say?" The marshal is now excited about this report of improvement and concerned that Barton might share information about the shoot-out in Rabbit Flat that didn't need to be shared quite yet.

The nurse chuckles, shakes her head, in an unbelieving fashion, and says, "He wanted to know if his horse was okay."

Tomes takes a moment to soak in this information, then busts out in laughter and states, "The man stood at the gates of Death for days, waiting to go in, you people were working hard to keep him out, I am worried about him, and the whole time, he is worried about that big, gray out there. That sounds pretty normal to me!" The marshal and Nurse Baird have a good laugh together at that thought.

Then, Marshal Tomes returns to the moment and asks, "How is Barton doing?

"To say that he is a lot better than when you brought him here would be too easy an answer. I will let Dr. Tilley give you all the particulars when you see him. He will be returning to the infirmary in an hour or so," replied Nurse Baird.

Marshal Tomes did not hear what he wanted to hear, in Nurse Baird's answer, so he asks her again, "How is Barton Anderson doing?"

The nurse got a furrow in her brow, pushed her plate away like something had taken her appetite away, and then comes a slow, carefully worded response. "Physically, the hardest part is probably over, if there are no surprise setbacks. We will, hopefully, see improvement over the next couple of days."

Marshal Tomes can tell that Nurse Baird has more on her mind, and he waits as she looks toward the door where Barton is kept. "I wouldn't say this to just anyone because I am held to the same confidentiality that a doctor is. But you seem to be a good friend and you are a lawman who is invested in all aspects of Mr. Anderson's situation. Dr. Tilley has another concern. I know he does, and he has kept it to himself for some reason. But I know there is something else that has his mind occupied. You don't work with a man for as long as I have and not be able to sense things. He doesn't think anyone else needs to know, including me, and I trust his judgment. Will you need to know? Only Dr. Tilley can decide that, and I will leave it to him to share with you if he feels he needs to."

Now, Tomes has gone from the reality of actual improvement to an unknown concern and has been given the chance that Dr. Tilley may not even discuss it, at least at this time.

Marshall Tomes stands up, thanks Nurse Baird for the information, and tells her that he will come back to the infirmary and talk with Dr. Tilley.

Nurse Baird said she would leave a note for the doctor, so he will be expecting Tomes when he comes back. She was sure that Dr. Tilley would be glad to see the marshal and could have a more in-depth discussion with Mr. Anderson's condition, prognosis, and future considerations.

Marshal Tomes tipped his hat, walked out the front door of the infirmary, where Smoke and Hickory stood, one tied to the hitching post and the big gray awaiting any news that the marshal might have. So Tomes rubbed Smoke's chin and shared a few words about Barton, and Smoke seemed satisfied, for now. Patience was not one of Smoke's shining qualities, but it is just a part of what made the big gray what he was, a rare jewel among horses and a fiercely loyal partner to the tall rancher.

The first stop was the telegraph office, and Tomes got there just as the clerk was locking up. Upon seeing the U.S. Marshal's badge of Tomes' chest, he put the key back in the front door and escorted his law guest back in and to the counter where the telegraph key, a pencil, and a pad of paper could be found. The telegrapher handed Tomes the pencil and the pad of paper, and said, "Here, Marshal, you know the drill."

Marshal Tomes has been in his share of telegraph offices, and he knew the protocol was always to be the same: keep it simple, keep it short. Most of the time, a lawman would not have to pay for the telegraph, but just sign the paper that the message was on, and then the telegraph office would send it to the U.S. Marshals office in Topeka, where it would act as an invoice to be reimbursed. Tomes never wanted to abuse the system, so this time would be no different.

```
In prestonburg few days, STOP.
Visit ford victim, STOP. Await
new info and orders from home
office. STOP.
```

Immediately after being handed the piece of paper, the telegrapher started sending the message. The clicks of the telegraph key were almost mesmerizing, and Tomes stood watching as, not doubting that the man at the key was able to do his job, but just having the peace of mind that the message was sent, and he could move on to the next stop.

"Marshal, it will probably be tomorrow morning before I hear anything back. I have sent enough messages from law men to know this one will not be a priority or will be sent to the appropriate official tonight. As soon as I hear something back from Topeka, I will find you and give it to you personally."

Tomes nodded his approval of this plan, as he still needed to get Hickory to the livery stable, and let the constable know that he was in town, just in case the constable's office has anything for a U.S. Marshall to handle or if they had heard anything new on Coy Newton.

Before taking Hickory to the livery stable, Tomes decided to walk across the street to make a short stop at Granny Ryan's eatery. Sissy, whom Tomes remembered as the young lady who served him last time, said if he was hungry that she could fix him a plate of the dinner special. Tomes, remembering that was what Nurse Baird was eating and how good it looked, said he would love to, but he had to get to the livery, the constable's office and back to the infirmary before it got too late. Sissy said she would have a plate sent to the doctor's office and it would be waiting for him when he got there. Tomes said he appreciated all the trouble she was willing to go to. With the nod of his head and the tip of his hat, the marshal stepped out the front door, grabbed Hickory's rein, and walked toward the blacksmith's stables, which were a few blocks away.

Tomes was about a block away from the livery when he could hear a hammer slamming against metal. He knew he would find a giant of a man at the end of that hammer. And, sure enough, there, swinging a ten-pound hammer like it was a child's toy, was Big Mike, covered in sweat, even though it was a cool fall evening.

"Hey, Marshal, I'm innocent! I promise I am!" was the salutation the blacksmith announced as Tomes opened the big entrance door to the stable building. Big Mike, with a big smile on his face, tossed down the hammer, took off his right leather glove and extended his huge hand with great anticipation. Tomes, having experienced one of Big Mike's handshakes before, put his hand forward and gritted his teeth. Big Mike didn't mean to hurt anyone. When he shook hands, the large man just never remembered that he had a size, and strength, advantage over everyone he met.

"Hello, sir!" Tomes responded, having a sincere appreciation for such a large man. For some reason, as they shook hands, Tomes thought of what a greeting would be like between Big Mike and Barton, the two men he had the most respect for, when it came to size and strength. Big Mike had gotten his strength from hard labor as a blacksmith, and the tall rancher got his from honest work on the ranch. Tomes chuckled to himself, as he was glad that both men could be counted as friends.

"You are keeping late hours. What could be so important that the owner of this fine establishment can't call it a day?"

Big Mike looked back at the anvil, and the piece of metal that was upon it, took a pause and said, "The

Smithview stage broke a wheel about a mile outside of town. I guess there were two bandits waiting on it, and when they came out of the bushes, the driver tried to outrun them and hit a chunk-hole and broke one of the wheels. Luckily, there were a couple of deputy sheriffs aboard, coming back from a trial in Loadstone and, along with the shotgun rider, they were able to turn the bandits back. As a matter of fact, one of the deputies said he thinks he wounded one of the outlaws. That the bandit was still sitting in his saddle, but his left arm was limp by his side, and he was slumped as he rode away. The only other damage suffered were a few new bullet holes to the stagecoach, and this broken wheel. I have to have it fixed by morning, as there is a passenger who is in a hurry to get to Smithview and is willing to pay extra if I can get him back on the trail. With five kids and Christmas coming up, I can use all the extra cash I can get. Are you going to be with us for a while, Marshal?"

Tomes didn't hear any of Big Mike's description of the day's events past the mention of two bandits. The marshal's mind raced as he contemplated if this could have been Coy Newton? Was he still in the area? Has he joined with a partner? Was the one bandit truly wounded and was that Newton? Should he leave and try to track down the bandits, knowing a wounded man will leave more tracks?

"Well marshal, are you going to be staying around Prestonburg for a time, especially since your friend over at the Doctors has finally woke up?"

When the big blacksmith mentioned Barton's plight, Tomes was reminded why he was in Prestonburg and that he needed to stay here for the continued search for answers, the handling of known facts and the preparation of the ramifications of "surprises" yet to come. The Anderson Family tragedy was his priority, and Barton was still the biggest piece missing from this puzzle.

"I'm sorry," Tomes finally answered to Big Mike's quizzing, "I don't know how long I will be here, but I am going to need to put Hickory up here, if you have the room? I will check with the constable for a sleeping spot at the jail."

Big Mike had already stepped around Tomes, taken Hickory by reins, and was leading the marshal's horse to a stall as the marshal was still occupied with the what ifs of the stagecoach attack.

"You, and this fine horse, are always welcome at Big Mike's Livery. And you might as well find you a soft corner here, as there will be no room at the jailhouse, as the town drunks and those two deputy sheriffs have taken all the beds in the cells there."

Armed with that information, Tomes figured to put off a visit to the constable's office until in the morning. Past interactions with this constable had proven, more times than not, to be less than fruitful encounters. Tomes simply performed these as acts of respect. The marshal had learned over the years that even if a local lawman wasn't able to contribute to an investigation or arrest, you never embarrassed a fellow officer by making him look inept or impotent. It is always better to have someone following you than get in your way. And Tomes' experience affirmed that an ignored local lawman is usually the latter.

"Thanks for the hospitality and the invitation. I will be back later this evening," Tomes shared as he took his saddle, blanket, saddlebags, and rifle sheath off Hickory and stepped out of the stall where Big Mike had placed

148

Him.

"I'll be here Marshal. Looks like it is going to be a late night for both of us." the huge man answered as he picked up his hammer and started back to work on the stagecoach wheel.

The marshal tipped his hat, as he walked out the big door of the livery, affirming that the big man had spoken true words, for Tomes didn't know what new information his visit to the doctor would uncover. What is the concern that Dr. Tilley has about Barton? If he won't share it with Nurse Baird, will he share it with Tomes? This question was still tumbling in the marshal's mind, like a gambler's dice, as he walked up the front steps of the infirmary porch.

Chapter Ten

"Dr. Tilley, it's U.S. Marshal Lyndon Tomes!"

Tomes announced his arrival as he walked through the front door of the infirmary. For some reason, the thought entered his mind that he would startle the doctor if he didn't let him know that someone was there. God forbid Dr. Tilley be performing a delicate procedure on a patient and he jerked his hands because he was caught off-guard by an unannounced presence in the infirmary. Tomes' concern was quickly quenched by the sound of a perturbed voice from across the dimly lit room.

"It's ten o'clock in the dang evening. I hate to be an inconvenience, but do you think you can make your entrance a little softer next time? This is an infirmary, not a blasted saloon!"

Tomes felt like walking back out the door and trying again in the morning. He recognized Dr. Tilley's voice, and he was fairly certain that he had accomplished the one thing that he was trying not to do, startle the doctor with his entrance. Tomes, suddenly, is presented with a possibility that the doctor was dozing in a chair, thus the low lighting in the front room, and he was awakened by Tomes' sincere attempt to avoid such a response.

Sure enough, as the marshal's eyes adjusted to the limited light in the room, he could see the form of a man leaning back against the wall in a cane-bottom chair. As fate would have it, it was a chair that the marshal himself had to sit in just a few hours earlier.

"Come on in, marshal. I have been expecting you, just not with such fanfare and flair", the doctor groused as he reached forward to turn up the coal-oil lamp that was sitting on the desk where Nurse Baird usually sat.

As the light started to fill the dusky room of the infirmary entrance, Tomes searched around the visitor's waiting room, found another chair, and pulled it up to the desk. Upon situating himself to where he was in front of the doctor, a smell caught his attention and his enraptured reaction must have been obvious, as Dr. Tilley smirked as he had some fun with the marshal.

"And I thought you had come here to enjoy my vast medical knowledge and charming personality; your face and growling stomach have betrayed your true intentions, Marshal. Your timing is impeccable as Sissy just dropped it off for you," the doctor said as he moved the globe lamp forward on the desk.

Tomes doesn't know what the proper etiquette is now, for he doesn't want to be rude and ignore Dr. Tilley by immediately diving into the meal that is, tantalizingly, sitting before him. But it has been a long time since his last meal, for he was in a hurry to get to Prestonburg to check on Barton. He hadn't even packed any beef jerky in his saddlebags to munch on as he traveled.

Dr. Tilley, taking his wire-rimmed glasses off and wiping them with a cotton patch he kept in his vest pocket, sensed the hesitation of the marshal to begin the consumption of this humble feast before him. So, he decided to give Tomes a nudge. "Marshal, I am going to wash up a bit, then put on a fresh pot of coffee. You're going to need something to go with your meal, and we are going to need something to help keep us awake. I think we have a lot to talk about and the evening is getting late already."

Tomes nodded his appreciation of the doctor's understanding, and grabbed the silverware by the plate,

151

and started to dig in. The job of a U.S. Marshal calls for sacrifices, whether that be time, rest, personal life and even something as simple as eating. Many meals are bypassed because performing his duty can depend upon being in the right place at the right time. And if the timing of apprehending an outlaw, or stopping an unlawful act, depended on something being forsaken, then taking time to eat too often got moved to the back of the schedule. But, for this moment in time, there was nothing that needed to push aside this savory opportunity to keep himself nourished and able to do his job. Even he didn't know when the next chance would come to sit down like this again.

Tomes was just getting to the apple pie when Dr. Tilley sat down with the coffeepot and two coffee cups. He first poured the marshal a cup and then grabbed the second cup, poured it full, set down the coffeepot and took a slow sip of the freshly brewed drink. The doctor felt a kinship and understanding of how precious this time was to the marshal, as doctors must make the same sacrifices to perform their callings, that many a needed meal had been missed while trying to keep a fellow human being alive.

"You go ahead and finish. We have all night, if we need it, to get caught up. Your friend isn't going anywhere tonight. I know you have many questions about him, so here it is, the best I can share it. He is a lucky man; some are calling him the miracle man. I can't ever offer false hope to anyone's situation, and I can't ever totally write anyone off. A lot of what I do depends on the ability to keep working, to keep trying, to keep reaching into my knowledge and my experience, hoping the next effort will be what turns it around and keeps a life this side of the pearly gates. There were a couple of times I didn't know if I had the aptitude, or the tools, to get Mr. Anderson to the next breath and the next heartbeat. But, between Nurse Baird and that big gray horse out there, I knew I had a support system that could get us to advance on, no matter how small that step seemed. In this business, you don't take any victories for granted. Size doesn't matter because it may be what turns the whole thing around."

Tomes, by now finished, takes a swallow of coffee, and prepares to join in the conversation.

"I will be honest, there were a few times I wouldn't have been surprised if someone had brought me a telegram stating that Barton had lost his battle, that someone needed to come and take him home to rest with his family. But, while my mind wanted to go there, my heart just wouldn't allow it to stay. You're a good doctor, never doubted that, but I know that tall man in there, and I know how strong he is. Fortunately, or unfortunately, I know he has a hurt inside him that is raging. That the tragic end of his family must be avenged, and that drive for vengeance can give rise to a man, whether that's right or not. Barton lost everything in his life that mattered, and all he has left is this one cause, and it may be the only Bible truth that he cares to live by right now: an eye for an eye. And that may have been what kept that man from succumbing to a freshly dug grave."

Dr. Tilley rubbed his chin with his hand and replied, "I thought I had heard of just about every evil there was in this world and Hell itself, until the news reached Prestonburg about the Anderson family. What happened to that man's family is beyond sad. It's unfathomable. And, however he felt his family needed to be avenged, whatever act he has performed to that end, then I don't know of many God-fearing people that will feel like he wasn't vindicated to seek justice, whatever form he felt like that needed to take. And, if that took place with or without the help of the law, maybe it's just something a person will have to work out with their Maker, when that time of judgment comes."

It is at this point in what has been one man's monologue that Tomes realizes that Dr. Tilley is talking in terms that implies that this has already happened. Could it be that the doctor is in possession of knowledge about the tall rancher that has been gleaned beyond what information that the marshal has felt he could share? Tomes had only discussed previously who Barton was, where he was from, and the bare facts of how he was wounded. But the medical man is talking of "vindication" and "justice" with or without the law. Why would the doctor feel Barton would need to be vindicated, unless... The only two people who have all the facts of what happened in the saloon in Rabbit Flat are the marshal and the patient in the other room. Could it be that Barton had been doing more than mumbling or asking about the big gray horse? Have Tomes' concerns and fears become realities? Where does he take this conversation to find out exactly what, if anything, Dr. Tilley knows? Will Tomes be given the same consideration as Nurse Baird and be placed into a need-to-know classification? And would now be the time for the marshal to know?

Tomes' concerns about where to direct this discussion were immediately resolved with Dr. Tilley's next words. "Yes, I know that the story that has been going around Prestonburg, about that day in Rabbit Flat, is not what happened. I am fairly convinced that tale is the result of some hot air from our nincompoop town constable. Our poor excuse of a lawman has a lack of ability to discern the truth from fantasy."

At this point, Tomes has a death grip on his coffee cup, and hasn't taken a breath for what seems like forever. But he knows to stay quiet and let the doctor continue down this path of discovery, confession or whatever this was that Dr. Tilley felt like he needed to release into the marshal's cognitive custody. Years of experience had taught Tomes that saying nothing was often the most profitable part of a lawman's communication, and often got him where he needed to go faster.

"It started out as mumbling," the doctor continued. "I couldn't make out but a word or two. Then, your friend started putting together one- or two-word expressions. This went on for a couple of days. I wondered if what he was saying or attempting to say was from the injuries? Was it from the medicines that I had given him to fight infection or ease his pain? Was he hallucinating or was he recalling actual things that happened? Whatever was causing these ramblings, it was also causing him great distress because it appeared that he was reliving some fierce things in his mind. At some point, I became very concerned about him relapsing or worse. I was also concerned he might go into some of these dynamic episodes while Nurse Baird was in the room. So, to ease his battle and to ensure that his rantings stay between him and me, I gave him something to comfort him and cause him to rest more than talk when I wasn't with him."

Tomes is now sitting on the front edge of the oak chair. "What did he say, Doc? What do you know that makes you think Barton needs vindication?"

Dr. Tilley reaches for the coffeepot and pours himself a hot refill, using this moment to gather his thoughts and his words. He knows that the future of Barton Anderson could rest upon where this discussion goes from this point, as the doctor knows he is talking to his patient's friend, but also a sworn U.S. Marshal. The doctor doesn't know which personality will take this information and run with it.

"First, let me say this," the physician restarts his story with his right hand up, almost in a stature to assure Tomes. "When I first became a doctor, I took an oath to protect the privacy of any person I may treat. So, it doesn't matter what you say, it doesn't matter what your friend in there says. Heck, it doesn't matter if that big, gray horse was to speak in perfect King's English. I couldn't repeat what he says. No matter what I have heard in the performing of my medical duties, I cannot, and will not, repeat it. Do you believe that?"

It takes Tomes a second to respond, because the marshal is trying not to laugh at the thought of Smoke talking.

"Yes, sir! I believe you and I trust you, especially after Nurse Baird told me that there was something concerning you, but you would not even share it with her," Tomes replies as he takes a sip of hot coffee and waits for the next revelation from Dr. Tilley.

The doctor gets up, turns, and stares at the door, behind which lays the man at the center of all discussion this night. One last moment, he considers if he is getting ready to cross the line of his Hippocratic oath. Because if he does, he knows he can't come back. Anything he shares now will be considered freely given information in any legal investigation or hearing.

"The first thing he said that I could understand, was a name, Jenny. He would say it in an anguished tone, never in a strong or hailing manner. I noticed that his lip would tremble when he would speak this name. It was the only name that he ever spoke. Having never met Mr. Anderson before you brought him here, I am going to venture to say that Jenny was his wife, right?"

The marshal nodded his head to affirm that the doctor's statement was right. Tomes hadn't spoken Jenny's name in a while, for his mind would always go back to that tragic morning when he walked in on Barton, holding the body of his precious wife. It was a gruesome picture that the marshal was sure he would never get out of his mind. But he could, at least, control its reappearance by not speaking of it. For now, Tomes could not let an emotional experience get in the way of letting Dr. Tilley continue with his recounting of what Barton had spoken.

The doctor, not noticing the struggle that Tomes was having to keep his composure, continued with his retracing of his encounters with Barton, that has painted a picture of that day in Rabbit Flat.

"The next thing that your friend seemed to be saying was, what I interpreted to be, an encounter of some sort. Or, maybe I should say his attempt to avoid an encounter, as he would repeat, 'Don't do it, don't do it. I'll give you the same.' Nothing more, just that warning. Could it have been a hope that he had, that whatever it was would not happen? He wasn't anguished about this, like when he spoke the woman's name, but more resolved and ready for this".

Marshal Tomes, in his mind, has an idea that this has

to do with Curt, the saloon owner's son. The marshal, recalling the scene at the card table, wonders if the boy was reaching for the gun that was lying on the table. Was there enough goodness, still left somewhere in Barton, to give the young man a chance to walk away that intense morning? If that was the case, then Tomes could report that Barton had reacted in self-defense in the shooting of all three men. No jury would find him guilty, and no judge would sentence him to any time in prison, considering what Ford and Beeler had done to his family. If Barton had to shoot Curt because the young man went for his gun, then Barton was, as the doctor had previously stated, vindicated.

Tomes, now feeling a little more encouraged about what he would report, asks Dr. Tilley if those were the only things Barton had uttered.

"I wish it was," the doctor responded as he curled his lower lip over his upper lip, in an act of apparent hesitation, "I would be remorse if I didn't tell you about this morning. It was about an hour before Nurse Baird got here to relieve me. I was sitting by the bed, listening to his heart, and getting ready to give him a drink of water. Then suddenly, he sat up in the bed, extended his arm out like he was holding something, and growled, 'Kiss the flames of hell, you son of a bitch!' Scared the living crap out of me when he did it. He hadn't moved before, hadn't spoken above a soft volume, and then he does that out of the blue. I got him to lie down, gave him something to calm him down, and that is the last thing he has said, or has tried to say, since. What do you think he was seeing, Marshal?"

"I don't know, Doc." Tomes is now wondering if this proclamation was directed at Ford, Beeler, or Curt. If he

158

spewed it at Ford or Beeler, then it could be understood. But if he is speaking to Curt, and the boy hasn't made a move for the gun, then this starts opening the possibility of a charge of a premeditated action. Tomes is starting to have concerns again about what future legal hurdles his tall friend may be facing. The only person who knows what truly went on that morning in Rabbit Flat is the man who lays beyond that door.

"Doc, where do we go from here? I mean, medically for Barton."

Dr. Tilley turns to face the marshal and answers, "My first thought is to not give him any more medicine to calm him. We won't truly know what condition he is in, unless we let all his faculties wake up and see what he is able to do, to move, to say under his own power. I will keep vigil tonight, and if he has any more dreams, nightmares, or visions, and they cause him stress, I will treat him. We will try to bring him to a greater state of awareness later."

"If I may suggest another thought," Tomes responds. "You haven't slept in your own bed in over a week, and I don't have any place to lay my head tonight, other than a pile of dusty straw in the corner of the livery stable. What if I take your cot here in the office, and you go home and catch up on your rest? I think, from this point on, Barton could greatly benefit from a physician that is at the top of his form, both physically and mentally."

"I guess I could show you what to give Mr. Anderson, if he gets wound up again," the doctor reasons. "My wife has probably forgotten she is married, no more than I have been home lately. If you do encounter any problems with the patient, the medicine will put him out until I get back in a few hours. I will try to return before Nurse

159

Baird gets here around seven in the morning."

Dr. Tilley shows Tomes the bottle of relaxant that he has been administering to Barton when he gets disturbed and tells him how much to give him. After receiving the doctor's final instructions and wishing him a good night, the marshal takes off his hat and holster and lays them on the desk and sits on the edge of the cot. The ticking of an old pendulum clock on the top shelf of a bookcase across the room reminds Tomes that time is slipping away, in more ways than one. Morning will come soon, and so will the next steps of a journey that no one at this point in time knows how it will continue, or what the eventual end of the trip will look like.

Dr. Tilley opens the door to Barton's room, a slight crack in case the tall rancher has any more episodes of distressing dreams. This will give the marshal a chance to hear him and go to his aid. As the doc reaches the front door, he turns to the marshal, who is now laying on the bed, with his hands behind his head.

"Can I ask you something, Marshal?" the weary eyed physician asks, as he prepares to go out into the cool night.

"Sure, Doc. What else could be on your mind tonight?"

"I know you are a man of principle and duty, and I know that man is a valued friend of yours," the doctor starts with an observation and then comes the inquiry. "When you take him back to Smithview, and I know you will have to, what is going to happen to him?"

"The when is up to you, him, and the good Lord, Doc. The what is up to a judge and jury," Tomes simply replies as he closes his eyes.

Chapter Eleven

It had been four days since Marshal Tomes had arrived in Prestonburg upon hearing that Barton had awakened from his unconsciousness. He had spread his time in checking on the tall rancher, riding to Rabbit Flat to talk with those who experienced the two-day rage of the outlaws, helping local law with a couple of skirmishes with ranch hands and trail riders, having the bodies of Ford and Beeler buried and staying in touch with the Marshal's office in Topeka. Up to this point, Tomes' reports about that morning in Rabbit Flat have stated the following: That the three dead men were victims of a gunfight, brought on by their own reckless actions and heavy drinking. Sworn witness accounts attested to hours of drinking, vandalism, and emboldened threatening of townspeople. Location of the fourth outlaw was still unknown. The citizen, wounded in his encounter with these men, still had not been able to recall all the facts of the events of that morning. That this victim continued to recover from his life-threatening wounds. And that he will continue to talk with the citizen victim and report any new aspects immediately.

The last part of his official report on the ongoing investigation had been accepted by the home office for now. Tomes knew it wasn't exactly a clear picture of the situation. For it wasn't that Barton wasn't able to recall all the facts of Rabbit Flat, but more like he was unwilling to say anything about what happened that deadly morning.

This morning might be a step in the right direction. Maybe not restoring the friendship, but at least enough trust to talk with Tomes. Dr. Tilley, against his own medical judgment, has agreed to let Tomes take Barton out on a short ride. Other than short sits on the front porch of the infirmary, Barton has been isolated to his room there. Tomes feels like if Barton can get away from there, just to sit on Smoke again for whatever short time and distance that might be, it could help. To feel his horse underneath him, to see the world again, might brighten the rancher's stone-cold attitude and give him reason to open up and communicate. At this point, Tomes is willing to settle for any conversation, even if it were weather conditions or cattle prices.

"Mr. Anderson, your friend with the U.S. marshal's badge seems to think that you are ready to get out of our fine infirmary for a bit and get some fresh air on that big gray horse out there. I know that fine steed would probably be up to it. But I have my reservations about such an endeavor. If you open your wound again, or show any signs of internal trauma, it will mean staying in that bed for as long as it takes to satisfy my professional opinion. I am going to leave it up to you, sir."

When Dr. Tilley presents Barton with the chance to sit on his old friend again, he doesn't act one way or another. The tall rancher slowly rises off the side of the bed and walks out of his room. Nurse Baird offers Barton a coat that belongs to her husband that she had brought from home, but he pushes it away. The nurse, and the marshal, then try to help him walk to the front door. But he jerks his arms away from both and continues his path to the outdoors that awaits. As they walk along, Dr. Tilley is walking behind them, constantly telling the marshal that he must conduct this little exercise in emotional and mental therapy exactly as the doctor has agreed: 30 minutes maximum, walking pace only, away from other people and horses, and return to the infirmary with rest afterward. If it all goes as the doctor has agreed to, they might try it again in the afternoon. Tomes assures Dr. Tilley that he will do his part to make this work, but there is no response from Barton, as he just stares at nothing in particular.

When the doctor starts to explain to Barton that this is not a joke and is against everything that is within him, it is then that everyone sees why there is no verbal answer to the doctor's statement. Barton was standing on the front edge of the porch, his left arm wrapped around a porch post to steady himself. With his other arm outstretched, he is cupping his hand while holding the chin of the big gray horse. Smoke had gently walked up to Barton, as if knowing this was not going to be a usual free-spirited ride, but his rancher friend would need some special considerations today. Barton said nothing as he stood there, just gently rubbing the soft underside of the great steed's muzzle. Smoke stood there with his eyes half-closed, and his right hind leg relaxed. It had been a while since horse and rider had connected like this. Nurse Baird put her hands up to her face and softly said, "Oh, my goodness." Tomes stood there, observing a sight that he had seen numerous times, and wondered if the big, gray horse could do what no one else had been able to do to this point in time, and that being reach inside a part of Barton's humanity that was still available to caring or concern. Dr. Tilley, turning to go back inside the infirmary, smiled and said, "Remember... 30 minutes, that's it!"

One of the stipulations that Dr. Tilley had about taking this ride was that Barton was not about to mount Smoke from the ground. The doctor had a fear of reopening the wound, getting bleeding started again, or Barton losing his balance and falling to the ground before anyone could catch him. So, Smoke allowed Tomes to position him against the front of the porch floor, where Barton could just simply throw his leg over the saddle and sit. Smoke didn't move an inch, as Barton slowly and carefully walked up to the side of his equine friend, gently raised his leg up over the saddle, and then sort of slid into the leather seat. Nurse Baird held her breath, wanting to help Barton, but knowing that he was not open to any kind of assistance. Once Tomes was convinced that Barton was stable upon the big gray horse, the marshal turned to get upon Hickory. Big Mike had brought the chestnut horse from the livery after the blacksmith heard of this endeavor to reunite the tall man with his faithful horse.

Tomes' plan was to take the back alleys out of town, staying off the main streets that would be more heavily traveled, and where more people would be able to watch them. Although almost everyone knew of the visiting patient at the infirmary, no one had seen him. Tomes was afraid, out of curiosity or concern, that there could be a lot of talking, staring, pointing and other displays that could cause Barton to become uncomfortable and unwilling to open up or relax, to the point that Tomes could establish some sort of conversation. Anything would be better than what had been offered up to now.

The first ten minutes were uneventful, and Tomes knows he must be patient, and let things play out. If this thirty-minute exercise only results in Barton and Smoke being reunited and his friend getting a feel of something that used to mean the world to him, a good ride upon the big gray horse, then that would be a foundation to build on. Tomes didn't want to antagonize Barton or make him feel like the marshal was trying to corner him into something or herding him into a direction that Barton didn't want to go or wasn't ready yet.

At some point, Tomes notices that Barton's hand, which had been holding onto the saddle horn to steady himself, is now rubbing Smoke's strong, smooth neck in a very simple, caring motion. Tomes makes it a point to remember that what Barton does may tell the marshal more than what the tall man says. The small things could let the marshal know if what was going on was relaxing Barton, or causing him to withdraw into that dark, emotional place he had resided in since coming out of his coma. Tomes fondly recalls how often when riding with Barton on a trail somewhere, that if he and the rancher ran out of things to talk about, then Barton would talk to Smoke. Not in broken sentences or childish gibberish, but the tall man would speak in a way he would speak to any person. And Smoke seemed to be listening to every word and would even make a sound or move his head to prove he was following along. Again, Tomes was always amazed at the relationship between the rancher and the big gray horse.

In keeping with the doctor's rules for taking Barton out for a ride, Tomes got him back to the infirmary with a couple of minutes to spare. Dr. Tilley, Nurse Baird, and Big Mike were all waiting on the front porch, all looking like they couldn't wait for a report on the outing. Tomes jumped down off Hickory, and Big Mike said he would take the chestnut horse back to the stable, feed him and brush him down. The marshal thanked him for his kindness. When Tomes turned to position Smoke close to the porch, where Barton could get off easily, he saw that there would be no need for the marshal's assistance. Smoke had already walked up to the front edge of the porch floor, and Barton was sliding himself out of the saddle with Nurse Baird's assistance. Tomes made a note that Barton was allowing someone to help him, where before he didn't want anyone's help, and jerked his arms away from any attempt. Could this first investment in trying to reach Barton's trust have paid off? Tomes could wait until they tried again in the afternoon.

While Nurse Baird was walking beside Barton as he returned to his infirmary room, Dr. Tilley handed Tomes a piece of paper. "The telegrapher brought this to you a few minutes ago. I haven't looked at it, nor anyone else. But the look on the telegrapher's face told me that it might contain information that you wouldn't find especially comforting at this time."

Tomes unfolded the telegraph message, and he sighed as he read it:

```
Governor    wants    rabbit    flat
solved.    STOP.    Saloon    owner
causing   problems.   STOP.   Get
surviving   citizen   to   hearing
asap. STOP. Judge likens ready
to convene in Smithview. STOP.
```

The marshal realized that his plan to be patient and wait upon Barton's retelling of the events of Rabbit Flat may be out the window with this revelation. As long as it was just him investigating and controlling the flow of the search, Tomes knew he could keep the case away from legal, and political, influence. The marshal has even been able to keep Barton's name out of it, simply referring to him as the "citizen victim" in his reports. Only Dr. Tilley, Nurse Baird, and Granny Ryan had any clue as to who he was and what part he had played in the Rabbit Flat shooting.

But now, this has reached the top office of the state government, and his bosses were not going to be as easy to put off now that they had executive pressure being applied to them to wrap this up. If Tomes can't show signs of progress, and soon, then the U.S. Marshal's office would be sending someone to check on why he wasn't getting anything accomplished. Then he would not be able to keep Barton in the shadows of a growing inquiry. Plus, Judge Jacob Likens was widely known as a charismatic, by-the-book adjudicator, who was not shy to publicity or the spotlight. He often ruled without showing any sign of compassion or consideration, but always had a smile for the newspapers.

"Doc, how soon do you think Barton will be able to ride back to Smithview?"

"Are you kidding me?" Dr. Tilley bellows. "The man was on death's door for almost a week and you're asking me when you can throw him on a horse and ride back to Smithview for whatever may be waiting for him. Marshal, you just got back from a thirty-minute casual ride and he's done in. Blast it, you had this on your mind all along!"

Tomes says nothing, just hands the telegraph to the doctor and lets it do all the talking. After looking over the message from the U.S. Marshal's office, Dr. Tilley rubs his chin, hands it back to Tomes and backtracks on his previous tirade.

"Well, I guess I should say I am sorry for bringing the heat on you, but you could have at least told me where that moronic idea came from. They can't be serious in thinking this man is in any shape to withstand the trip to

Smithview. Especially not now, are they?"

Tomes, having worked with those in high government offices, and knowing that his supervisors often bent to their political whims and wishes too easy, just shakes his head in mock disbelief, folds the paper and puts it in his coat pocket. "I don't know who this saloon owner is, but he has the attention of the governor. The governor has the attention of my bosses. They have my attention, and I have now brought it to your attention. How long until he is ready to ride? I am sure they will respect your medical opinion up to a point."

"Maybe I should send them a telegram and tell them I don't give a damn about what they think or want," proclaims Dr. Tilley, who is starting to sound like Reverend Sutton when he gets started on one of his stem-winding sermons. "These political hacks and office law dogs don't sit and hold a man's guts together, trying to stop the bleeding and keep the breathing going. Nor tell a man he is going to make it when I know he probably won't. They haven't listened as grown men cry for their wives, mothers or anyone who might be on their minds and hearts at that moment. Sorry, he will leave here when I think he is ready and not a second sooner!"

The marshal lowers his head, so the doctor can't see the slight smile on his face from listening to the saw bone's blistering diatribe. "Doc, you are preaching in the choir. I don't want to get halfway to Smithview and Barton start having a relapse or some medical event that is far beyond my simple abilities to slap on a bandage or administer a dose of medicine. I share your concerns, and some of your opinions, of our political office holders and some of my bosses who seem to have gotten overcome with the smell of their fancy office furniture and lost what it's like out here in the dust and the daylight. But here is a truth that can't be wished away: your patient's future is a legal situation, as well as a medical situation. And I have got to find a way to keep the balance between keeping him healthy and keeping him ahead of a mess that could be built. Here is my promise: whether it takes two, three or four days; whether it takes a horse, a buggy, or a stagecoach; I will do my best to get my friend back home and honor your wisdom and experience in doing so. That is what I promise."

Dr. Tilley leaned back against the porch post, took off his wire-rimmed glasses and looked at Smoke, who was standing there like he was ready to start the journey immediately. "That horse may be the best friend Mr. Anderson has, but he is an awfully lucky man to have a friend like you on his side. Do you get this attached to all the people you encounter, marshal?"

"No. Doc. Because I have never met anyone like that man in there. Anytime I have needed help, Barton has never said no. And, more than once, he has put his life on the line, that he might save mine. He's never asked for anything in return, except my continued friendship. The man I once knew may be gone, and that is a shame that I wish me, you, the Good Lord, or someone could overcome. But one thing is for sure; Barton Anderson is still my friend until he gives me reason to believe otherwise. And whether I like it or not, I may be all the help he has left. If that is the case, then I will stand with him for as long as he needs me. I feel like I owe it to him. I know this. I owe it to him to help him find what you said once before: vindication."

"Marshal, if it was any other lawman, I wouldn't even consider a plan short of what I know he needs. But you offer a compelling argument, and I believe I can trust you with my patient. You get in touch with those knot heads at your home office and tell them this is how it's going to work, and there are no negotiations. We will continue to monitor him, treat him, build up his strength with your horseback outings for three more days. If he meets my examination for travel, you and he will take a slow trek to Smithview, taking no less than two days to complete it. I trust that big, gray horse more than I do any stagecoach or buggy, so that will be how you transport him there. Nurse Baird and I will pack you a special bag of medical supplies in case you encounter any minor episodes or occurrences. That is the deal. If they can't live with that, then tell them it may be spring before I give him medical clearance to travel. You just can't tell how many setbacks he might have between now and then," Doc Tilley groused with a wink, then turned to walk back into the infirmary to check on his patient.

"Oh, I think my superiors can live with that. Especially if they think their other possible option is waiting until spring for a closure to this." Tomes smirked, as his mind starts racing with the things that would have to be done over the next 72 hours.

The marshal has two goals to achieve in the next few days: get Barton prepared for the long trip ahead and get him prepared for whatever awaits them in Smithview. The trip seems to be the lesser concern, as Tomes has a pretty clear idea of how to take his friend back. But until Barton starts talking about what happened at the saloon in Rabbit Flat, Tomes' hands are tied when it comes to a plan to maneuver his friend through the legal loopholes and legalese, praying it doesn't end in incarceration, pronounced by a judge looking for a legacy.

Yes, adequate time is not a luxury the marshal has, and it is becoming more valuable by the minute.

Chapter Twelve

It was a cool November morning, as preparations were being finished for the trip to Smithview. The three days of arraigning, and re-arraigning, had gone by quickly. Tomes had gotten approval, from the U.S. Marshal's office, of the plan to return to Smithview. Judge Likens would be waiting to hold a hearing on the happenings at Rabbit Flat. The judge had already announced that it would be held under the rules of a bench trial as Barton's standing in the community would make it near impossible to find a jury that would not be partial. Curt's father, who owned the saloon where the shootings took place, was demanding that his son get justice and he wanted his say in court. This added more concern for Tomes as he had counted on the hometown people to give Barton a compassionate ruling, considering what had happened to his family. But now, Barton's future rests in the hands of one man. Tomes now has two days to get the story out of Barton, if there is any chance to keep his friend from a ruling that could be punitive, rather than merciful, under the circumstances.

Dr. Tilley had reluctantly given his approval for this journey. He said that Barton's outer wound was healing well, considering all that the tall man had been through. But the doctor still had concerns about any internal trauma that might still be tender and susceptible to the travel. Barton's strength had shown steady improvement, which Nurse Baird attributed to Barton's appetite returning. Between Nurse Baird's cooking, and the occasional surprise delivery from Granny Ryan's place, the patient was getting good nourishment regularly.

Barton always ate alone, but he ate well, and that was a good sign.

During the seventy-two-hour period of preparation, the thirty-minute walk on Smoke had evolved into three hours of casual riding. Tomes had promised that they would keep their trek to Smithview on level land and roads, no shortcuts across the hill country. And that they would take periodic rest breaks to check Barton's wounds and condition. Tomes also knew of a couple of vacant shacks where they could spend the night and get in out of the cooler November air. He had used these rustic shelters on previous rounds as a U.S. Marshal and didn't think the owners would mind. Maybe in the quiet of the evening, both men relaxing next to a warming fire, that conversation that Tomes sought so desperately would offer itself. Somehow, Barton would take another step to normal if normalcy would ever be a part of his world again.

Big Mike showed up around sunrise at the infirmary with a suggestion for the marshal, which Tomes was grateful for. The blacksmith, in addition to bringing Hickory saddled and ready to go, also brought a pack horse to take along. Everyone, up to this point, has been thinking of all the supplies that would be needed to take this journey: medical items, clothes, blankets, water, food, cooking utensils, and the like. But Big Mike suggested the third horse, as to keep Smoke and Hickory as fresh as possible. Tomes asked the huge blacksmith if he trusted this horse for the task. Big Mike chuckled out loud and responded, "If I didn't, wouldn't have suggested it and wouldn't have brought it." Tomes reached out and shook the blacksmith's huge hand and thanked him for all he had done during this time. Big Mike just nodded his head and started loading the supplies on the packhorse.

Tomes turned just as Dr. Tilley came out onto the porch of the infirmary.

"Well, Marshal, here is your passenger. It's up to you now!"

Within moments, Barton walked out with Nurse Baird following behind him, her eyes locked upon Barton's every step and movement. He still refused any hands-on attention or direction, but he would, reluctantly, allow Nurse Baird to assist him if he felt he might falter. Maybe it was her soft voice, or her gentle way, but she was gifted with the ability to manage patients without them feeling lessened or manipulated. Again, the signs of personality change may be small, but they were real and, hopefully, would lead to that place Tomes needed to go before they get to Smithview.

Up to this point in time, Tomes hadn't established any talk with the tall man, other than the marshal trying to start a conversation and being met with a usual response of "I guess" or "doesn't matter", or that cold stare that told Tomes to give it a rest for a while. Tomes was learning that Barton may not be willing to have talks for old times' sake, but he could communicate, and Tomes was rapidly learning this new language.

Smoke had learned this routine of Barton getting on from the porch. Tomes didn't even have to show him or lead him. When he saw Nurse Baird and Barton standing and waiting on the front edge, the big, gray horse would walk over and position himself as close as he could. Barton was getting more stable and confident each time he mounted Smoke for one of their therapy rides, as the doctor would call them. Tomes was thankful for the improvements that Barton had experienced in such short

174

a time. No matter though, he would not push it, take any chances, or get foolish in the return to Smithview. He owed a successful journey to Barton, to Dr. Tilley, to Nurse Baird, and to himself. In one way or another, they all had something to gain, or lose, by how this adventure played out.

When Big Mike had finished loading the pack horse and Barton has mounted Smoke and appeared ready, Tomes walked over to the front of the porch, where Dr. Tilley and Nurse Baird stood, extended his hand, and said, "I can't say it's been a total pleasure, but I can say it has been an experience I will never forget. Thank you, don't seem like it's enough, but I offer it with all sincerity. I didn't know if this day would come. But you two rose to the need, and far surpassed it. I will let you know when we get to Smithview. When you figure up the cost of Barton's stay, send the bill to the sheriff's office there, and I will get you reimbursed as soon as I can."

"I think I speak for Nurse Baird and myself," Dr. Tilley started as he firmly squeezed the marshal's hand. "There are times when we wonder if we really make a difference, other than the occasional cut, bruise, or broken bone. Today, we are proud to be medical practitioners and glad we were entrusted with this man's life. As for the bill, it has been amazing how money would show up on the front porch, in cans, jars and envelopes, simply marked 'for the stranger'. You, and your friend, haven't been here a great period, but you leave having made a great impression upon the people of Prestonburg."

"Heck, Doc! Even corn, oats, and apples would mysteriously show up for Smoke and Hickory. Don't forget them!" joked Big Mike, as everyone laughed.

175

Everyone but Barton. And when Tomes had noticed that he realized it was time to cut the goodbyes short and get started on their way. So, the marshal mounted Hickory, gently applied his heels to the chestnut's sides, and headed east toward Smithview. As they were getting to where they would be out of sight, Tomes turned to wave goodbye. Everyone waved back, with Nurse Baird waving with one hand and covering her mouth with the other. The marshal was pretty sure that she was crying. And then they were out of sight.

Chapter Thirteen

The first four hours of the two men's trip went well. Nothing out of the ordinary popped up, and Tomes was relieved with that. The schedule that the marshal had formed in his mind was to ride for an hour or two, depending on how Barton was enduring the ride. They would stop, let the horses take a break, and Tomes would let them drink some water out of a coffee cup that he had put in the supply pack. The marshal would tell Barton to just rest on Smoke, so he wouldn't run the risk of opening his wound or get any other injuries from getting on and off his horse. Once the horses and riders were rested, they would resume their trek to Smithview.

When he noticed that the sun was straight up in the sky, Tomes turned to Barton and said they would stop long enough to have lunch. Before they left Prestonburg, Granny Ryan had sent food for them to take with. The goodwill basket contained some pan-cooked chicken, corn-on-the-cob, and fluffy biscuits stuffed with strawberry jam. Nurse Baird had filled a canteen with black coffee, so they would have a break from drinking water alone. Tomes got down from Hickory, took the basket from the packhorse, set it on a nearby rock, and started to prepare a meal for Barton. The marshal took a piece of chicken, a cob of corn and a biscuit, placed them in a cloth checkered napkin, and handed it to his tall friend, still sitting astride Smoke. Barton didn't say anything. He just took the napkin with its contents, and placed it between the saddle horn and the butt of his rifle, which was placed in its sheath. There it would sit securely as he ate with one hand and held a cup of coffee with the other.

Once he saw that Barton was satisfied and steady, Tomes returned to where he had set the basket and doled out some lunch for himself. For the next twenty minutes, both men concentrated on their meals. The horses munched on a few oats out of bags Big Mike had sent along. All was quiet and good on the road to Smithview. Tomes said a little prayer that this would be the theme of the rest of the trip, no matter how long it might take to get there.

After Tomes got everything placed back on the packhorse, he mounted Hickory, and the little caravan resumed its journey. The marshal figured this would be a good time to enjoy a post-meal cigarette, as Barton didn't seem interested in any kind of conversation. So Tomes reached into his pocket to retrieve his tobacco pouch and papers. It was then that he remembered that he had put a telegram there, one that the constable of Prestonburg had given him before they left the infirmary that morning. He hadn't looked at it because there was so much going on in preparing to get Barton ready for the trip. Tomes figured it was just another approval of his plans for the upcoming ride. The U. S. Marshal's office didn't always have new information on their telegrams; they were more reminders that they were expecting reports and results. Tomes almost dropped the tobacco pouch as he unfolded the yellow piece of paper and read:

```
Coy    Newton    robs    proffitt
freight    wagon.    STOP.    Kills
shotgun    rider.    STOP.    Thirty
miles from your location. STOP.
```

Not that it would have made any difference in their current plans, but Tomes now has an unexpected factor to keep in the back of his mind. Proffitt was a freight company that operated in the area between Prestonburg, Smithview and a few smaller towns that dotted the map. The family-owned company dealt in hauling farm hardware, mine equipment, bulk sundry items and the like. If it was convenient to their main delivery and destination, they were known to transport smaller amounts of gold and silver retrieved from the mines. On the rarest of occasions, Proffitt Freight would convey a payroll to one of the larger ranches in the area. Mostly, they hauled plows, tools, pickaxes, and items that would not be worth a bandit taking the risk of getting caught or killed over. But Coy Newton may be so desperate that he would settle for the watch in the wagon driver's pocket. Arnie Proffitt, the owner of the company, would usually drive the freight wagon. One of his sons would serve as shotgun rider. Tomes grimaced as he realized that the Proffitt family had probably suffered a tragic loss at the hands of Newton. Any other time, this would be an issue for a U. S. marshal to investigate. But today, Tomes' attention will have to be directed to the matter at hand, getting Barton safely to Smithview.

An idea did cross the marshal's mind; could the information in the telegram be a way to start a conversation with Barton? Tomes had not informed Barton about Coy Newton, at least by name, as being one of the Ford gang that was at his ranch that morning. Nor had Tomes shared with him that Newton had, apparently, slipped away during the shootout at the saloon in Rabbit Flat. The marshal had resolved to not give that particular information to his friend, for fear of causing Barton to become upset over the thought of one of the Ford gang still on the loose. Also, Tomes would have to worry about the tall man planning to continue his one-man quest for vengeance for his family. For now, Tomes had the situation with Barton under control. That is what he will try to protect and preserve.

"Hey Barton, I was handed a telegram before we left this morning. I had forgotten all about it. Seems like a fellow named Coy Newton held up the Proffitt Freight wagon sometime yesterday. They say that the shotgun rider was killed. I am sorry to hear that. Usually, one of Arnie's boys rode shotgun with him. Sorry if anyone got killed. I feel for the family, if that is the case. Arnie is a good man. Give you the shirt off his back if you needed it. He had six sons, but I think they lost one a few years ago; he got pneumonia, or something. Ms. Mable took that one hard. She almost grieved herself to death. If one of their boys was riding shotgun on that wagon, this will tear their hearts apart again. The community will be there for them. That family has served that area well, seeing that the train doesn't reach a lot of those smaller towns and a freight wagon is the only way they must get goods. If I am not mistaken, you used to have them deliver things for your ranch, didn't you? Barton, didn't the Proffitt freight wagon run out to your ranch? Barton?"

When Tomes turned to see why Barton wasn't answering him, the marshal was prepared to get the cold stare that Barton would usually give him when the tall man had no desire to engage in the marshal's conversation or quizzing. But, this time, Tomes wasn't prepared for what he saw.

Barton and Smoke were gone.

"Barton! Barton, where are you? Barton, can you hear me? Barton!"

Tomes yanked on Hickory's reins, and the chestnut

horse spun around in its tracks. When they had gone a couple of hundred yards back from the road they had traveled, Tomes saw Smoke walking out of a stand of oak trees off to his right. Barton was not on him.

"Big gray, where is Barton? Big gray, where is Barton?"

"Will you quiet down? I am right here," answered Barton as he followed Smoke out of the stand of trees.

Tomes, in a slight panic, jumps down off Hickory and runs to where Barton was standing. "Are you alright? Did you fall off? Do you feel bad? Are you bleeding?"

"I needed to piss."

Tomes, whose mind had been racing with hundreds of possibilities of what had interrupted their peaceful journey, was not quite ready for such a simple answer.

"What do you mean, you needed to piss?"

The cold stare that the marshal had anticipated earlier was firmly displayed across Barton's face now. He let a couple of moments pass before he responded, "Do I really need to explain it to you? Over five hours of riding, rest stops, water breaks, lunch, the nurse's coffee, get it?"

Tomes' heartbeat is slowing down, his breathing is near normal. He realizes that Barton appears alright. He also realizes that he had prepared for everything, every need that they might encounter, but had overlooked one important one. When nature calls.

"Why didn't you say something? I would have helped you," Tomes states innocently.

Barton responds as he walks toward Smoke, "That is what I was afraid of. You have mother-henned me this entire trip. You help me get on the horse, you help me drink water, you help me eat lunch. I was afraid if I had told you I needed to take a piss, you would have wanted

181

to help me with that. If you had tried, I would have shot you dead!"

Tomes stands stunned. Not so much at the thought of what Barton has suggested, but the fact that this is the most Barton has said since that fateful morning on the Anderson ranch. After all the attempts that Tomes had made to find common ground with his friend, it took something as basic as needing to empty one's bladder to get more than a grunt or a one-word response out of the sullen one. Suddenly, as if a great weight had been lifted from him, a weight that he had carried for weeks, Tomes started laughing.

"HAHAHA!"

He couldn't stop it. He wanted to. He tried to. But it just made him laugh that much more, and that much harder.

Barton just stood and watched. No response, no expression, nothing but that cold stare at the laughing lawman.

Tomes, wiping the tears from his eyes, slowly regained his composure. His impulse to laugh was quickly quenched, however, by what he saw next. Barton was getting ready to get back on Smoke without any assistance. This could have nightmare results. This trip could be greatly interrupted if Barton were to cause any damage or trauma to his injuries. Even if it had been a couple of weeks since he was wounded, Dr. Tilley had made the marshal promise that Barton would not have to endure any unnecessary physical actions or activities while traveling to Smithview.

"What do you think you are getting ready to do? You've had already gotten off without any help. You will not be getting back on that way. Let's find a rock or something that I can help you up on, and you can get back on Smoke that way," urged Tomes as he looked around for something for Smoke to stand by, so Barton could get back into the saddle with as little effort as possible.

"No need for that," Barton simply replied.

Noticing a rock formation nearby, the marshal gives his tall friend a stern look and announces, "Let's get one thing straight. You can decide whether you want to talk or not, or whether you want to try to catch me not paying attention. But, from now on, I will be watching you like a hawk, and you won't be able to spit without me knowing it. So, get over there by those rocks. Let's get you on your horse and quit wasting time."

Once he was satisfied Barton was securely stationed upon Smoke, Tomes got back upon Hickory, grabbed the lead rope of the packhorse, and rode up to where he was. Even with Barton feeling he needed to keep this newfound banter going, the marshal spoke in hopes that Barton would feel at ease now.

"Man, you scared me to death. I was thinking about where to make camp tonight, telling you about the Proffitt Freight killing. I didn't even notice that you had fallen back and out of sight. Yep, you had me worried there, Barton!"

Barton just looked ahead, his eyes were set like flint, not giving Tomes any idea whether he was willing to chat with the marshal, until…

"You had better quit worrying about me so much and start worrying about those three riders that have been following us."

Tomes turned around in his saddle and looked back down the road. He didn't see anything or anybody.

Could Barton be imagining this sudden piece of news? Is he just playing games with the marshal, realizing that Tomes was honestly concerned about not knowing where Barton was?

"I don't see anybody. What gave you the idea that we were being followed?"

He continued to look forward, his unshaven face frozen in a stern expression, speaking in a calm, impervious voice.

"I noticed them when we left Prestonburg. Didn't think much of it, just figured they were heading in the same direction as we were, going to travel the same road. But when they never caught up with us, or passed us when we would stop for breaks, I knew they were following us. Back in the woods just now, I noticed Smoke was a little uneasy and figured they were working their way closer to us."

Tomes is now frustrated that he has not discerned this new challenge. He realized that he has been so locked in on getting to Smithview, making sure Barton was traveling alright, putting forth all the effort of stopping and starting from the rest stops. But he is the marshal, and all aspects of this journey are his responsibilities. One thing is for sure now, whomever is back there, they are doing their best to not be detected. Barton was right. If these riders were just traveling in the same direction, they would have passed by and traveled on by now. Tomes' instincts told him that is not a good sign.

Tomes' mind considers the possibility that it could be Coy Newton behind them. The Proffitt Freight wagon incident happened in this area. The holdup happened yesterday, so the time frame might work out that it is Newton. But he realizes that doesn't make any sense for

Newton would be traveling at a fast pace, not being content to start and stop on the road. Newton has killed at least one person and no doubt there are lawmen looking for him and the outlaw is aware of that.

When he turned to ask Barton if he had any ideas about who it might be, or what they might want, he was surprised to see that Barton wasn't staring out in front of them. Instead, the tall man was looking at his Henry rifle, which he had pulled out of its saddle sheath. Barton slid his hand in the lever and pulled down and back to see if it was loaded. It was, as proven by a shell ejecting out the side, which he caught and placed in his pocket. Barton didn't put the rifle back in its sheath, but laid it across his lap.

"And exactly what are you planning to do with that?" Tomes asked, not anxious to hear what Barton's answer was.

"Whatever it takes," was the tall man's certain reply.

The two men rode for a few more hours until it started getting dark. Tomes figured if the trailing riders had bad intentions on their minds, they would try them in the dark, and when Tomes and Barton were in the open. Luckily, the marshal saw some familiar landmarks and realized that an old surveyor's shack was up ahead, about a hundred yards off the road. At some time, in the past, the railroad had discussed putting in a spur line in that area, but politics and money kept it from ever happening. Lawmen, bandits, hunters, nature lovers and anyone else who needed shelter would take advantage of its offer of a windbreak or a dry place to sleep. Tomes had used this one, and another one, a couple of times, usually when he had a prisoner, or he was just too tired to continue his journey.

As they rode up to the shack, Tomes yelled out to see if anyone was already in the weather-beaten building. Hearing no response, the marshal got off Hickory and tied him to an old wagon wheel that served as a makeshift hitching post in front of the structure. Although he knew what Barton's response would be, Tomes walked over to where Smoke was standing, with Barton still in the saddle. The marshal extended his hand in a gesture of assistance, but Barton waved him off. Even though he couldn't offer any immediate help, Tomes made sure to stand close by, just in case. Only thing that provided was a close view of another example of the trusting relationship between the tall man and his big equine friend. Barton gently worked his way backwards, out of the seat of the saddle. Smoke stood perfectly still, knowing what his rider's next move would be. Barton, with his rifle still in his hand, let gravity take its course. With his free hand, he pushed on the back of the saddle and slid over Smoke's behind until his feet touched the ground. Tomes just shook his head and started unloading the pack horse.

The surveyor's shack offered very little in terms of comfort. Because it was left deserted by the railroad crews, the only furnishings that it offered were a table, a candle holder, and a small wood stove. Tomes figured if it had, at one time, been furnished more fully, those things were pillaged over time. What was left was too heavy, too bulky, or too unnecessary for anyone to take. For their purpose on this night, the shack would do just fine.

Tomes' thoughts were two-fold this night: them spending the night inside and the trouble that was waiting for them outside. The marshal had brought in all their tack, their supplies, and other belongings. The horses were secured just outside the front door, so any attempt to take them could be easily thwarted. Tomes laughed to himself at the thought of someone trying to take Smoke against the big gray's will. That might even be entertaining to watch at another time. But tonight, he is going to have to stay aware of every sound that comes from outside the shack.

Once Tomes had arraigned the saddles and blankets into adequately sleeping spots, he started a fire in the small wood stove. The heat would be welcome as the air got chilly outside, as the November dusk swept over them. The stove, also, would serve as a source of light with its door slightly ajar. The marshal figured it wouldn't be a good idea to make it too bright in the shack. For anyone outside in the darkness, that would make them easier targets, if that was what the mysterious riders were looking for.

Barton settled himself onto his saddle and blanket as Tomes removed the last of Granny Ryan's food from the basket. What remained wasn't a lot, but it would do and would keep him from having to try to prepare something on the small stove or on a fire outside.

"Here, it's not much, but it will hopefully tie us over until I can fix us something tomorrow," Tomes said as he handed Barton a piece of chicken and a small, not so fluffy biscuit with a little strawberry jam still in it. Tomes took the canteen of coffee and set it upon the stove. The top of the stove is now glowing from the fire inside. "As soon as this heats up, I will get you a cup of Nurse Baird's coffee. It may not be as good now, but at least it will be warm going down."

Both men, quietly and quickly, ate their modest meals. Tomes, walking stooped over as to not be as noticeable to anyone watching outside, gathered up the cups and napkins. In the years of being a lawman, he had been in a situation like this before. He may not know what is waiting ahead, but he has that familiar feeling in his bones that there was a brush with the unknown waiting. Hoping it will pass is never enough. That is the dream of a fool that usually ends in an unsatisfactory, and permanent, ending.

The marshal sat down on his own his bedding spot. As he pulled his Colt revolver out of its holster and spun the cylinder to assure it was loaded, he heard these words from across the room.

"You get some shuteye; I will take first watch tonight."

Tomes looked across the dimly lit room, and there, his eyes focused in on Barton, with his arms wrapped around his Henry rifle. The tall man had placed his saddle up against the wall, and he was firmly planted with his back against it. The cold expression was still upon his face, his hands firmly clasped together, cradling the long gun in front of him.

Tomes was too tired to argue with a man who didn't want to talk, and who wasn't going to move now, anyway. As the marshal arraigned the blanket that was covering his saddle, and as his eyes slowly closed, one thought crossed his mind; if this is his last night on earth, there is no one he would rather entrust it with than the tall man across the room. No matter who Barton Anderson is now, in heart or in mind, Tomes knows one thing: he will take his chances with the man holding the mighty long gun.

With that thought, Tomes closed his eyes and fell asleep.

Chapter Fourteen

The sun was coming up as Tomes finished loading the pack horse. The night had been quiet, the marshal and Barton had traded lookouts a couple of times overnight, and while their chance for rest wasn't perfect, at least respite had come in some parts and parcels. Barton was standing by Smoke, checking the cinch straps and other tie-downs to make sure they were secure. Tomes threw his saddle on Hickory, and as he went through the routine of snugging it down on the chestnut horse, he noticed that Smoke was doing that thing with his front hooves, where he slaps them down on the ground and makes that high-pitched whinny. Then what was going on hit Tomes like a brick.

"Smoke is telling us our friends are close by, isn't he?" Tomes quietly asks as Barton continued with his tasks with Smoke.

"To your left, about fifty yards or so, look for the blackberry bushes and they are just beyond them, slowly heading our way."

Tomes carefully reaches down and removes the small leather strap that keeps his sidearm in its holster. He places his fingers around the elk-bone handle and lifts it slightly to insure it is loose and ready. The marshal hopes that his gun will not be needed, because the odds may not be with him and Barton on this given day. First, they are outnumbered, three to two. Second, Tomes realizes that Barton is not physically at his best. And third, he realizes one important factor that could play the biggest part in them surviving: he has never given Barton his Colt pistol back.

"Now is probably not the time to share this information with you, but your handgun is in the saddlebag on the packhorse. If you think you can get it out, try now. We may need it."

Barton pulls the big Henry rifle from its sheath and replies, "Don't plan on them getting close enough to need a sidearm."

Tomes, takes a big breath, and turns to his left as the riders emerge from behind the blackberry bushes. They are rough looking. Probably in their thirties, adequately armed, and their facial expressions do not give the marshal the feeling that they are out for a casual appreciation of the countryside.

"I am Lyndon Tomes, U.S. Marshal. State your business. If you have need of this shack, we are leaving. If you have need of assistance, we don't have much in the way of food or supplies. Whatever it is, tell me your purpose for being here!"

The strangers rode up within a hundred feet of where Tomes and Barton were standing. The way they were aligned, still on their horses, they were blocking any chance of anyone leaving. That is, unless a person wanted to take their chances riding through the brushes and bushes. Tomes is now convinced that this is a confrontation, and not a coincidence.

"Are you the coward that killed Angus Ford in Rabbit Flat?" the one in the middle asks, in a tone that gives the impression he already knows the answer. Each of the other riders remain silent and still for the moment.

"Angus Ford was a murderer and a robber," Tomes replies." He was wanted by numerous jurisdictions, including the United States government. He killed lawmen, innocent men, defenseless women, and children.

I don't think anyone is grieving the loss of such a man. What is your concern with how he died, or who made it happen?"

The spokesman for this rugged ensemble re-arraigns himself in his saddle, then checks Barton to see what he is doing. Barton is still standing behind Smoke, hiding the fact he is holding a great rifle between himself and the big gray horse.

"Tall man, this has nothing to do with you. Get on your horse and we will give you passage out of here. This is between us and the coward with the badge. Mount up and git, now!" barked the middle rider, growing bolder by the moment.

Barton, knowing that these men have arrived with the intention of bringing hurt upon someone, lifts the Henry rifle up and lays it across his saddle. Smoke firmly sets his feet in the dirt, giving Barton a solid support from which to fire his gun. The big gray horse has assumed this position before, during times when Barton would go hunting for big game to bring home to feed his family.

"I think I will stay," Barton informed the loudmouth in the middle.

Tomes, following Barton's lead to put all the cards on the table, repeats his earlier inquiry. "What business is it of yours how Angus Ford died and who killed him? State your intentions or move on. I am tired of wasting time with you!"

"I am Vernon Ford, Angus Ford's brother, and these two gentlemen are Angus' cousins. We heard that some chicken-crap marshal had killed Angus and a couple of his friends while they were drinking and unable to defend themselves. Me and my family declared this was a cold-blooded killing, and we have been chosen to carry out the deserved justice. You, yellow law-dog, have been found guilty by the Ford family council. The sentence is death. And, unlike you, we aren't going to wait until you can't defend yourself. We could have ambushed you on the trail or shot you through the window last night. We want you to know why you died and who did it, you gutless trash."

Just as Tomes was preparing to respond to the charges being leveled at him, Barton pulled the hammer back on his rifle, and said, "You are, without a doubt, the stupidest bastard in Kansas today. He didn't kill your brother! I did!"

It didn't take long for the look on Vernon Ford's face to go from total confusion to total rage, causing him to scream, "Kill them both!"

It was all over in a matter of seconds. The cousin on the left was the first to pull his gun, but just wasn't fast enough, as Tomes cleared leather first, fired his Colt and the marshal's bullet found its mark, mid-chest, causing that Ford cousin to fall backwards off his horse.

Kaboom!

While Tomes was drawing and shooting the assailant on the left, he knew that loud sound meant that Barton had gotten a shot off, and having not heard a responding shot, the marshal knew that Barton had not missed. Tomes had learned two things from riding with Barton. One: at that close of a range, Barton never misses. And two: a Henry rifle leaves no survivors. Sure enough, upon looking to his right, the marshal saw Vernon Ford was lying on the ground, with his chest gaping open from a .44 rimfire bullet hit.

What Tomes observed next was Barton, who had quickly cocked the lever action on the Henry, preparing the gun to fire again. The tall man was aiming straight at the remaining Ford cousin, still mounted upon the horse he rode in on. The young man, whom Tomes figured couldn't have been much older than twenty, was clearly in no position to take this confrontation any further. The young man's hands, which were out of his body, were shaking. His lower lip was quivering. This wasn't a violent criminal. He was probably just someone who was pressured into going on this search for vengeance for the sake of family pride. Now, Tomes must convince Barton of that.

After making sure the other two were not going to be any further concerned, the marshal walks over to Barton, who is looking down the long barrel of his gun, the butt of his Henry rifle firmly pressed against his shoulder. Barton has that look that says Tomes will need to be careful with his actions, and his words.

"Barton, I think you can lower the barrel on that cannon of yours. Can't you see that this young man isn't cut from the same cloth as the other two? The first two deserved what they got. They announced their intentions, they made their moves, and they paid for it. I have no problem with their demise, but the situation has changed. This one knows he is outnumbered and outgunned. This dust-up is over."

Barton continues to stare through the sights that are lined up on the remaining rider, not lowering the gun an inch or saying a word. Barton offers nothing that might give Tomes an indication of what was running through the tall man's mind.

"Look at him. I wouldn't be surprised if he hadn't crapped his pants after what he had seen here. I am sure the boy has been pressured into joining these other two.

He didn't want to be here. Did you, boy? Did you want to be here today? Did you want to kill somebody today?"

The young man, still trembling, answers in what voice he can get out of his throat, "No, sir. No, sir, I didn't want to come with them."

Tomes turns to Barton and tries to encourage him to take a moment to think about what happens next.

"Now, can you give me one good reason that we should do something like causing this boy's mom to grieve her son's death? Give me one good reason why we ought to put this boy in a grave next to his worthless cousins."

Barton, without any hesitation, coldly answers, "He is a Ford. That's good enough for me."

Tomes understands why Barton could have so much hatred for a name because it was a Ford that took his family away from him. But Tomes quickly counters, "Yes, it was a Ford that brought hell to the Anderson ranch that morning, but you can't kill everyone named Ford. This boy wasn't there. If he has three brothers and four sisters, are you going to kill all of them, too?"

Barton stands still, and silent, for a couple of moments. Then, he puts his rifle back in its sheath, puts his arms over his saddle to steady himself, and says, "He is your responsibility. I am tired."

Tomes, not wanting to revel in this small victory too long, turns to the young man and asks, "What is your name, boy?"

"Calvin. Calvin Ford, Sir."

"Calvin, do you understand that you are getting a second chance that your two cousins didn't get because they were too stupid to know better?"

"Yes, sir."

"And are you willing to make sure that I am not going to be sorry I didn't let that tall man over there kill you and send you home to your momma laying over the back of this horse?"

"Yes, sir. You won't be sorry, I promise."

"Then, today is a day to learn a valuable lesson, son," Tomes says as he returns his Colt to its holster and pulls the strap over the hammer to secure it there. "You ride out of here and take your cousin's bodies with you. Tell your family that when they bury these family members, they need to bury any more ideas of self-declared justice with them. Angus Ford got what he deserved, whether it was by a bullet or a rope. And these two did also, by coming here today full of hate and vinegar. Whatever the Ford family feels like it's owed, the price is just going to keep rising unless they move on. You understand what I am saying, boy?"

The young man nods his head "yes" and slowly gets off his horse. Once the lifeless corpses are secured upon their horses, Tomes takes a pencil and paper, and writes out a statement on how the marshal was confronted by unknown riders, that the riders gave the impression there was imminent danger from them, and that the two Ford cousins died in an ensuing gunfight, the results occurring while Tomes was defending himself. He handed the statement to Calvin to sign it. This will be turned in to the U.S. Marshal's office to serve as an official record of what happened this day.

Tomes asks the young man if he has enough supplies to get home, and if he will be alright. Calvin says that he should be alright, clumsily tries thank you the marshal, then gets on his horse. With two horses hauling two bodies following behind, the young man slowly rode

195

away.

Tomes turns and walks toward Barton, who is still leaning on Smoke. Not in a mood to tarry any longer, on resuming their trip to Smithview, Tomes grabs Barton by the back of his pants' belt and says, "Get your rear end up in your saddle, the day is getting away from us." Barton, not resisting the offer for assistance this time, puts one boot in the saddle stirrup and lifts himself upon Smoke, who has not moved one inch this entire time. Tomes mounts up on Hickory, leans over to grab the lead rein on the packhorse, and they are on their way again to Smithview.

They had ridden around two hours when Tomes remembered that, due to the unexpected run-in with the Ford family, he and Barton had not taken time to prepare breakfast. So, the marshal informed Barton they would get off the road, take a break from riding, and he would throw some beans and jerky together for an early lunch. Barton just nodded his head to confirm his approval of the marshal's plans.

The men found a suitable place to stop just off the main road. It was a nice clearing with plenty of grass for the horses. There was no need for shade, as it was still cool on this November day and the sun felt good on humans and horses alike. Tomes noticed the one tree close by, once a mighty elm, was lying on its side, lifeless and decaying from years of exposure to the extremes of the Kansas weather. But, for today's needs, it would serve as a sufficient source of kindling wood for a cook fire and a place for them to sit. Barton slid off the backside of Smoke and took a seat upon the fallen tree. Tomes gathered some limbs and got a fire going. Lunch would be simple today, not like the more ample fare that

Granny Ryan had provided them with. The marshal retrieved some beans out of one of the pack horse bags, along with some beef jerky to add some flavor. With the crackling fire rising, Tomes placed a pan over it, added the beans, jerky and some water from a canteen. In the time while their meal was cooking, the marshal checked on the horses and then shifted his attention to Barton, who was sitting on the downed tree, rubbing the area where he had been wounded during the shooting at Rabbit Flat.

"You doing alright?", Tomes asked with growing concern for his friend.

"Yeah, rifle recoil jarred me a little back there, but I'll be ok."

"Didn't shake you near as much as it did Vernon Ford," Tomes replies, trying to interject some humor into the conversation and relieve the tall man of his current discomfort.

Barton doesn't react to the marshal's attempt of levity, just gives him a look that tells Tomes to move the dialogue along.

"That was a pretty bold thing you did, taking responsibility for Angus Ford's death. I had been given credit for it or blamed for it until this morning. That boy knows the truth, or at least your version of the truth," Tomes says, trying to go fishing for a way to get Barton to open up about what happened at Rabbit Flat.

"If you had let me shoot the boy, you would still get the credit, or blame, for Ford's death. You are the good Samaritan that let him go," comes Barton's retort back.

"No reason to kill that boy just so a version of Rabbit Flat could be protected," the marshal says with some displeasure in his voice. "Especially if you are going to be so liberal and free with your telling of it."

Barton lowers his head and then looks back up at Tomes. "You know it's the truth."

Tomes points his finger at Barton and proclaims, "I don't know what the truth is. You won't talk to me. I know what I saw when I got there. But I don't have any clue what happened before that. You won't tell me what you know. And there is a judge, waiting in Smithview, who is ready to strut like a stud rooster for the newspapers, so he can add to his resume at your expense. I can't help you with what I know!"

Barton calmly leans back and asks, "Do you want to know what I know?"

With his building frustration pouring out, Tomes responds, "Yes, I want to know!"

Barton, as if he is not convinced, asks again, "Do you want to know what I know?"

Tomes stands up and angrily answers, "Yes, dammit. I want to know what you know!"

Barton, leans to his left to look around Tomes. "I know that if you don't get that food off the fire, we won't be eating lunch anytime soon."

Tomes, looks around, and sees the humble meal starting to burn. The marshal had gotten so caught up in this chance to open the door to discover that he had forgotten about their lunch, awaiting on the fire. He reaches and pulls the pan off the flames, burning his hand in the process. Feeling the pain of his blistering hand and the burn of his patience with Barton, Tomes let out a stream of expletives that causes the horses to lift their heads abruptly.

"Is that your way of saying that lunch is ready?" Barton dryly asks, with just the slightest smirk in the corners of his mouth.

Wrapping a wet handkerchief around his singed hand, Tomes notices and thinks, *'If that is what it takes to get through, then it's worth it.'*

And with that, Tomes dishes out beans and jerky. They eat and another word will not be said.

Until that evening.

Chapter Fifteen

Tomes figures that they are sixteen miles from Smithview, when they finally stop for the evening. If he has his bearings right, and they don't encounter any setbacks, they should arrive within the city limits around late morning. He still is undecided as to where they will go first. He needs to check with the telegraph office for messages and send Dr. Tilley a word that they have arrived safely. The marshal considers the possibility that he could go straight to the sheriff's office to let him know that the marshal is in town and if there is any news of Seth. Is the timing right to take Barton to the cemetery to see where Jenny, Adam, and Nate are laid to rest? Does he bypass the city and ride out to the Anderson ranch, which has been watched over by Jenny's brother Jeff? Will Barton even want to go out there anymore? These are decisions that will not have to be made right now.

With the horses unsaddled and unloaded, and grazing in a meadow by a stream, Tomes has taken on the task of preparing a campsite for himself and Barton. Unlike the previous night, they will not have the luxury of a shack to protect them from the outside elements. The marshal sets out to gather enough wood to suffice for a cook fire, as well as a source of warmth throughout the night. Barton has offered to be of assistance, either with gathering wood or preparing a meal. The marshal, whose objective is to get Barton to Smithview in the best condition possible, thanks the tall man for the offer and suggests he make himself a comfortable place to bed down. Tomes points in the general area where the campfire will be, and Barton starts arraigning his saddle, blanket, saddle bag and rifle in a configuration that will be handy to him.

It has been thirty-five hours since leaving Prestonburg, and Tomes has seen a change in his traveling companion. Barton started the journey silent and sullen, not even willing to acknowledge that Tomes was even riding along. But, from the incident of not knowing where Barton was; to offering to take a watch last night; to the incident with the Ford's, to Barton's attempt to be a smartass about the burning lunch; there has been progress in the disposition of the tall man. At this point, Tomes wasn't going to be greedy about how little or large that shift was. Barton was now responding with full, legible sentences, and the marshal could work with that and was willing to wait for more.

"Looks like supper will be beans again. With a potato sliced up in it, and a little salt for seasoning and flavor," Tomes announced as he dug in a pack bag for the needed ingredients and a pan to prepare the evening's meal.

"I don't think I am in any position to be picky about the menu," Barton replied.

"Yeah, I don't think Granny Ryan, or Nurse Baird, are going to surprise us with their presence or their cooking talents here tonight," Tomes joked as he positioned the pan over the campfire.

Both men consumed their modest meals slowly, and without banter. Tomes took Barton's plate and fork from him, grabbed a canteen, and proceeded to wash the remaining morsels off each item. Tomes placed each one strategically by the fire to dry. While it wasn't a meal that would bring back culinary memories in the future, it would sustain them this night.

As was his habit after a meal, Tomes sat down and reached in his vest pocket for his tobacco pouch and

201

papers. He, adeptly, held the cigarette paper between two fingers in one hand as he poured the tobacco onto the awaiting wedged casing. Once he was pleased with the amount of tobacco dispensed, Tomes grabbed the pouch string with his teeth and gave it a pull, closing the pouch and saving its contents for another time. Upon returning the pouch and papers to his vest pocket, the marshal ran his tongue along the edge of the paper, then quickly folded and rolled the configuration until it was the desired product: a cigarette to enjoy as a post-meal treat. Tomes, for no particular reason, handed the newly shaped item to Barton, then drew it back.

"Sorry, but I don't think I have ever seen you smoke before. You can start now, I guess, if you have a mind or an urge to."

"They were drunk when I got there that morning," Barton says softly.

Tomes didn't understand what his friend had said at first. But when he did discern what Barton had just shared, it grabbed his attention like a blacksmith's vice. By the light of the crackling campfire, the marshal could see Barton was sitting with his legs crossed, looking down at his hands. He was rubbing the rugged palms together in a way that might help him find the strength he would need to continue this story.

"Take your time, we have all night to go down this road," Tomes responds in a reassuring tone as he sits down facing his friend.

"I had tracked Ford for over three weeks," Barton starts as he opens his memory to the events of that morning in Rabbit Flat. "It wasn't hard to follow him, for he leaves heartache and havoc everywhere he goes. It seemed like I was always a day late, no matter where I would be. They would hit some town, some farm or something, and be gone by the time I would get there. Then, I rode into Prestonburg the day they had robbed the bank there. I believe they killed a few people before they left. One witness said they thought they had ridden out in the direction of a little town called Rabbit Flat. This was the closest I had been to them, so Smoke and I rode hard, trying to close the gap and not lose them. I just couldn't live with the thought of losing them again."

Barton pauses, as if assembling the facts of the next segment of his tale, before continuing with his telling of that morning. Tomes reaches for the coffeepot, which is sitting on a rock in the campfire. He stretches over to Barton's cup, fills it with the hot refill, then sits back on his blanket and patiently waits for his friend to continue with his version of his encounter with Angus Ford.

"It was sunrise when Smoke and I got to Rabbit Flat. I sat there for a minute, observing where Ford and his partners could be. There were really only two places that offered any possibility: the general store and the saloon. Then, I heard something from inside the saloon, sounded like someone groaning or something. So, I jumped off Smoke, sent him on his way up the street and out of the way, and I walked into the saloon. It took my eyes a couple of moments to adjust to the dimness, and then I saw three men sitting at a round table in the middle of the room."

Tomes is hesitant to interject anything , but inquires, "At this point, did you know it was Ford and his associates?" Tomes was fishing to see if Barton had, noticed that the saloon owner's son was sitting there, instead of a harden outlaw.

Barton shakes his head no, and continues. "It was too

dark to see exact features of the men sitting there. I could just tell there were three of them, and from the size of them, adult men. At that point, I figured it was Ford, because it had been reported that three men had been doing the ravaging and robbery along the way."

"Did they say anything when you walked into the saloon?" The marshal is feeling more comfortable inserting a timely question while Barton is feeling the need to share his encounter.

"No, they were passed out, dead to the world," Barton continues, "I stood there, waiting for one of them to look up and see me. I wanted to get this over. But they were out. I waited for what seemed like forever. When I thought none of them was going to sober up, I started to go outside and wait to have it out with them out there. Then…"

Tomes leans forward, anxiously waiting for the next words to come forth. When Barton continues to withhold the next bit of the account, Tomes tries to give the storyteller a nudge.

"And then what?" the marshal presses gently.

Barton takes a breath and his tone changes, as if preparing Tomes for the next part of this revelation to get darker and more complicated.

"Someone said, 'Hey, ranchero! Don't even think about walking out that door!' I turned around and the one in the middle, the one I took to be Angus Ford, was sitting there, leaning on the arm of his chair, pointing his gun right at me. From time to time, he would let his gun barrel drop down, but he would recover his senses and lift it back on me."

"What are the other two doing? Isn't this talk getting anyone else's attention?" Tomes is now feeling more emboldened but remembering that there is a fine line between investigation and interrogation.

Barton, still looking down and wringing his hands, looking for that source of strength to continue this path of recalling what led to the deaths of three men, apparently from Barton's gun.

"The one to my left with a bandana on opened his eyes. He was listening, but he couldn't participate yet. The one on my right was still out. He would continue his whiskey nap until later. The one in the middle was the one who was interested in doing all the talking. I was reminded of that when we had that dust-up with his brother this morning."

Tomes lifted his eyebrows, leaned back, and remarked, "There is no comparison between Angus Ford and Vernon Ford. Vernon was a fool; Angus was evil and criminally insane. Absolutely nothing even close between those two."

Barton takes a sip of coffee, rubs his bristly chin, then continues. "He asked me what my name was and what was I doing there. I told him my name was Barton Anderson, and I was going to kill him, and both the men with him."

Tomes, again, shakes his head in disbelief at his friend's recklessness and disregard for who was sitting in front of him, an outlaw who had killed people out of boredom.

"I honestly don't know who the crazier man was, him or you. Did it even enter your mind how serious the situation was that you were in? Or how over-matched you probably were, especially if the other two come to their senses?"

Barton looks up at the marshal, peering right straight

into his eyes, and exclaims, "I didn't care! Do you understand that? I didn't care! That bastard killed everyone I cared for. He killed everyone I loved. He killed everything I lived for. I have nothing to live for now. I had nothing that morning. I had nothing to lose except the chance to send that trash to hell and do society a damn favor! Do you understand that, Tomes?"

Tomes is now worried he has pushed Barton too hard, too far. The tall man has never talked to him in such a state of hopelessness, devoid of any reason to care. Barton was always the one everyone else looked to for inspiration. But the tall man is unable to even inspire himself to any levels of recovery or healing.

Barton slowly lifts himself up and walks over to where Smoke is standing, running his hand over the big gray horse. Smoke nickers at Barton repeatedly, as the tall man strokes his strong back. Tomes wonders if the horse can sense Barton's state of mind and that was an attempt to calm his friend.

Tomes gets up and proceeds to gather some firewood to put on the campfire, which is starting to die down. At this point, the marshal figures there is nothing to lose by trying to rekindle Barton's willingness to recount of the events of that morning in Rabbit Flat.

"What did Ford say when you said you were there to kill him?"

Barton continues to stroke Smoke, then in semi-amazement, he responds, "He laughed. Can you believe that? He laughed and bragged that he had killed quite a few families. That I was going to have to be more specific."

Barton turns and goes back to his spot by the fire. Tomes, with the flames dancing up again, grabs the

206

coffeepot, tops off Barton's cup, sets the pot back on the fire and then takes his place on his blanket. Barton takes a sip of coffee, looks into the fire as if he is looking into his own soul, and continues.

"I told Ford it was my ranch that he and his scum was on when they tied an old man to a corral gate and hung an innocent boy in the barn. He elbowed the one with the bandana as the memory came back to him. They both laughed like it was an amusement for them. Ford said I should be proud of Adam, that the boy didn't go without a fight, even killed one of his gang members. The one with the bandana slapped his hand on the table and said that Ike was really surprised when he opened the barn door and the kid was standing there with that shotgun and blew his guts out. That kid must get killing from you, stranger. Then, Ford said he really admired Adam. At least, he did until the boy started kicking and crying for his mama while he was hanging there."

Tomes feels his stomach churning, remembering the sight of the ten-year-old boy hanging from the support beam in the barn. "Is that when you shot Ford?" the marshal asks.

Slowly, Barton's eyes narrowed, and the corners of his mouth tightened. He swallows hard, clenches his fists, and takes a big breath. Tomes finds himself bracing for what set Barton's rage off that morning, although deep down inside he knows that the hate in his friend was conceived that day at the ranch.

"Ford got a big smile on his face, and he said, 'Oh, Ranchero, speaking of his mama, that was some mighty fine—'" Barton threw his coffee cup into the fire, bent his head forward, and placed his face in his hands. By the light of the campfire, the marshal can see that Barton is shaking uncontrollably. Tomes wanted to go over and put his arm around the shoulders of his friend, but the marshal was at a loss as to what was needed. The tall man remembers the confrontation with Ford but is reliving the hell of finding his precious wife in the bloody bedroom. His sanity is on the edge of shattering, and one misinterpreted gesture could shove Barton over the brink.

The marshal got up, put a couple of logs on the fire, then checked on the horses, hoping this would give Barton some time alone to gather himself. For now, Tomes didn't care if he heard any more of what happened in Rabbit Flat, ever. It just wasn't worth watching this man being dragged through the pain again. To watch the emotional scars, left by the tragedy at the Anderson ranch being torn from his soul.

Tomes slowly worked his way back to his bedding site and sat down. He could see that Barton was staring into the fire, a gaunt look now upon his face. His hands are clasped together between his legs, his fingers intertwined like he is holding on to life itself.

"I am going to tell the rest of this once, and only once. Do you understand?"

The marshal replied, "Yes, I understand."

"That bastard didn't deserve to talk about Jenny. I wasn't going to stand there and listen to him brag about it like he had been with a two-dollar whore. So, I pulled my gun, and I shot Ford. Immediately after that, I saw the one on my left go for his gun and I shot him. I guess I was hoping that Ford had been wounded so bad he wouldn't be able to get a shot off. As you know, that wasn't the case. As Ford was losing strength and his arm was dropping, he squeezed off a shot that hit me in the side. I didn't know how bad I was hit; I just knew that I wasn't going to die without the peace of knowing that scum wasn't going to hurt anyone again. So, I walked around the table, placed the barrel of my pistol between his eyes, said something that I don't remember now, and pulled the trigger."

"Kiss the flames of hell, you son-of-a-bitch," Tomes added to the narrative.

Barton stared at the marshal, confused that Tomes would know something that the marshal had never experienced in person.

Tomes raised his hands and shoulders, in a gesture that insinuated that he didn't obtain that information all by himself.

"Dr. Tilley said you tended to talk and ramble while you were unconscious. But I am the only one he shared that bit of chatter with. He can be trusted; he is a good man who is sympathetic to your story."

Barton solemnly continued. "I was standing there, wiping the blood off the end of my gun, when I noticed the third outlaw had recovered from his drunken stupor. His eyes looked at me, then they would look at the gun laying on the table. Back and forth, he looked. Then he fixed his eyes upon the gun, his hand coming up from under the table. I don't know why, maybe it was because I was starting to feel woozy and weak, but I told him, 'Don't do it! don't do it, I'll give you the same.' He kept on looking at the gun and sliding his hand toward it. The only thought that was crossing my mind at that point was that if I passed out, he would kill me. So, I shot him where he sat. His head fell forward, and he took one last, long breath. When I realized I had done what I had set out to do, kill the three devils that had taken my family from me, I limped to a table, sat down, and waited for death to come and end it all."

"But what about Seth?" Tomes asks, hoping that Ford had given Barton some idea of where the youngest Anderson was. "You had to live so you could find Seth. Didn't you think of that?" But the marshal was not prepared for the answer that followed.

"Seth is dead," Barton grimly replied.

For a second, Tomes couldn't get his breath. Seth was that glimmer of hope that there was some sort of light at the end of the tunnel, some motivation to keep this story from ending in total tragedy.

"How do you know that Seth is dead? Is that what Ford told you? Can you believe him about something like that?" Tomes asked, desperately wanting Barton to be mistaken.

"You know," Barton begins. "Ford seemed sorry about it, as if his dark soul could care about anything but himself. He said they took Seth in case they ran into trouble. They would use him to bargain or as a shield. But, that night when no one was looking, Seth slipped out of camp and tried to run away. In the darkness of the night, he stepped on a rattlesnake and it bit him a couple of times. When they did finally find him, he was dead. They quickly dug a hole and put him in it. My baby boy is buried in an unmarked grave in the middle of nowhere. A final resting place that was dug by the hands that killed his family. Hell of an ending, isn't it, marshal?"

Now, Tomes feels like throwing something in the fire, frustration sweeping over him. The marshal's "ace in the hole" was that if Barton had a motive of finding Seth, that would give him the desire to handle whatever happens at Smithview and take up the search for the last remaining Anderson.

Barton, reaches over, takes a last sip of cold coffee, and says, "That's it. All my family is dead. The ones who played a part in it are all dead. I did what needed to be done. And now, it's over."

With a pressure building in his chest, Tomes realizes there is no good time to share the reality that Barton has missed in his telling of Rabbit Flat, and there is no way of knowing how his friend will react. But the truth is waiting for them in Smithview, and Tomes feels that Barton needs to know it now, and not be ambushed by it when they get to town.

"It's not over, Barton," the marshal eases into this next exchange. "You think it is, but it's not. You didn't kill the last three in Rabbit Flat, only two of the three that were left. One, named Coy Newton, wasn't in the saloon when the shooting started, and it looks like he may have gotten away during the melee. The last one you shot at the table wasn't a member of Ford's crew but was just the young son of the saloon owner."

Tomes watches as the solemn look that had been on Barton's face is replaced with a look that the marshal has seen before. It is the look that was on the tall man's face when he knocked Tomes down that morning on the Anderson ranch and took off in search of the ones that had killed his loved ones.

"Well, all I can say is whoever that was that I killed picked his poison when he chose to associate with those murdering vermin," Barton says, his voice and eyes cold with vengeance again.

"Look, I can't say I disagree with you about him being in the wrong place with the wrong people. But the last time I looked; it is not a capital offense to be piss-poor at picking your friends!" Tomes emphatically tries to bring

Barton back to that place where they could talk.

Barton wouldn't say another word until they get to Smithview the next morning. But his face told Tomes everything he needed to know. As long as there was still one left, that would be enough to drive Barton through whatever hardship, setback or penalty he had to face to finish his pursuit for retribution.

And, with that thought in his head, Tomes throws one last log on the fire, rolls up in his blanket, and tries to go to sleep.

Tomorrow, it all starts again.

Chapter Sixteen

The clock on the front of the Smithview Savings and Loan building was showing almost ten o'clock when the men rode into town. It was a Friday, and the town was already buzzing with activity. Word had been passed around that Barton Anderson would be returning home after being gone for almost two months. Tomes wondered what the reaction would be to their arrival. Most likely, many understood why he left, and the mindset he left in. Some wouldn't understand why he wasn't there when his family was laid to rest. A few will feel like he could have taken the time to join the search for Seth. The marshal does not know if all the facts of Rabbit Flat were floating around the gossip circles. Tomes figured there was no need to go looking for trouble. That if there was any lurking about, it would work its way to them eventually.

"Hey marshal," yelled Jason Nash, running up the street with something in his hand. "This came early this morning. It's from the U.S. Marshal's office in Topeka."

Tomes took the telegram and read it:

Need final report on rabbit flat shooting. STOP. Condition of survivor. STOP. Hearing to start upon arrival in Smithview. STOP.

Tomes tells Jason to send a message, back to Topeka, that shooting in Rabbit Flat was self-defense, and that the survivor is recovering. The marshal also asks that a telegram be sent to Dr. Tilley in Prestonburg to tell him that the patient is improving. When he finishes with his requests, Tomes notices that Jason is standing there, staring at Barton. The marshal realizes that Barton is not, visually, the same man that people have been used to seeing. He is scruffy looking, his clothes disheveled, and his withdrawn manner will be confusing to those who knew him as a man free with a conversation, a compliment, an encouragement.

"Son, it's Barton Anderson. You have known him your entire life. Say hi to him and then get back to the gun shop and get those telegrams sent off."

"Hi, Mr. Anderson. It's nice to have you back. If there is anything I can do for you, look at your gun, or anything, just let me know, sir. It's good to see you, sir," Jason stammers and stumbles as he tries to say something that would entice Barton's response to the young man's act of goodwill.

Barton didn't say a word, just nodded his head as a gesture of approval of Jason's greeting. As he turned to head back to the gun shop, Jason remembered another message he was to deliver to the marshal upon Tomes' arrival in Smithview.

"Oh, Marshal. Judge Likens was in the telegraph office this morning, and he told me that if I saw you, I was to tell you to go to the jailhouse immediately, and you were to bring your prisoner with you. He wasn't talking about Mr. Anderson, was he?"

Tomes just closed his eyes and sighed. The marshal, upon hearing that Likens would oversee this legal proceeding, was afraid that the grandstanding adjudicator wouldn't be happy with keeping this in chambers. There wouldn't be press coverage there, and that will be important for a man, whom many say has his eyes set upon the governor's job. While a full, public trial might not play well in Smithview, the ambitious arbiter knew

214

how to milk it to the "tea and cucumber sandwich" crowd that controlled the hefty purse strings that could make, or break, a campaign for the state mansion.

As Tomes and Barton rode up Main Street, people started to gather and watch them. Some would wave in a manner that suggested it was a gesture of their sympathy for their neighbor and the loss he had suffered. Some would yell out, "We are praying for you, Barton", or "Justice is on your side, Barton". Others just pointed and talked among themselves, not willing to make a public statement on the matters at hand. A few could not hide their impressions of the tall man on the dark, gray horse. These citizens were looking for penance to be paid, and their facial expressions proclaimed that they had already passed a verdict and sentence upon Barton.

About a block away from the jailhouse, someone stepped out of the general store and walked toward the two men riding up the street. Tomes' first instinct was to place his hand on his sidearm, just a reaction that he had developed over years of being a lawman. But it didn't take long to realize that a gun would not be needed as the smiling, elder man drew closer.

"Reverend Sutton, it is good to see a friendly face," Tomes said as he extended his hand toward the approaching preacher.

"Same with me, Marshall. Good to see both of you in Smithview," the clergyman responded, as he grabbed the marshal's hand and vigorously shook it.

Then Reverend Sutton turned to Barton. The preacher always seemed to be able to sense what was an appropriate approach, or word, when it came to people. Reverend Sutton took a couple of steps toward the tall man, placed his wrinkled hand upon Smoke's neck and

215

gently stroked the big gray horse. Smoke also had the ability to sense a situation and offered no resistance to the preacher's act of kindness.

"Let me share something with you, Brother Anderson," the reverend started. "Only one person knows why things happen in life, what the results of those things will be, and where life goes from those points. That person is the Lord Himself. I am not capable of such great insight, nor am I entrusted with all the correct words that lay a path to follow in such times. All I can say is the Lord is never absent, is never slow, and is never short of redemption to those who warrant it. The Anderson family always stood with the people of Smithview, and the people of Smithview will stand with you, sir."

Barton looked down at the old preacher and answered, "We will see, won't we?"

Then, the calm of their meeting was shattered by a voice so loud, it echoed off the business buildings that lined Main Street. Even nearby horses flinched at the sudden vocal onslaught.

"Marshal Tomes! U.S. Marshal Tomes! I order you to surrender your prisoner to the local authorities! I order you to comply with the wishes of the court!"

Tomes didn't have to turn around to know that the bombastic venting was coming from Judge Jacob Likens. Sure enough, when the marshal did swivel around in his saddle, there stood Judge Likens, hands on his hips and dressed more like he was going to the theatre than preparing to sit behind a legal bench. The judge never wore his court robe while overseeing a proceeding. Some thought maybe it was because he would get too hot. Most figured that he wanted all to see his propensity for fashion and flair.

"Your honor, Mr. Anderson is not a prisoner, nor in my custody. He has been in medical care due to being the victim of a gunshot wound during a fight in which Mr. Anderson defended himself against his attackers. I am sure it is not against the law in the state of Kansas to defend one's own life from those who wish to take it from you," Tomes proclaims, as a crowd starts to assemble around them.

Judge Likens, quickly, steps down from the sidewalk, pointing his finger at the Barton. "Well, I am pretty sure it is against the law in the mighty state of Kansas to take the life of an innocent young man, and such a charge has been leveled against you, Mr. Anderson. I have issued a bench warrant for your arrest. You are to be confined in the sheriff's jail. I am commandeering the church to be used as my courtroom and trial will start Monday morning, eight o'clock sharp."

"Wait a minute, your honor," Reverend Sutton protests, garnering a few amens from the growing crowd. "This man has the right to a hearing to decide if there is evidence strong enough to hold a trial. He has the right to prepare an adequate defense for such a trial and he has the right to have bail set during such a hearing."

"There will be no bail. That is my ruling. He has two days to find counsel and prepare a defense. The charge will be murder, the sentence will be the full extent that the state of Kansas will allow, up to and including hanging, if I so rule," Judge Likens snapped at the clergyman, and then added, "Preacher, I suggest you stick to the issues that are dealt with in the Heavenly courts and leave the laws of this land to people who know what they are doing, namely me!" the judge barked,

217

placing his thumbs under the lapels of his jacket, as to sell his proclamation with his posture.

With the assembly of citizens increasing by the minute, and growing more restless, Tomes gets down from Hickory and walks over to Barton, who is still sitting on Smoke, the big gray horse growing agitated by the tone of the surrounding voices.

"Barton, I am so sorry. I was hoping we could avoid this. But Likens isn't going to let it go. I am concerned about the potential of people being arrested, hurt, or worse today. Until we can find out the specifics of who has brought the charge, we are going to have to play his game for now. But, as an old soul told me recently, 'Only thing that matters is letting the truth work its way toward the final goal, which should be justice.'"

"Sheriff Harris, arrest your prisoner and take him into custody. Time is a wasting, and I haven't had my lunch yet," Judge Likens ordered.

Cliff Harris was the sheriff of the county territory that included Smithview. He, along with two deputies, approached Barton as he dismounted from Smoke. As he was placing the handcuffs on the tall man, the local lawman kept saying that "I don't agree with this, Barton. You've got to know that I don't agree with this one bit."

As Barton was being led away, Smoke started lunging at those who grabbed Barton and were leading the tall man away. The dark, gray horse repeatedly slammed his hooves into the dirt and commenced to making that low, growling noise that he made at Dr. Tilley's the night Barton was brought to the infirmary. The sheriff and his deputies jumped to get out of the way of the irritated equine as the crowd laughed and shouted its approval.

"Mr. Anderson, I order you to get that animal under

218

control or I will have it lassoed and taken to a stall. If no one can accomplish such a feat without being injured, then I will have that menace shot and drug off. I am not hesitant to order either one," Judge Likens blustered, waving his hands to accentuate his outburst.

Barton stops, turns, and looks back at the judge. The expression on his face tells Tomes that his tall friend is rapidly losing patience with this legal windbag.

"Don't worry," the marshal assures Barton. "I will see that Smoke is taken care of. Big gray and I have an understanding now. You go with Sheriff Harris. I will have Jason send a wire to Senator Jim Richards. You and he have done a lot of state business together and he will want to be your legal counsel. I have seen him go toe-to-toe with Judge Likens when Jim was an attorney, he can hold his own against that showboating old goat."

Barton sighed. "Let Likens have his show. If justice were really the priority, Coy Newton would have a Henry bullet in him before the sun goes down. The only crime I am guilty of is failing to avenge my murdered family. As long as one of those murderers is still out there, I will live in a personal hell worse than any prison Likens can put me in."

As the sheriff and his deputies led Barton off to jail, Tomes urged the crowd to break up before things got any worse. Reverend Sutton announced that the church would be open for anyone who wanted to come and pray for Barton, Senator Richards, Smithview and for the Lord's grace to be the deciding factor in the upcoming trial. Whether by accident or on purpose, the pastor didn't mention any spiritual supplications for Judge Likens, and no one who was present seemed concerned about the omission.

219

For the next seventy hours, the jailhouse was the center of attention in Smithview. From ladies keeping prayer vigils around the structure, to kids who brought treats for Smoke, who would not leave the location where the tall man was being held, to those who wanted to personally offer encouragement but were not allowed to enter the local lockup. Barton had given Sheriff Harris instructions that he did not wish to have any interaction with anyone except Marshal Tomes. Many who considered the tall man a friend did not understand why Barton would ask that, rather they reasoned that it was another of Judge Likens' outrageous rulings. There would be no visitors allowed in the jail, nor desired by Barton, until an unexpected person showed up on Sunday.

Barton was sitting in his cell. He had just finished his Sunday lunch meal when Marshal Tomes came into the jail. The lawman grabbed a chair, drug it over to the front of Barton's cell, and sat down facing his confined friend inside.

"I would ask you about how you are doing, but I think I know the answer to that. You are spending your entire time in here thinking about unfinished business out there, aren't you?" Tomes asked, hoping to build up to the purpose of his visit.

Barton responded by the method he finds adequate, and that Tomes has learned to interpret. Barton gave the marshal a look that forced the lawman to get to the point of his visit, which was not checking on the conditions of the tall man's confinement.

"I have a favor to ask," Tomes preparing to move into the act of imploring if his request was turned down.

"I don't think I really owe you any favors, seeing you have played a part in my being here," Barton answered, in a tone of astonishment that the marshal wanted to try that manner of approach.

"You are right, you owe me nothing after everything you have been through," Tomes continued. "But, I think you owe someone else something, and they are here to appeal to your sense of allegiance."

Without waiting for Barton's objection, Tomes got up and walked to the front door of the jail house. After stepping outside for a moment, Tomes returned, and following the marshal was Jenny's brother, Jeff.

For a moment, the expression on Barton's face showed that the appearance of his brother-in-law had thrown him off guard. Barton had encountered a lot of people since that morning at the Anderson ranch. But this was the first time he had faced what Jeff represented, family.

"Hey, Barton. Sally and the kids said to say hi. They love you and they are praying for you," Jeff shares as he looks as if he is prepared for a rough reaction.

But one does not come, which surprises Tomes and Jeff. While Barton does not return a vocal recognition of the young man's greeting, he does not turn his back or give the impression that this is totally a bad idea.

Tomes walks over to Jeff, puts his hand upon Jeff's back and gently pushes in a manner to suggest that Jeff sit in the chair that is still in front of the cell door.

As Jeff slowly lowers himself into the chair, he keeps his eyes on Barton, hoping that the man, in the cell, will give his approval.

Barton nods his head in the direction of the chair in apparent concession.

"Don't blame the marshal for me coming here. It was my idea," Jeff starts, feeling more at ease with each moment that Barton does not object. As Tomes heads

221

toward the front door, he waves his hand to the deputies standing guard, signaling for them to follow him, and let these two men have some time alone.

Jeff takes a big breath, releases it, and then pours out his heart to the only person on earth who may understand what he is about to say.

"I lost my dad, my sister, and two nephews that morning. You weren't the only one that wanted to kill those murderers. I would have ridden with you; I would have hunted them down with you. I would have killed them, too. But I knew that time was the enemy, so I moved Sally and the kids to the ranch so we could keep it going for you. So you would have a place to come home to when you had done what needed to be done. Jenny will always make us family, whether she is here or not. We will always have that binding us together. I know she would have wanted it to be that way."

Barton gets up and walks to the tiny window in the jail cell. As he looks out, he responds in a resolute manner. "I wouldn't have let you ride with me. You made the right decision to stay with your family. You see, I wasn't there when my family needed me the most. I can blame those butchers for what they did. I can blame Marshal Tomes for asking me to leave them to join his posse. I can even blame God, and I blame them all. But I blame myself the most, and I am prepared to live with that thought for the rest of my life. As for the ranch, your father gave it to Jenny and me, and I give it to you and Sally. I have no need for it, and I have no want for it. When Jenny died, the dreams died with her. When I get out of this, and I will get out of this, I will kill Coy Newton or he will kill me; that is the only reason I will ever want to see another day."

222

As Jeff started to protest the fact that Barton had given up on what he and Jenny had built together, Barton walked to the front of the cell, reached through the bars, and grabbed the agonizing young man by the arm.

"There is one thing you can do for me, if you will?" Barton softly requests.

"You name it, Barton. If I can't, I will find someone who can," Jeff says, so thankful that his brother-in-law still has faith in him.

"I don't know what this judge has in store for me, but it could mean going away for a while. Or, when I have that run-in with Newton and he is the better man when the air clears, I want you to take Smoke back to the only home he has ever known. The marshal has learned how to deal with the big gray, he will show you. If family is important, then you will be the only family he will have then. That is all I ask."

Jeff, fighting hard to keep his composure, answers, "Yes, sir, I will. I promise that Smoke will always be family on the Anderson ranch."

Barton smirks and suggests that Jeff be thinking of a new name for the ranch.

Jeff shakes his head no and replies, "No, sir. It is the Anderson ranch and always will be. For you see, you may not have any dreams, but Sally and I do. And if she was here, I am sure she would agree. It's our dream to see you and Smoke roaming those hills and valleys again, helping us keep Jenny's dream alive. She loved you and she loved that land. You made it a home for my dad when life got hard for him. And no matter what happens, it will be your home, always."

Barton squeezed Jeff's arm, cleared his throat, and replied, "Dreams should be things that are within reach, that have paths to achievement, no matter how impossible it may seem. Smoke will return to his home there, but that land will never be home to me again. Go be with your little family, go back to the ranch, and go dream with them. I want to be alone now."

Barton gives Jeff a pat on the shoulder as he returns to look out the small window of his cell. Jeff walks out the front door of the jailhouse, where he finds the deputies sitting on the front porch and Marshal Tomes leaning against a porch post.

"Did he talk with you, son?" Tomes asks, hoping that their gamble has paid off.

"Yes, sir. But you are not going to believe what he said. He told me that he was giving me the ranch and he wants Smoke to come and stay at there." Jeff tries to explain what happened and keep his composure. "He sounds like he has given up, marshal. What is going to happen to him tomorrow?"

"I wish I knew, Jeff. I truly wish I knew," Tomes answers as he looks at Smoke, who is still standing in the street, looking like he is waiting for someone to explain all of this to him.

Chapter Seventeen

It's a brisk autumn Monday morning, and Smithview has been awake since before sunup. Whether by horse, wagon, or foot, people have been arriving for the trial of Barton Anderson. While the expected crowd will not approach the numbers of the Anderson family funeral, there is a pensive feeling in the air that this will affect this close-knit community in a very heartfelt way. One of their own will be put on display for a judge to make a self-surmised verdict on, rather than a judgment by a jury of Barton's peers. Will the bombastic jurist listen to all the facts, consider all the implications, and rule from a position of neutrality? Or will Judge Likens push all those things aside and use this legal action as a showcase to inflate his political hopes? Those are just two of the topics of talk being debated on this November morning.

As eight o'clock approaches, the church is already packed. Not only are all the pews filled, but there are people standing against the walls and the windows are all open, so those outside can try to hear the proceedings. Bonfires have been started to keep the outdoor participants warm, and the woodstove is glowing orange in the church house to combat the chilly air coming in the open windows. Smithview School has been called off for this significant occasion. Along with the adults, there are plenty of children present. Some of the older kids will be drafted to act as messengers, taking the latest court news around town to those who are sitting in the eateries, the saloons, the library, and any place where two or more can gather. In return for their efforts as Junior Town Criers, the young couriers will be given pennies which will, likely, wind up at the candy counter at Vincent's general store.

After yesterday morning's church service was over, Judge Likens had cornered Reverend Sutton and ordered the pastor to have the choir area roped off, preventing anyone from sitting in that area. The judge said he wanted everyone sitting in front of him, where he could keep an eye on the malcontents of Smithview. No one knew if it offended the preacher or not, but Reverend Sutton had the preaching pulpit moved and an old table and unpadded stool replace it. Someone said they heard the old preacher say that the Holy Desk was not to be used for anything but seeking the truth, and not for personal puffery.

At the request of Marshal Tomes, the sheriff had Barton escorted into the church through a back door about an hour before the trial was to start. Because he knew that tension would be running high, the marshal had deputized Jason Nash and Mark Miller to assist with crowd containment. Tomes had ridden with both young men, and he trusted them to listen to him when needed.

Barton was taken to an area in the back of the church, which was used for meetings, bible studies, and a bride's changing room on days when there was a wedding. When the tall man got there, Senator Jim Richards was waiting for him. The respected statesman was a native of Smithview, had operated a law office from the room above the gun shop. Senator Richards was an elected legislator, in large part due to the encouragement of Barton and the public endorsement that he had gotten from the much-respected rancher. Upon hearing of Barton's situation, the senator rode all night, both on train and carriage, to get to the trial. Senator Richards, like most people, was shocked upon seeing Barton, and equally concerned for the tall man's lack of concern about what might happen to him. But the senator promised that he would do everything he could to get Barton the vindication he deserved.

When the clock on the fireplace mantel rang eight times, Sheriff Harris stepped inside the room and said, "Barton, it's time we go in for the trial."

So, surrounded by the sheriff and three deputies, Barton walked into the sanctuary, which, on this day, will serve as an interim courtroom. Tomes and Senator Richards walked behind them. Once inside the courtroom, Barton, Richards, and Tomes sat on the front pew to the right of the judge's table. The county attorney, Rance Embree, was sitting with an unidentified man on the other front pew. They would later find out that this man was Carter Sanders, the father of the young man Barton shot in Rabbit Flat. He has a look which tells Tomes that this is the man who has caused the trial to be necessary.

No sooner had Barton, Tomes, Richards, and the other legal players taken their seats, a great commotion broke out in the back of the sanctuary. Every head in the large room turned to see Judge Jacob Likens making his grand entrance, waving his gavel like a mighty sword at the assembly of citizens. The judge was demanding them to keep quiet, to mind their manners, and to give him the respect he was due. The throng of partisan attenders sympathetic to Barton's cause and concern let their sentiments be known as the jousting justice continued to berate and belittle them. Some in the crowd booed, some shook their heads or their fists, and one made the not-so-Christian suggestion of what Judge Likens could do with his gavel. Deputies Nash and Miller, novices at law enforcement, had their hands full as they escorted the judge to the table where he would oversee the proceedings.

Once the trial was declared in session, Rance Embree stood and shared that he had been appointed to represent the state of Kansas in the matter of bringing murder charges against Barton Anderson. The county attorney shared that Carter Sanders, the father of the deceased Curt Sanders, would share that his son was killed by Mr. Anderson for no reason other than acting out of a hateful heart. That Curt was in his father's saloon, tending to the business in his father's absence. The elder Sanders would portray his son as a gentle soul, incapable of hurting anyone or anything. Mr. Anderson, uninvited, came in and started blasting away without provocation. Mr. Sanders will also share that his son was limited in his mental capabilities and was beyond an innocent victim, that he was a young man incapable of violence or hurt.

Once Attorney Embree finished his opening statements, Senator Richards stood and established that they all sympathized with Mr. Sanders' loss, that they could understand the challenges Curt may have had in his life, considering whatever cognitive limitations he may have had. But mental illness is not a free pass to act however you want and inflicting harm and hurt in a haphazard fashion. Curt made the decision to involve himself with violent criminals and, thereby, positioned himself to experience the peripheral consequences of such an association.

Bang! Bang! Bang!

Judge Likens hammers his gavel on the table, leans forward on his stool, and proclaims, "Dear Senator. You

228

must have been out of the legal realm at the state capitol to the extent that you have forgotten, but in the mighty state of Kansas, a man is allowed to pick his friends!"

Before the Senator can respond, an unsolicited comeback rises from the crowd. "Evidently, in the mighty state of Kansas, an asshole is allowed to become a judge, too!"

As the laughter, approving applause and whistles thundered in the courtroom, Judge Likens slammed his gavel down, so angry that it broke in half, with the head of it flying into the audience. Jason sheepishly retrieved it from the still giggling crowd and, upon returning to the judge's table, tried to put the gavel parts back together. Having no patience for the deputy marshal's fumbling attempts, the judge orders, "Son, just give me the damn thing!"

Immediately, like an arrow being released from a bow, Reverend Sutton rises from his seat and emphatically exclaims, "I object, your Honor, to your language in the House of God!"

The flustered justice rises from his stool, points his finger at the rattled reverend, and erupts, "Sit down and shut up, Reverend! Today, this is my house. God will have to wait until I am through to have it back!"

A different tension overtook the crowd, as they murmured among themselves. Many of them were members of this very church, were God-fearing people and had never heard a public figure ever commit such an irreverent claim in a religious institution. While the murmuring continued, Judge Likens gazed over the group, slowly waved his hand back and forth, and then declared, "I will say this once, and only once. This disrespect of the bench, and the discharging of my duties as a legal adjudicator, will not be tolerated any more. If there are any more outbursts while this court is in session, I will declare the entire courtroom in contempt. I will have chains put on the doors of this building, and you will each get your future square meals, courtesy of the sheriff's department, until I deem you repentant of your actions. Don't believe it? Just try me."

Tomes wasn't sure that the judge had the legal right to do such a thing, but he was sure that Judge Likens was mad enough to try it. The marshal looked back at his temporary deputies and nodded for them to keep doing what he told them to do. Once calm was restored, Senator Richards stood up and continued with his opening statement:

"Your Honor, thank you for your understanding of the emotions of this hearing and your guidance upon it. The defense's desire is to, rationally, replicate the events of that morning in Rabbit Flat, with the help of people who were there. With signed affidavits of citizens who saw things. Marshal Tome's will give reliable testimony of what he discovered at the actual scene. And we will hear an account of the actual shooting from the defendant, as told to a sworn U.S. lawman, who will reprise that narrative under oath. We know, when presented with actual evidence and testimony to consider, this court will find its way to the obvious conclusion, that Barton Anderson is sitting here today, by the grace of God and his ability to defend himself, as afforded by the laws of the state of Kansas."

Applause and amens quickly go up in the courtroom, and just as quickly die down, as the assembly observes the fierce look that Judge Likens is casting over them. The judge thanks both attorneys for their opening statements, then calls for an early lunch break, considering the events of the morning and the work still yet to be accomplished. With the sound of his broken gavel hitting the desk, the judge announces that the court is adjourned until one o'clock that afternoon.

Seeing that Senator Richards did not arrive in Smithview until minutes before the trial began and had not had a chance to discuss the case with Barton and Marshal Tomes, the statesman suggests that they have food sent to the jail. While they ate, they could talk over what they wanted to accomplish in the afternoon session and how they would reach a satisfactory verdict for Barton. Tomes agreed and looked to Barton for his approval. The tall man got up from the church pew, walked over to the open window and watched as some kids were playing kick-the-can. The marshal came over beside Barton, and with a voice that betrayed the lawman's concern for his friend, asked, "Barton, do you even care what happens this afternoon? Won't you help Jim defend you against this unfounded charge?"

Barton continued to look out the window, taking in the antics of the laughing youngsters. "You see that bean can those kids have? That piece of tin has more of a chance of getting away from their romping than I do leaving here a free man today. This whole thing is a waste of time. Judge Likens had his mind made up before he got to Smithview, and the grieving father didn't look too broken to me. The only people who are going to benefit from today are the newspapers and the stories they will get from it."

Senator Richards, quickly, steps over by the two men and pleads, "You are wrong, Barton. The prosecution has nothing but the unwitnessed guessing of Carter Sanders. And, you are right, something just doesn't feel right about him being here today. After learning who had brought the charges against you, I sent a telegram to the state attorney general's office seeking any information that they might have on this man. With what the attorney general finds, with Marshal Tomes' signed statements from the people of Rabbit Flat, his eyewitness testimony of the aftermath, and your statement of what happened, I know we have a good chance of presenting a favorable case.

Barton turns to the imploring statesmen and asks, "And what about the blowhard politician posing as a judge? Won't he have the last say when it's all said and done?"

Senator Richards sighs, looks up at the table where the verdict will come from, and replies, "Politics can absolutely be a cad to Lady Justice when the two cross paths. She stands there with her blindfold on, making sure the scales are not tipped in anyone's favor, holding her sword to fight for the rights of all men. Then politics comes racing by, riding rough-shod over her in the name of personal gain, governmental profit, and electoral votes. Afterwards, she is left in the dust to clean up the mess. I don't know if the verdict is signed and sealed in Judge Likens' mind, but I know we will tell our story. And, if he isn't convinced that it is the truth, then we will appeal to other options and benches."

And with that thought, the men leave the church for lunch, preparing and pondering what the afternoon will hold for Barton.

By one o'clock, everyone is back in their seats. Whether it is the chance of another verbal onslaught from Judge Likens, or the fact that everyone is culinarily satisfied, the gallery seems a little more subdued. Even when Sheriff Harris announces for everyone to rise, Judge

Likens tries for a more low-key entrance into the court proceedings. After a few careful taps with his broken gavel, Sheriff Harris states that everyone may be seated and the judge, immediately, instructs country attorney Rance Embree to begin his case for the prosecution.

"Thank you, your Honor," the impromptu prosecutor begins. "I call as a witness for the state, Carter Sanders."

The father of Curt Sanders makes his way to a chair that has been set to the right of the judge's table, facing the gallery.

After Sanders is sworn in by the sheriff, Embree thanks the witness for being there, considering the distance Rabbit Flat is from Smithview, the emotional state the grieving father is in, and having to face the man who is accused of murdering his son.

"Your Honor." Senator Richards slowly rises from his pew. "I think we spent the biggest part of the morning explaining the people who will have a part in this proceeding, the defense would appreciate it if Mr. Embree would get to his case and his witness' part in it. Thank you, your Honor."

Judge Likens, with a frown on his face, signals for the county attorney to stand closer to him. When the temporary prosecutor steps over, the judge, after rolling his eyes for all to see, says, "I know you got ambushed into taking this responsibility, and you probably don't have any experience at this sort of legal area. So, let me help you. You ask the questions; the witness answers them. When you have asked all your questions, and the witness has answered all of them, then I give the defense a chance to ask some questions. Does that sound fair? You can do that, can't you?"

The gallery erupts with laughter, and the judge is slow

233

to stop them, as this is the first positive response he has gotten all day, and he will revel in it for a moment.

Embree, feeling like a child who has just been admonished in front of the whole class, thanks the judge for his understanding and tutelage. Then he turns back toward the witness and starts his questioning.

"Mr. Sanders, would you describe your deceased son as a peaceful person, a fun-loving young man, someone that you took great pride in?"

"Yes, sir," the witness responds. "That boy meant the world to me. He wouldn't have harmed no one. The town acted like he was one of their own, just like he was one of their own kinfolks. Yes, sir. That boy was the pride of Rabbit Flat."

"So, Mr. Sanders. Your son never would pose any kind of threat to anyone, stranger or known, that approached him in your saloon or anywhere, for that matter?" Rance Embree continued with his questioning.

Sanders looked at the inquisitor with an expression of surprise. "Why, that boy was gentle, kind and wouldn't know which end of a gun to hold. He was pampered by his mother and was kind of a sissy, if you know what I mean. He wouldn't hurt nobody. That man over there killed my boy, and I deserve some damages for my heartache and loss of help at the saloon."

When Sanders makes these statements, Marshal Tomes leans over, whispers something in Senator Richards' ear, and hands him some papers. The senator looks at the papers and nods back at Tomes, with a confident look on his face.

"Your Honor, I believe the prosecution has done what it needs to do, to show that Curt Sanders was an innocent bystander who posed no threat to anyone. But Curt was, tragically, gunned downed in his father's business, by a man who had no regard for Curt's life and took young Sanders' life out of hatred and rage. The prosecution rests, with the right to question any witnesses, or evidence, that the defense may present in the continuance of this murder trial," the interim prosecutor proclaims to the judge and all in the courtroom.

"Senator, do you have any questions for the witness?" Judge Likens asks.

"Oh, yes, your Honor. We most certainly need to solicit the witness' help in explaining some things that we are a little cloudy on," the senator remarks as he continues to look at the papers that Tomes had handed him.

"Mr. Sanders," the statesman begins his inquiry. "You say that Curt was peaceful, loving, caring, a timid type, never to cause anyone any harm or hurt. Did I understand you to describe your son as such a person?"

"That's what I said, I think I was pretty plain. If you don't believe me, you can ask anyone around Rabbit Flat," Sanders retorts with a huffy voice.

Senator Richards lifts the papers up in the air, turns to the witness, and starts his cross examination. "It's funny you would say that, because United States Marshal Lyndon Tomes did just that. I hold in my hands the signed statements of citizens of Rabbit Flat. They picture your son as a bully, a malcontent, a vandalizer, as one whom some were afraid of. Some had even observed your son shooting household pets and innocent animals. I also hold a report that, while your son attended a special school for the mentally challenged in Prestonburg, Curt sent a couple of students to the infirmary with apparent knife wounds. Sir, I don't think your son held such a lofty

235

place of admiration in the eyes and hearts of the citizens of Rabbit Flat, do you?"

"Those self-righteous people need to mind their own business. From time to time, I have to leave town to conduct business and Curt, being a boy, would act up from time-to-time. It's not easy raising a boy alone, since his whore mom ran off with that drover. She should have taken her halfwit son with her," Sanders proclaims unapologetically as a gasp comes from the gallery.

"Your Honor, the defense has no more need for this witness," the senator states as he looks at Barton, who shakes his head in amazement at what just happened.

"Mr. Sanders, with the bench's blessing, would you please go back to your seat and try not to add any more to this proceeding?" Judge Likens orders in an exasperated tone.

"Your Honor, if we may, the defense calls United States Marshal Lydon Tomes to testify on the behalf of the defense for Barton Anderson."

After sitting in the witness chair and taking the oath, Tomes explains the circumstances of the shooting in Rabbit Flat. That Barton was trailing the murderers of his family, that the outlaws had been vandalizing and terrorizing Rabbit Flat for many hours, that Curt Sanders had participated in the actions of the outlaws, even taunting the citizens to try to stop them. Tomes said, that according to Mr. Anderson's statements, that he entered the saloon to confront the outlaws, not knowing that Coy Newton was not present, but assuming that Curt was the third murderer. Upon seeing that all three were highly inebriated and armed, Mr. Anderson decided to leave the saloon, but was stopped by Angus Ford, who had awakened and was pointing a handgun at Mr. Anderson in a threatening way. After words were exchanged, a gunfight ensued, in which Mr. Anderson was severely wounded and the three males at the table were killed.

"Marshal Tomes," the senator follows. "Upon your examination of the scene, does what you found back up the story of the defendant?"

"Yes, senator. Upon my findings, it is highly probable that the events happened as the defendant has shared with law enforcement, and that is the report I filed with the Topeka office of the U. S. Marshal bureau there," Tomes replied as he looked at Barton and smiled.

"Thank you, Marshal. Your Honor, the defense is grateful for the marshal's help, and we have no more questions for him at this time."

Judge Likens acknowledges the statement of the senator, then turns and asks if the prosecution has any questions of the witness.

"Yes sir, we do," Embree answers as he rises and looks at Tomes, still sitting in the witness chair.

"Marshal, as a lawman, I am sure you are trained to use your many talents to carry out the keeping of the law. Would you say that knowing the thoughts of a dead man was one of your strong suits?" Embree asks as murmuring sweeps over the gallery.

Tomes has a puzzled look on his face as he carefully responds, "Sir, I don't know if I fully understand your question. I have simply testified to what the scene indicated, in conjunction with the statement of the defendant. I have not said I know what anyone thought, just what the physical evidence implied."

"But, Marshal Tomes, the defendant has claimed that he acted in defense of his life, that he felt that he was in danger and had to shoot everyone there. But isn't it true that you only found one gun in the hands of those sitting at the table?"

"Yes, Mr. Embree. I found a gun in the hand of Angus Ford and another gun, recently fired, lying in front of the body of Curt Sanders. That is true," Tomes answers hesitantly.

"And the defendant claims that he saw the young Sanders reaching for that gun on the table. Is there a chance that Curt mistakenly reached out in the direction of the gun?" Embree inquires, feeling he has Tomes cornered.

"Well, Mr. Embree, I don't claim to be the smartest person in the world, but I think most people would agree that it's not the wisest thing to do to be reaching in the direction of a gun while a gunfight is in progress," Tomes comes back as the gallery agrees with responses of "That's right, Marshal," and "You tell him, Tomes."

Judge Likens taps his gavel, imploring the gallery to keep silent. The jurist asks the prosecutor if he has any more questions of the marshal. Upon getting a nod from Embree, the judge turns to Senator Richards and asks, "Do you have more witnesses you would like to call today?"

The Senator looks at Barton, who shakes his head as to discourage the statesman from continuing with his duties, replies, "No, Your Honor, I believe the defense rests."

Judge Likens pulls his watch out of his pocket, and after assessing the time, announces, "We will take a break for supper. This court will reconvene at six o'clock, at which time I will give my verdict in the matter of the charge against Mr. Barton Anderson. Court is adjourned."

While the crowd starts to file out the front door, Tomes turns to the Senator and voices his hope that the Judge would have wanted to sleep on the decision and give it the following morning. The senator shakes his head in agreement.

Barton, while standing as Sheriff Harris places the handcuffs back on him, simply replies, "No need to take the night when you already know the verdict."

Later, as the supper adjournment winds down, people file back into the church building. The conversations are lively as to what the expectation is for the verdict against their neighbor, Barton Anderson. Most seem to think the judge should let him go, that he has paid a high price with the loss of his family, and his near loss of life. Some aren't so sure, concerned that the judge may still use this as a political step into higher professional desires. A few simply want all this to be over and the normalcy of Smithview be restored.

At six o'clock, Sheriff Harris asks everyone to rise for the entrance of Judge Likens. Once the judicator seats himself, and all other follow suit, the judge starts his remarks with the pew containing the prosecution party.

"While it has nothing to do with the focus of this legal proceeding, I just want to say that I have never seen a sorrier example of fatherhood than you, Mr. Sanders. Absolutely an abominable picture of parental worth. By your ignorant remarks, you, sir, feel you are owed something, evidently. Well, sir, you deserve to be taken out back of the nearest building and shown the errors of your ways. I don't believe you would profit from such an action, but I am tempted."

Then the judge turns and looks at Barton, sitting with Tomes and Richards.

"Mr. Anderson, as for you. I would have to be one cold son-of-a-gun to not be moved by what happened to your family. I am a family man, and I can't even imagine experiencing what you have experienced. I don't know where your mind was after that. I am sure it wasn't on what was the judicial approach to those who perpetrated this travesty. And, sir, Angus Ford and Willie Beeler got what they deserved, and I will even say it's a shame that scum, Coy Newton, wasn't there to receive his come-uppance. But unfortunately, it seems he wasn't, and Curt Sanders was sitting in his place. You didn't seem to know that, and in that moment, you weren't greatly concerned with sorting out the identities of those at that table. With your mind raging and a gun pointed at you, choices weren't plentiful as to how to handle the situation, were they, Mr. Anderson?"

Judge Likens pauses for a moment, folds his hands together, rests his chin on his hands, and continues. "But, in Kansas, it is not against the law to be in the wrong place at the wrong time, just painful sometimes. And it's not against the law to be flawed at picking your friends, which Curt Sanders seems to have done. It's all sad, but not against the law. Ford and Beeler deserved what they got, and more. But we will never know what the young Sanders was thinking. Was he going to use the gun, or did he want to hand it to you, to show he didn't want to participate in the violence? We will never know, Mr. Anderson, will we?"

After another pause to go over his notes and deliberate, the judge instructs Barton to stand for his verdict. As the tall man rises, Tomes and Senator Richards stand up with him in unison to show their support for their friend.

"Mr. Anderson, after listening to the testimonies, viewing statements, and considering the circumstances of the last few months, by the legal powers given to me, by the state of Kansas, I reduce the charges of murder to involuntary manslaughter, and I find you guilty of such a charge. By the judicial guidelines of the state of Kansas, the minimum I can sentence you to is two years' incarceration, so that is your sentence, to be served in the Lansing State Prison. You are to be taken there tomorrow morning, and I believe that U.S. Marshal Tomes would like that responsibility, would you not, marshal?"

"Yes, your Honor. I will take the duty of delivering Mr. Anderson to Lansing."

"Then, it is the pronouncement of this bench that this trial is over," the judge says as he taps his gavel, gathers his papers, and exits out the back of the church.

With some women weeping, some men cursing under their breaths, Senator Richards promising to not give up, and others filing out of the building with thoughts of their plans for tomorrow, Tomes turns to Barton and asks, "Don't you have anything to say? Do you have any thoughts running through your mind, at all?"

Barton looked at Tomes, his eyes narrowing and the corners of his mouth tightening. Then, the tall man coldly responded, "The judge just bought Coy Newton two years. If you don't kill him, then I will in seven hundred and thirty days."

And from that moment, Barton Anderson counted the days.

Chapter Eighteen

The Kansas winter had been an unusually harsh one. So, a sunny, cool spring day was welcome on this fifteenth day of March at Lansing State Prison. It had been four months since Barton Anderson's trial. The time seemed to pass quickly. For the tall rancher, time is not something he considers as something he has lost, but it is something that impedes him from the only thing that consumes his mind, finding Coy Newton and finalizing his quest for his fallen family.

Barton, staying true to his persona after the loss of his family had not sought friendships or associations in prison. He is a quiet loner, distancing himself from any chance of conversation. Among the convicts, he became known as The Mute, which was jailhouse lingo that meant he had a reason for not talking, and the cons were willing to accept that. The fact that he, single-handedly, killed his family's assassins procured him status among the general population too. One braggart, a onetime cohort of Angus Ford, let it be known that the new prisoner executed one of the great outlaws and he was going to avenge their brother in crime. Such talk fell on deaf ears, because even in a prison full of killers, thieves, arsonists and the like, there is a line that most criminals will never cross: you never touch a child. Whether the concept of honor among thieves is a real thing or not, Barton is allowed his space and, so far, it has not been breached or challenged.

Although he was not aware of it, Barton had acquired an unlikely ally within the prison walls. Warden Walton Millsap had taken a measured interest in the plight of the new inmate. The warden was a fellow law student with Senator Jim Richards, and the statesman had stayed in touch with the penitentiary superintendent from the early days of Barton's term. Warden Millsap, like most people, felt for the tall man and the path that life had forced him to travel. The warden, after years of being the steward of this penal institution, had developed an ability to gauge what a person was bringing to the prison. Most were void of goodness, compassion, or the ability of having a trait that would be minimally valuable to society. He had learned that you never toss away the paperwork on a released inmate because they will be back in time. While he felt that some of the fault was due to some failure of the prison system, the one truth that could never be dismissed was that being a criminal was just who they were. No amount of discipline, educating, or preaching was going to change that.

But the warden had a different feeling about Barton. After considering the correspondences from Senator Richards, talking with Marshal Tomes upon the tall mans' arrival, and Millsap's gut feeling about the new prisoner, the warden came to an assessment of Barton that he was willing to live with. Until the day he walked out of Lansing Prison, Barton would be approached as an inmate who would not be one to start a situation but would be quick to end a situation if confronted with one.

So, within a short time of Barton's arrival, Warden Millsap informed the guards that the newest inmate was to be assigned to the prison farm. The prison, under the warden's progressive leadership, had developed an agricultural program that allowed it to grow its own food, provide product for an inmate boot and saddle shop, and generate the prison a steady revenue flow through a venture with the nearby army garrison to sell cattle, horses, and boots. With Barton's experience as a rancher, this would be a natural environment for him to be in. And it would provide a result that everyone could live with; that Barton would not have to make any new friends or, hopefully, any new enemies.

Marshal Tomes visited Lansing Prison from time to time when he would escort a prisoner there on behalf of the U.S. Marshal's office. These official sojourns usually involved arriving with the prisoner, signing what paperwork was needed, visit with Barton for the allotted time, and then return to his lawman responsibilities. Tomes usually planned on a fifteen-minute encounter with Barton in a controlled visitation area. The two men would sit across from each other, a table in between them. The meetings consisted of Tomes telling of what experiences he had had lately, sharing the latest from Jeff and the Anderson ranch, and any other news that the marshal felt his friend might be interested in. The marshal hoped these tidbits might give Barton something else to think about than just Coy Newton. Barton's participation in these meetings was usually to listen, offer a two-word response occasionally, and then inform Tomes he had to get back to the livestock. By now, the marshal knew what to expect and accepted them as good visits.

But today is going to be different. Instead of arriving on a horse with a prisoner, Tomes is in a stagecoach, that is being escorted by four armed military riders. Rather than be taken to the visitation area, the guard will take Barton to the warden's office, where he will wait until the marshal shows up with an unexpected traveling companion. The warden excuses himself and leaves

Barton alone in his office for what seemed like a long time but was only a few minutes. The tall man is suspicious of this change in the prison visitation routine.

After hearing a commotion of people walking down the hall, the office door opens and there stands Tomes with an impressively dressed man positioned next to him.

"Barton, I want to introduce you to a man who has a desire to talk with you," the marshal starts. "And I hope when you hear what he has to say, you will consider what he has to offer you."

Barton looks at the visitor, then looks at Tomes and responds, "I don't think I have much choice, do I?"

The stranger stepped forward, confidently threw his hand out and said, "Mr. Anderson, my name is Anthony Hayes. I am the governor of the great state of Kansas, and I believe that you and I can be of assistance to each other's situations."

Barton, not returning the offer of a handshake, calmly responds, "Let me guess. You have been caught being a bad boy in Topeka, and you are going to be getting your mail here at Lansing, and you need a friend on the inside, right?"

Tomes, sensing that the opening greeting has not gone as smoothly as hoped, enters the exchange. "The governor has been following your story and believes that, if given the right opportunity, you could be of more value to the state of Kansas outside these walls. He has an idea that can get you out of here if you are willing to listen to him and just consider it. Will you at least listen to what he wants to propose?"

Barton looks at the governor and says, "You have fifteen minutes. I have livestock to tend to."

While it took more than the fifteen minutes he was

allotted, Governor Hayes laid out a classified plan that at least kept Barton's attention throughout the presentation. The state boss, with Tomes giving his support, spoke of a strategy to help the state with a rising problem within its borders—the number of homicides performed by fugitive outlaws. With law enforcement spread thin with all matters of enforcement, from burglaries to land grabs, from range wars to drunk cowboys, there weren't enough badges to focus on those dregs like Angus Ford, who always took lives no matter where they went. The governor spoke of selecting a special individual whose only purpose would be to seek out these fugitive butchers and eliminate these elements before they could take more innocent lives. Conservative estimates showed that three to five respectable citizens could be saved by the elimination of one soulless assassin.

Barton, after listening to Governor Hayes, looks at Tomes and inquires with a mystified tone, "And you think I am the man to do this task for the great state of Kansas?"

The marshal shrugs his shoulders and remarks, "Well, you do have some experience at killing felons without asking very many questions."

As Barton ponders the thought of not waiting another twenty months to get out of prison, Governor Hayes steps up his effort to solicit the tall man's help for this project. "Sir, you are someone who understands what it's like to lose loved ones to evil men who don't care why they pulled the trigger. Sometimes it is just for the devilish pleasure it brings them. Mr. Anderson, those hurting families have no way to do what you did, to just go and cut off the snake's head before it can bite someone else. The only people who would know about your actions

246

would be me, Marshal Tomes, and Senator Richards. You would answer to Marshal Tomes, and him alone. If you agree to this, the expectation is for you to spend the rest of your days performing these covert chores for the state. In return, you will be released on special parole as soon as the ink dries on the paperwork that Warden Millsap is putting together, as we speak."

Barton turns to Tomes, and with a smirk says, "You were pretty sure of how this was going to work out, wasn't you?"

The U.S. lawman answers, "I could only hope. I knew one thing, in twenty months, you were going to walk out of this prison with killing Coy Newton on your mind. You can walk out now and go after Newton with something you didn't have the first time: the support of a governor, a senator, and a U.S. marshal. Along the way, if it takes ten days or ten years to find Newton, you can do some good for some families who have been hurt and try to keep some families from being hurt. That wasn't a bad thing to hope for, was it?"

While Barton is still trying to absorb what has been presented, Governor Hayes interjects. "While I support this completely, there is one thing you need to know. You are not being given a free pass to go out and just start shooting people. There is no expectation of you arresting any fugitive that you, and Marshal Tomes, choose to pursue. As a matter of fact, the state would appreciate saving the time, and money, of incarcerating and trying the vermin again. But, Mr. Anderson, collateral damage will not be tolerated. In other words, if any innocent bystanders are hurt, or killed, by you, and it is determined it could have been avoided, then you will be back here in Lansing pronto. And, not just for twenty months, if you

247

catch my meaning. Again, the removal of these thugs is the goal and a careful pursuit will be instituted in accomplishing that course. Remember, the effort is to decrease the loss of innocent life, not increase them through reckless actions."

Barton, having quickly considered the aspects of such an undertaking, makes an observation. "If this goes as planned, you are going to come out of this looking pretty good, aren't you, Governor?"

Governor Hayes shakes his head, in an affirmative manner, and answers, "Yes sir. I am not going to act as if I won't. I am up for reelection in eight months and reducing the number of violent homicides is going to play well with the public. But don't get too reproving of what this can do for me, because you are going to benefit too."

Barton's eyes narrow as he is caught off guard by this slant to the governor's response. "Exactly, what am I going to get for doing this? A Christmas card from the governor's mansion or, perhaps, a bullet from one of these fugitives that are going to cost you votes?"

"Well, Mr. Anderson. The obvious benefit is you are not going to spend the next twenty months feeding someone else's livestock, sleeping in a cold prison cell, and wearing state-issued clothes," the governor replies as he hopes to close his presentation on these next words. "There is, also, a financial return for you if you are successful at completing your assignments. Only three people will know of this strategy, therefore only three people will know of your involvement. There will be no paper trail, no public contacts, no state sponsored acknowledgements of it; just you "cleaning up" the territory of these "stains on humanity". You will not be on staff, nor a paid employee or a contracted service.

Nothing will connect you with the state government. But you must exist, and you will have expenses in performing your duties. Thus, your benefit is that there is an excellent chance that each mark that is to be eliminated,will have a reward for them. Once the task is done, you will make arraignments with Marshal Tomes to turn over the remains to him. In his official capacity, he will make a report, obtain the reward, and get it to you. Everything stays nice and tidy and you move on to your next objective. Sounds like a plan, doesn't it?"

Barton, with a slightly disgusted look on his face, answers, "Hell, it sounds like I would be a government sanctioned bounty hunter, if you just cut through the political horse crap and be honest about it!"

Tomes, feeling they are starting to lose the tall man, jumps in. "No, Barton. Not a bounty hunter for the state, but more like a janitor, cleaning up the state so people can live safer and better, keeping families intact. As a matter of fact, in our discussions about this entire undertaking, it has been referred to as just that: The Janitor Project. Unlike a bounty hunter, who works according to his own rules and is willing to rewrite those rules for his own benefit, you would be a monitored resource of corrective justice, swinging the scales of justice back in favor of the citizens and the law. The monetary part is what will get you to the next job and, hopefully, save another life. As the governor has stated, there will be no pay, no expense account, no paper trail. You will live off the legally compensated reward money that you will receive. This isn't a bad thing, Barton, just something that will take a special person to do it. There are three men who are willing to put a lot on the line for that to be you."

Barton runs his fingers through his scruffy beard, looks at the marshal and says, "I think the governor better watch out, you are starting to sound like one of those bureaucratic chinwaggers in the state capitol."

Governor Hayes laughs and responds, "Mr. Anderson, I have tried to get the marshal to join my cabinet in Topeka, but he seems to think he can do more good riding the state, wearing a badge and trying to keep the peace that way. I am convinced that Kansas has a good lawman in Marshal Tomes, and I know you have a good friend in him."

Barton does not respond to the governor's statement, just keeps rubbing his hand against his face and contemplating what has been presented to him. After a few minutes, the tall man gets up from his chair, walks over to an outside window, and asks, "If I agree to this hare-brained idea, when do I get out and when would I start my job as... what did you call it? The janitor?"

Governor Hayes, feeling that he is on the verge of accomplishing his goal of coming to Lansing, spells out what the next steps are.

"As we mentioned, Warden Millsap is putting together the paperwork to get you released. I gave him a signed special pardon from my state office to sanction such an order. Once that is done, there will be a twenty-four-hour period between my leaving Lansing and your release as to prevent anyone suggesting the two are connected. As far as my office is concerned, I came here today to see the fine job the warden is doing with his prison farm system, nothing more. Your special pardon will be one of many executive orders I signed one day. It will be filed away somewhere, and, if all goes well, it will never be needed again. Of course, that all depends on if you say yes. Will you work with us, Mr. Anderson, to be a center piece of something that can keep people from going through the heartache and suffering you have been through?"

Barton stood silently for a moment. Tomes and the governor stood waiting for an answer. Then, the tall man turned to the marshal and said, "If I do this, I am going to need two things as soon as possible. There isn't any chance you were prophetic enough to be working on them, is there?"

Tomes, taking that as a yes to their proposal, smiles coyly. "Jeff left Smithview this morning, and he should be here sometime tomorrow afternoon. When you walk beyond the gray walls of Lansing tomorrow, you should find Smoke, saddled up, and your Henry sheathed and ready to go."

When the marshal notices a look of great concern come over Barton's face, Tomes laughs and assures his friend that in the last four months, the young rancher and the big gray horse have learned a couple of things. One, Smoke has learned to tolerate Jeff, and two, Jeff has learned that it's best to let the Smoke have his way and just hope for the best.

With that understanding, Barton turns and heads for the office door. As he walks out, he yells back, "See you tomorrow, lawman!"

It was around four in the afternoon when the guards came to get Barton. He didn't have much to pack, because just as Barton wasn't one to accumulate friends, he didn't amass any belongings or mementos during his stay at Lansing Prison, either. As was the policy of the prison, any released inmate would be provided with a jacket, a clean shirt, clean pants, a new pair of boots from the prison leather shop, and five dollars in living money.

251

The token funds were an effort to keep the newly freed from reverting to old habits to survive on the outside. It usually was effective for a few days, until old skills would be revived and used, resulting in a ticket back to Lansing Prison.

Barton was, as usual, subdued as he walked toward the main gate. Maybe the fact there was so much unknown waiting for him, on the other side of the wall. He showed no emotion as he walked through the gate until he heard a high-pitched whinny that he had not heard in a long time.

For the first time in six months, Barton Anderson smiled.

Upon seeing the tall man walking outside the prison gate, Smoke started rearing up on his hind legs, making that high-pitched sound he would make on certain occasions, and doing that front foot dance that he was famous for.

After Tomes and Jeff did their best to restrain excited equine, the marshal finally let go of the lead rope, and approvingly announced, "Go on, big gray! Go see your friend! Get on to him, boy!"

Jeff would later state that he had not seen that much energy from Smoke since the day that Barton got on the Smithview stagecoach and left for Lansing Prison. The big gray horse ran with all his heart to his friend, who was standing there with his hand extended, waiting for a chin to rub. Smoke was running so hard that he almost ran past Barton, but the mighty steed gathered his feet, and slowly walked up to Barton. The tall man put one hand under Smoke's chin and wrapped his other arm under his strong neck. The two stood there, in no hurry to break the embrace, in no rush to move on to the next thing in their lives. This moment had been long anticipated and would be completely appreciated.

As Tomes observed the touching reunion, the marshal leaned back in his saddle and sighed. For the first time, since he, Senator Richards, and Governor Hayes had their first meeting about an idea that involved the incarcerated rancher from Smithview, a new feeling came over the watching lawman.

This thing may actually work.

Chapter Nineteen

The first twenty-four hours of freedom for Barton were spent on things the average person takes for granted, like the smell of nature coming to life on a spring day, drinking cool water from a rippling stream, eating campfire food, loading and holding your favorite rifle, and riding a dark, gray horse who wanted to run like the wind. The next day was spent listening to Marshal Tomes explain this thing called The Janitor Project. The lawman did all the talking, and for the first time since that devastating morning at the Anderson ranch, Tomes felt the tall man was listening to him. Barton understood that some good men were taking a big risk at getting him involved in this operation. He also understood that if he did not do his part well then his ultimate goal would never be achieved. The goal of locating and consummating retribution on Coy Newton.

The unofficial formula for this operation to work was pretty simple. Don't miss your shot, don't get shot, don't make your move in a crowd, and don't get recognized. The first two were pretty simple to understand. The objective of the third rule was to cut down on the chance of someone innocent getting hurt or someone feeling they needed to get involved and coming against Barton. Each action was about one outlaw, so keeping it between that fugitive and the tall man would make it a lot simpler, and cleaner. As for the last rule, the thought was to try to keep the element of surprise in play, cut down on the possibility of anyone linking the tall man with the state, and to eliminate any chance of reprisal against Barton or anyone tied to him.

Tomes instructed Barton that each encounter was to be as close to legal as possible. The marshal explained that Barton was not to take on the role of sniper, but that of a swift confronted of each wanted man. Every fugitive would have one thing in common: that their careers were to be ended by means of their arrest or by their death. As the tall man was not a sworn lawman, arresting someone was not an option. The latter part of this judicial edict allowed Barton to cut out the middleman and just end the outlaws' felonious vocation coldly and permanently. Tomes tried drawing a comparison between the public service that Barton would be providing and the biblical principle of an eye for an eye. But Tomes stopped when Barton would give the marshal a look that expressed that he had no problem with closing an outlaw's record once and for all.

Upon locating his subject, Barton was to observe when the best time would be to make his approach, establish how to take away any edge the outlaw might have, and never shoot from the rear, if possible. Most citizens would be grateful for the demise of another cold-blooded murderer, but back shooting always seemed to leave a bad taste in a lot of people's mouths. Finally, Tomes explained, after years of marshaling, one of the keys of getting a job done was to be patient. While time is always important, when trying to save innocent lives, getting in too big of a hurry could prove fatal, and allow the outlaw to continue with his bloody crimes.

Once they agreed on how each plan was to be carried out, Tomes shared another big concern that he had, one that Barton was going to have to work at assuring the tall man would walk away alive. While no one questioned that Barton was a master with a Henry rifle, Tomes pointed out that most scenarios would lend themselves to the skilled use of a Colt sidearm. Barton initially protested the marshal's contention that his Henry rifle would not be the best option. Tomes, in making his case, reminded Barton of what happened that morning in Rabbit Flat. The reason that Barton almost died wasn't because he chose the wrong gun, but because he wasn't skilled enough with a sidearm. Once Barton accepted the marshal's assessment of the weapon of choice for this undertaking, Tomes would look for places to practice as they traveled the countryside. Initially, Barton was not smooth in drawing and firing a Colt handgun, it just wasn't a skill that a rancher needed in his daily life. But with Tomes' encouragement and coaching, the tall man got to the point where he could clear leather and fire before a rock dropped from the marshal's outstretched hand could hit the ground.

"You are getting pretty impressive with that Colt," the marshal observed during one practice. "but there is one more thing you have to master before we can turn you loose for real."

Barton, growing frustrated with vying for the marshal's final approval, replied, "I am wondering if you are so good at this. Why do you even need me, lawman?"

Tomes, sensing his friend's impatience with the process, answered, "Because you have something I do not have and I wouldn't want it for any amount of money. You have this hunger for vengeance, and I don't know if it will ever be quenched for you. So, maybe we can use it as the spark that helps others find their healing from tragedy. You have the opportunity to bring a sense of closure to some very good folks. And, while it will never justify what your family went through, if you will control this spark from becoming a flame, then you have the chance to do something that none of us can do, and that is to adjust the scales of virtue. And maybe if we are lucky, the balance of life for some people.

"My word!" Barton exclaims as he shakes his head. "There you go talking like one of those government windbags again. What is the one thing that I must master before you turn me loose on the unsuspecting villains of Kansas?"

Tomes drew his pistol, pointed to a dead limb on a nearby tree, and said, "Being fast is only half of the skill. Being able to hit what you draw on is what will move you on to the next outlaw." When he had finished talking, he pulled the hammer back on his sidearm, pulled the, trigger and shot a section of the dead limb off.

Barton, with a sense of fake enlightenment, remarked, "So, if I encounter a wanted felon, I just pull my gun and shoot the end off of a dead tree limb. He is just going to drop dead. Then I throw his rear-end over a horse and bring him to you. This is going to be easier than I even imagined."

"No!" Tomes answered angrily, refusing to see the need of Barton's flippant banter. "If you are not going to—"

Before the marshal could complete his infuriated commentary, Barton stepped over, grabbed Tomes' hat from his head, threw it in the air, quickly drew his Colt, and discharged six .45 bullets into it before it could return to the ground.

While Tomes stood there stunned, Barton picked up the tattered hat, handed it to his lawman friend and announced, "It has never been about whether I can hit anything with a pistol, the question has been how fast I could do it. Thanks to your expert guidance, would you say that will suffice?"

Once the marshal gathers his senses, after Barton's display of his newfound, lightening marksmanship, he sternly asks, "And what about my hat, Wild Bill Anderson?"

As he turned to get on Smoke, Barton replied, "Get you a new one, take it out of the first reward money you will be bringing me."

Tomes could almost swear that he heard his friend chuckling as the men got on their horses and rode toward what would be a new period in both of their lives.

Over the next five months, law offices across the state got dispatches informing them that wanted posters for hunted murderers could be taken down. These reports simply stated that the designated outlaw had met their doom, the city that it happened in, and that further information was unknown. In all, six killers had been erased from the landscape and the public was breathing a little easier because of it. No one knew who to give credit to for this sudden wave of crime control. But, slowly, reports of a tall man on a dark, gray horse started making the rounds. This unknown rider became the subject of conversations everywhere. To the public, the opinion of the tall man fell between a hired gun and an avenging angel. No one was going to be quick to invite this silent sentinel to the church social, but they would remember him in their prayers each night.

To the law enforcement community, the report of a hard-case criminal being taken out was always good news. It meant one less troublemaker to come to their towns and cause destruction and despair. But, if a bad seed were to come to their cities, would this chastising stranger be far behind? While almost all of those wearing a badge wished him well, they also hoped that he would get his business done and move on as quickly as possible.

To anyone with their picture on a wanted poster and a price on their murderous heads, Barton became a to keep one eye out for. Fugitives were always looking over their shoulders for this man who was, single-handedly, thinning the ranks of the most wanted in Kansas. Whether it was actually the truth or just wishful thinking, lawmen and politicians spoke of how it seemed crime as a whole was down since the tall man had ridden his big, gray horse onto the scene.

Up to now, it seemed like everything was going as planned. Tomes would share information about where a fugitive had been seen, Barton and Smoke would ride there. Barton would take the time to locate the subject, observe him as much as possible, isolate the murderer away from unsuspecting citizens, engage him in a confrontation, then leave town with the outlaw dead and as quietly as possible. Upon completion of the assignment, Barton would send a telegram to Tomes at the telegraph office in Smithview. The marshal, without revealing the identity of the sender, alerted Jason Nash that there would be these short messages coming to him. Because of the sensitivity of the situations, Jason was to tell no one about the reports nor about what they said, and to get them to Tomes as fast as possible. Jason assured the marshal that he was the man for the job. The marshal agreed.

Apart from one time when Barton buried an outlaw in a stand of trees because of circumstances beyond his control, the two men would meet at Rooster Pass just outside of Smithview. Because he had ridden through this part of the country many times and knew of isolated places where they could meet, Barton would bring the dead fugitive to the marshal, turn the body over to Tomes who would take it to Smithview, make a report with Sheriff Harris, wait for the reward money to arrive, then return to meet with Barton a couple of days later. The pre-agreed arraignment with handling the reward money was that Tomes was to return to Rooster Pass with just enough expense money for Barton's next endeavor. The rest was put in a special account at the Smithview bank to be available to Jeff and his family if they ever encountered hardships on the ranch, or with life itself. Jeff didn't know about the account, which was how Barton wanted it. His new line of work would benefit Jenny's family, and that helped put a different spin on where the money came from and why.

While Barton waited for Tomes to return each time, he found solace in the hill country of Rooster Pass. He used to come here with his boys to hunt deer and fish in the freshwater stream. He and Jenny had brought picnic lunches on sunny summer days to just be alone for a few moments. When he would sit on the highest ridge of Rooster Pass, he could see a large part of the Anderson ranch below. Barton never went down there while waiting for Tomes to return. He would just sit up on the high ridge, looking over the impressive herd of cows that Jeff was raising. When the spring colts would run across the flat ranch land, Smoke would do his foot dance, wanting to join in as he did in past days. Barton would calm him down with the promise of "Maybe someday, big gray, maybe someday." When he would catch a glimpse of Jeff's kids playing and their mom hanging laundry in the back of the house, Barton would get on

Smoke and return to the campsite. Nothing against the family that lived there now, it was just a reminder of what he once had, how it was taken from him, and why he would never walk the land of the Anderson ranch again.

As Barton and Smoke returned to the campsite, Tomes was there, waiting. It didn't take long for him to see that Tomes had a look of concern on his face, which usually meant that the marshal had encountered unwanted news in Smithview.

"Let me guess," Barton started, "they didn't have your favorite on the lunch special and you are never going back there again?"

When Tomes didn't look up from the campfire, Barton abandoned his attempt to lighten the mood. "What is wrong, Tomes?"

Still not looking up, the marshal replied, "Remember when we started this thing, we established that there were four things that would have to be maintained for you to have your highest chance of success and survival?"

"If my memory serves me right, they were shooting quicker and straighter, not getting shot, keeping away from crowds, and not being recognized. Did I not keep with the program, somehow?" Barton ponders as he awaits what has the marshal so uneasy.

Tomes looked up at Barton with a facial expression that gave the impression of surprise, then acceptance. "It wasn't really anything you did. It is more just who you are. To be exact, who you and Smoke are. Evidently, over time, the talk of this tall man on a dark, gray horse has been making the rounds all over Kansas. Some people don't like when the picture isn't complete and tend to start filling in the blanks. This thing has gotten increasingly twisted as far as who people are saying is

261

taking out the bad seeds of society.

"Okay, so what is the story now? What is being passed around the bridge clubs and the social circles?" Barton asks as his curiosity is growing by the minute.

"Well," Tomes begins. "It didn't take the citizens of Smithview long to figure out who it was. These people have known you, and Smoke, for years. So we should have realized that it was inevitable. But when it spread outside of the city, and others started realizing it was the rancher whose family was slaughtered by devils, their imaginations started shoving reality into the shadows. Many have concluded that it was too much for you to handle, that you have gone insane. They say that you are roaming the country, out of your mind, looking for blood to spill with your gun. Some are even saying that it's an act of God that you have only disposed of vicious fugitives and no one else. You, according to others, are so unstable that even the law is afraid of you. Can you believe this?"

Barton thinks for a moment, and then asks Tomes, with a tone of seriousness, "Aside from the act of God thing, can you say that they are terribly wrong in their assessment of me?"

Tomes answers in a troubled manner. "Look here, Barton, this is serious. The newspapers, starved for good stories, have taken this, and are running regular stories about you. After taking witnesses' descriptions, they have had pictures drawn of you which aren't very flattering. There are contests to see if anyone can guess who will be your next mark. They are even doing special kid's sections about this big, gray horse that the crazed, gunslinging tall man rides."

Barton looks at Smoke and says, "Hey, big gray, maybe you ought to be getting a share of the reward!"

262

Smoke shook his hea, like he was agreeing.

After letting Tomes settle down for a moment, Barton returns to his original observation. "Be honest, lawman. You going to tell me that you haven't had the same opinion that these people are having. That you haven't thought I am broken in mind, out of control, and that is why you approached me with this janitor thing, because you were hoping I was crazy enough to do it?".

Tomes responds, "I may have, at some point, questioned your wisdom or your actions, but I have never questioned your sanity. If I had any reservations about your mind, I would have never come to Rabbit Flat, Prestonburg, or Lansing. I would have just let someone kill you and put you out of your misery."

Barton, with a smirk, responds, "Well, I am glad I have had you fooled so far, lawman. If I start drooling or talking crazy, you have my permission to put me out of my misery."

Without responding to Barton's facetious retort, Tomes tells the tall man that, in his opinion, this puts everything in a new light. Before, Barton was just one in the crowd, could move around without raising suspicion or concern. But now, as soon as people see him, and the big, gray horse, come into their town, there will be a realization of who he is. And when that happens, they will have to make an immediate decision about how they are going to handle being around him. Will they be comforted, or will they be afraid of him?

Barton's response caught Tomes by surprise. "Is that such a bad thing, especially being afraid of this unknown rider? Fear has kept a lot of people from doing stupid things that they would be sorry for later. Usually, things that I have been afraid of, whether a bear or bad weather, I have tried to avoid because I didn't want to see who was bigger, badder, or better. I say, let them keep talking. That is all it is, just talk that is played out in simple minds."

"Let's just not feed their fantasies anything. Let's not allow their chattering to paint this as anything more than it is, and that you don't become the hunted, instead of the hunter," Tomes surmised, and added, "If you become at greater risk of not completing each task, you will have to walk away from being the janitor and find a newer, safer line of work."

Barton, upon hearing the last part of Tomes' discourse, sharply replies, "Until the day that Coy Newton, or myself, lays dead on the ground, I will continue to search for that butcher. Whether as a secret appointee of the government, cleaning up the state's messes, or just on my own, taking care of unfinished family business. And, if anyone, including you, tries to keep that from happening, then I can't promise what will happen. Lawman, don't ever think that our working together has forged some kind of unbreakable bond between us. I started this alone, and I am prepared to finish it alone, if that is the way it must be."

Disappointed that their relationship had not grown beyond an indifferent business arraignment, Tomes sighs deeply and hands a telegram to Barton that the lawman found waiting for him in Smithview. Barton reads what is on the paper, then gives the marshal a look that displays a sense of skepticism.

"It can be trusted," Tomes says to reassure Barton of the contents of the message. "Topeka office says it has confirmation that Coy Newton has been seen around an area known as Dog Creek in the last month. That is all they know."

Upon hearing this, Barton puts the telegram in his pocket, throws his saddle upon Smoke, gets upon the big, gray horse and the duo head in a northwest direction. Smoke was moving at such a pace that his feet barely made a dust trail.

As Tomes watched them riding off, an uneasy but familiar feeling swept over the marshal. The last time he stood on this land and witnessed his tall friend leaving in such a rush, the marshal wondered if he would ever see Barton alive again. He did see the tall man again, but he was barely alive and was not the man that the marshal had ridden with so many times before.

Tomes closed his eyes, and although he was not an outwardly religious man, the marshal said a little prayer. "Lord, may the next time that I see Barton Anderson, let him be sitting astride of the big, gray horse, running like the wind."

When he opened his eyes and realized that Barton was already out of sight, he softly uttered one last word.

"Amen."

Chapter Twenty

"Well, Smoke, Jack was right, there is the sign on the bridge!"

Barton took the time to read the entire placard, for Jack's anxiety at the Dog Creek Saloon foretold of a danger beyond this point. The tall man discovered that, while the road was used for public travel, the land on each side was not to be tread upon by human foot, let alone be disturbed by wagon tracks or horse's hooves. And, sure enough, the last line was very plain about the ramifications awaiting those who felt they didn't have to honor the desires of the owner of this section of Kansas.

Trespassers will be shot on sight without warning.

As Smoke trotted over the bridge, his feet making a rhythmic cadence upon the timbered floor, Barton thought of what might be awaiting him. He felt that if he could talk to Asa Givens, he might be able to reason with the recluse rancher. But Jack and Will, the card players at the Dog Creek saloon, had both been adamant about the old man's intolerance of fools, foreigners, and the footloose.

After traveling a mile or so up the main road, Barton took notice of a trail that split off the main road out of Dog Creek. From the collection of wagon tracks, sled skids and horseshoe prints left upon it, the tall man had a strong feeling that this was a well-traveled passage leading to the ranch house and other dwellings of the Asa Givens spread. The number and variations of the impressions displayed in the dirt let Barton know that the Givens operation was served by an adequate number of ranch hands. And whether for protection from dangerous critters or enforcing the wishes of the landowner, the tall man knew that each one would be reasonably armed. With that thought in mind, Barton reached down and slipped off the small leather strap that secured his Colt in its holster as he turned Smoke up the trail.

It did not take long for Barton to experience his first contact as three riders appeared in the path and blocked his way. Seeing that they had their hands upon their holstered sidearms, he was convinced that this was not a welcoming party sent on behalf of Asa Givens.

"Alright, stranger," the one in the middle yelled out. "It doesn't matter who you are or what you want. You turn that horse around and get off this land or you will be put face down in the dirt of it. We don't usually give warnings, so you are lucky today."

Barton, sitting easy upon a steady Smoke, sized up the situation and replied, "If you don't move aside and let me through, I believe that you will find it is your unlucky day that you brought only two associates with you,."

Ever since that morning in Rabbit Flat and since he had taken on this function of purging Kansas of butchers and murderers, Barton had learned that when confronted by more than one opponent, the one who does the most talking will be the one to make the first move. Within seconds, this confrontation will prove to be no different.

Bang! Bang! Bang!

With a rapid draw and three shots, Barton's three challengers were taken off their horses and were now laying on the ground. As the tall man urged Smoke to step up closer, he noticed that two were rolling in obvious pain, still trying to get their guns from their leather gun belts. As for the spokesman for the trio, it was plain to see with blood oozing through his shirt pocket that he would not be expressing his opinion again.

The sound of more approaching riders convinced Barton to reload his Colt revolver as quickly as possible. This time, he was approached by a party of five horsemen, being led by an older gentleman. Barton's pistol was still in his hand, which was resting upon the saddle horn. There it would stay, for now, as he observed that the new arrivals had their sidearms already drawn and pointed in his direction. The old cowboy rode over by the ones laying on the ground, two still agonizing from their encounter with Barton.

"Damn, drifter," the elderly rancher proclaimed with a cigarette hanging from the corner of his mouth. "It's hard enough to get help around here without having strangers riding up and shooting em' like it's some kind of carnival game."

Silently, with his eyes fixed upon the old man, Barton remained upon Smoke. His casual posture gave the portrayal of someone who was unfazed by the events of the previous minutes. Likewise, the big, gray horse was standing firm in anticipation of more action to follow.

One of the other riders moved up beside the older cowboy and asks, "Mr. Givens, do you want us to kill him and throw him in the north canyon like all the other trespassers and vagrants before?"

The old man takes a draw on his cigarette, throws it aside and said, "No, Carl. I didn't get this old by being impetuous and stupid. A man who can shoot three men off their horses before they can even clear leather is a man who deserves a little more deliberation before we decide our next play. We know he can take at least a couple of us before we take him. Who among you are volunteering to prove my point?"

268

"Sir," yet another rider joins in. "He is on your land. He is just one man."

The white-haired man with a look of sudden realization coming over his rugged face, responds, "Yes, he is just one man. That big, gray horse that he is riding tells me he is not just any man. Am I right, Mr. Anderson?"

As he remained calm and restrained upon Smoke, Barton placed his Colt revolver back in its holster, sensing that one simple act of goodwill might open the door to more productive communication and less gun play.

"I am Barton Anderson. I need information about a former ranch hand of yours. Tell me what you know, and I will be gone. Or we can continue to fill the air with needless gun smoke. It's your land, and it's your decision.

The old man puts his pistol back in its holster. And with a gesture of his hand, the other riders follow his lead and do likewise. Then he looks back at Barton and says, "You have a lot of brass riding in here today. I have heard that about you. Mr. Anderson. You may scare a lot of other people. I am too old and have seen too much to be scared anymore. But you do have my attention. I am willing to hear your questions today. I find that most discussions are best accomplished while appreciating a drink and a Mexican cigar. Are you open to either, or both?"

Barton, with his facial expression now easing and his tone less surly, answers, "Get rid of your friends and I will follow you for both, sir."

"Carl, take the wounded to the bunkhouse and do the best you can patching them up. As for Toby, I don't think he will be complaining too much if you don't get to burying him in the next few minutes. When you get ready to put him under, find an appropriate place around the west grove of trees, out of sight of the main house. Gather his belongings up and save them for the pot for this Saturday's bunkhouse poker game. His horse belongs to the ranch now," Givens orders as he waves his hand, signaling for Barton to follow him.

After they had ridden about a mile back down the trail, they arrived at the Givens ranching operation. It was large compared to the place that Barton had once watched over. Other than the main house that looked as big as a Topeka hotel, the complex included various barns, sheds, corrals, and ponds. Barton was impressed with what he saw. He and Jenny had dreamed of growing their place into a formidable homestead, but this ranch was something that their imaginations could have never been beheld.

Both men rode up to the front of the big house, tying their horses to a mighty oaken rail that spanned a good fifty feet across the front of the yard entrance. When Asa noticed that Barton was not following him toward the house, he looked back and observed the tall man still standing by Smoke, his eyes and hand upon the Henry rifle that was still in its sheath.

"You won't need it and no one will touch it," the old rancher assured his visitor. "There are three things you don't touch on the Givens ranch: another man's woman, another man's horse, and another man's gun. They all are given the same respect, and all come with the same penalty if mishandled; the chastising end of a strong rope that is tied to a low limb. You have my word on it."

As the men walked into the large residence, they were met by an elderly Indian gentleman dressed in formal attire. Barton guessed that this person was part of the

270

house staff as opposed to being a ranch hand or the like. Asa instructed the awaiting attendant to bring them good drink, the better cigars, and to tell the kitchen to prepare their guest nourishment to be enjoyed now, and to be taken on the trail when the tall man leaves. At this point, Barton is sure that any objections that he would show to Givens' hospitality could end in not getting what he came for; that being leads to where Coy Newton might have ridden off to.

Each item that was brought for Barton's pleasure was accompanied by a story of its origin. Asa said that the bourbon was from Kentucky, the cigars from a little tobacco plantation outside of Tijuana, the ham biscuits were from Missouri, and the garden vegetables were grown by a tribe of Shawnee natives, whom he allowed to live in the northern part of his ranch land. The old rancher found great joy in the fact that his arraignment did not sit well with the federal government, who had tried to force this tribe to a reservation far away. Asa shared that his agreement with the natives was simple: they could live there unbothered, hunt buffalo and deer, fish the streams and lakes on the ranch, and market their native products to him and his ranch hands. In return, the Shawnee would help with handling the livestock, provide persons to staff the main house, and act as sentinels for the northern parcel of the ranch. They were not to engage anyone, just to watch and to alert him if anything was out of the normal.

Once the meal had been finished, the men moved to a large sitting area, where a young Shawnee woman passed a box of cigars that possessed an aroma that said this offering was going to be better than anything Barton had ever known. His anticipation was rewarded, as he took a long draw from the leaf-wrapped stogie, held it in to fully embrace the essence of the quality, and then slowly released the cloud of contentment. So far, this ordeal has gone better than expected.

With his curiosity reaching its zenith, Asa's booming voice breaks the casual atmosphere with an abrupt inquiry. "You were willing to put your life on the line and was willing to take a life to ask me a question. What is it you have such a craving to know about one of my former ranch hands, Mr. Anderson?"

Barton takes another puff of his Tijuana cigar, lays it aside, and says, "A few weeks back, you had a bad hombre come through here, worked for you a while, and then left suddenly. His name would have been Coy Newton. Do you remember him?"

The old rancher's eyes widen, and he takes a big breath before responding, "One of the meanest son-of-a-bitches I have ever hired, was glad to see his gear packed and gone. Had no skills when it came to working with cattle, but he was strong as an ox and about as smart. When he wasn't getting into scrapes with the other workers, he could be found fixing fence, loading supplies, clearing creek rock, that sort of thing. In other words, he had more strength in his back than he had between his ears. What in the world are you looking for him for?"

It didn't take long for the old man, after seeing the sudden change in Barton's expression, to know exactly why the tall man would be looking for such a callous individual.

"Oh, no." A sense of regret enters Asa's voice as he realizes the motive that compelled this visitor to take such a chance at coming there.

"If I had known that he had partnered with Angus

Ford and that he was one of the butchers that killed your family, I would have gut-shot him myself. Let him suffer awhile before he died. You would have found his carcass nailed to the main barn, stretched out and waiting for you, if I had only known."

Barton waits a moment, then softly responds, "I didn't need for you to kill him. I will take care of that. I just need to know where he went when he left here."

The old rancher, suddenly, gets up, walks out onto the sprawling front porch, yells something, and then steps back into the sitting room, where Barton is waiting for some kind of response that will help with his search for Newton.

"As I said," Asa started. "I didn't care for the cretin, didn't like him, and was glad to see his butt riding up the road. But Carl might know something or heard something, while the trash was here. Carl is the foreman of the ranch, and he is involved in just about everything that goes on out here."

Just as Asa finished his thought, the foreman stepped through the front door. "You want me, Mr. Givens?"

The old man explained who Barton was, and why he was there, and that he was looking for their help in finding the whereabouts of Coy Newton.

"Well, sir. After that big blowup he caused at the saloon in Dog Creek, he couldn't get out of here fast enough. The men were willing to put up with his mulish ways around here, but when he danged near killed one of them, I think the writing was on the wall for his days on the Givens ranch to be over."

Barton stands up, takes a sip out of his bourbon glass, and asks, "Did he ever talk about where he might go? Anywhere he might go back to? Any plans that he had if he ever had the chance?'"

Carl thinks for a minute, and then with a hope that what he just remembered might help, shares that the rough man would talk about being his own boss someday. He would put together his own outfit and no one would stand in his way with him calling the shots. He would go on about how Prestonburg would be easy because they had a simpleton for a constable. Carl added that Newton was usually drunk when he would spew these ramblings, so no one really paid him any attention.

Barton takes one last puff from his cigar, another sip of Kentucky bourbon, and heads for the front door. Asa hurries to get in front of the tall man, reaches in his pocket, pulls out two fifty-dollar gold pieces and hands them to his visitor. When Barton tries to refuse them and hand them back, the old man shakes his head no and signals for him to put them in his pocket.

"Mr. Anderson, I don't feel like it's just happenstance that you are here today." Asa is now almost pleading for Barton's compliance. "You see, forty-two years ago, I was married to a beautiful Shawnee girl named Aylen, which meant 'happy flower'. I called her my Rose of the Ranch. I loved her and we talked of filling this big house with a family. One day, a bunch of drovers were in Dog Creek getting drunk and tearing up the town. They had just finished a big cattle drive and were filled with nature's need to be men. Aylen had gone to town to pick up a few things at the general store, wasn't bothering anybody. Those drovers, in a drunken frenzy, grabbed Aylen and drug her into the saloon. For two hours, they took their turns with her. She screamed for help, I was later told, but the townspeople offered no help. Oh, they heard her, but because she was an Indian, they didn't find the

274

courage to get involved. Once the drovers were done with her, she tried to get back to the ranch house. But after starting to miss her, I found the tiny body of my Rose of the Ranch in the buggy about a hundred yards up the trail, and…"

While the old man was taking a moment to compose himself, Barton slipped the gold coins in his pocket, placed his hand upon the elderly rancher's shoulder, and softly promised, "If I ever come across some old cowboys bragging about a time they were in Dog Creek, I will kill the bastards for free. I will use your money to come back and tell you how good it felt to bring Aylen some justice for what they did to her."

As Barton walks out the front door and heads for Smoke, the foreman follows him out and shares that his grandfather was the foreman of the Givens' ranch when Aylen died. Carl said that his grandad told stories of how Asa drank away his memories of finding his wife dead in the buggy for weeks. The ranch hands tried to find the drovers and bring them back, but they had scattered from Dog Creek. Carl said, with the time of year and with the responsibilities of the herd, his grandfather put his efforts into getting Asa sobered up and put back together.

As Barton listened to Carl's account of the tragic events of the Givens' ranch, he watched as a young Shawnee girl placed some food along with a few Mexican cigars into Smoke's saddlebags. Once she was finished, Barton got upon the big gray horse and told his equine companion it was time to go.

As Smoke turned and headed toward the trail out, Carl yelled to Barton.

"Hey tall man! You are welcome if you ever come back this way. For now, where are you headed?"

Barton turned in the saddle and answered the foreman, "I heard the name of a place mentioned in your stories of Coy Newton. I spent some time in that place once. I think it may be time to go back and visit Prestonburg."

And with that announcement, Barton pressed his heels into Smoke's sides, and the big, gray horse took them both, like the wind, out of sight.

Chapter Twenty-One

When Barton first started carrying out the assignments that marshal Tomes would give him, it was fairly easy to ride into a town, stay in the back of the crowds, stand in the shadows of daytime, and not draw a lot of attention to himself. But as he was riding toward Prestonburg, he was thinking of what Tomes had said about people talking about the tall man on the dark gray horse. Only Dr. Tilley, Nurse Baird and Big Mike had ever seen him during his medical stay in Prestonburg, so that might not pose a problem. But Smoke was an entirely different story. He had become quite popular around town, with the young and not so young alike. For that reason, Barton decided to keep to the back alleys and side streets once he got to Prestonburg.

The first stop on Barton's arrival in the city was Dr. Tilley's office. Barton remembered hearing conversations between the doctor and his medical assistant while they ministered to his recovery. It seemed like the physician and his nurse kept their hands on the pulse of the affairs around Prestonburg. If Coy Newton had been around Prestonburg, there was a good chance that the outlaw's presence would result in someone needing a doctor eventually.

When he walked in the front door of the infirmary, Nurse Baird didn't recognize him at first. She had never seen Barton standing up straight, walking strong, or willing to invoke conversation. But, when realization came to her mind as to who the tall man was, she gasped and then smiled.

"My Lord, is that you, Mr. Anderson? The doctor and

I were just talking about you yesterday. How are you doing? I am willing to bet that there is a big, gray horse standing outside, isn't there? Oh, I am asking too many questions, aren't I? Especially to a man who was always one to be sparing with his words."

Barton, with a slight smile to one corner of his mouth, told her that he was doing good, that Smoke was outside waiting for one of her apples, and that he needed their help in possibly locating a man who may be in, or had been in, Prestonburg.

Just as Nurse Baird started to answer, Dr. Tilley stepped into the room and in his gruff, candid manner, cut right to the question of the day, "Are you looking for this man to buy him a drink, or are you looking for this man to kill him? It would be kind of hypocritical of me to help keep you alive, and then help you take someone else's life, wouldn't it?"

Barton feels frustration building up inside himself. Not that the old sawbones might not help him, but that Dr. Tilley's words carried the weight of legitimate consideration, especially for a man who took an oath to save lives.

"You see, Mr. Anderson," Dr. Tilley explained. "A lot of people come through Prestonburg daily. It's people who have arrived from all places across our fine state. And the three things they seem to be talking about these days are Topeka politics, the Kansas fall crop predictions, and the expanding narrative of a tall man on a big, gray horse. I can't say I am as captivated by the lore of your actions as others seem to be. As a matter of fact, I had hoped that your gun would never be brought to Prestonburg. But, by you standing here, I see my wishes have not been granted."

278

Nurse Baird stands, silently, as the air is filled with the reality of contrasting ideals and opinions between the two men in the room. Barton, reminding himself that the man in front of him is a big reason that he is standing at all, asks the medical man a forthright question.

"Doc, are you sorry that your efforts saved someone like me?"

Dr. Tilley walks over to a chair and sits down. He takes a long breath, closes his eyes as if lost in contemplation, then finally speaks.

"No, Mr. Anderson, I am never sorry when I play a part in continuing a person's life. But sometimes I am concerned with what I may have played a part in, when that person walks out that front door and back into the world out there."

"Then, Doc, I will take no more of your time. I didn't come here today for your approval, just taking a chance on your help," Barton shares as he turns to walk out the front door.

As Barton steps up to where Smoke is standing, he hears footsteps coming up behind him. From the lightness of the sound, he is confident it is not the doctor. Sure enough, he turns to find Nurse Baird standing there, holding an apple in her hand.

"Well, you did say that this fine-looking boy was in need of one of my sweet apples," Nurse Baird remarked, as she sliced up the apple and offered a piece to the awaiting Smoke. While she continued to watch the big, gray horse devour the fruit in the nurse's hand, she suddenly whispers.

"If the man you are looking for is named Coy Newton, you are not the only one looking for him. Your friend, Marshal Tomes, rode into town two days ago. He said he had solid information that this Newton fellow might be riding into Prestonburg, leading a gang of outlaws with the intention of taking the bank or the freight office, which is rumored to have a payroll run to the Hix mines. The marshal also said there was a chance that you might be show up."

When the soft-speaking nurse finally looked up, she noticed the look of confusion on Barton's face. She felt an explanation was needed.

"Don't feel hard against Dr. Tilley. It's his commitment to the living that makes him such a great physician. A lot of doctors would have given up on your situation, but he never did. He knew it wasn't going to be easy, but he never laid his tools, or talents, aside and gave up. He is a gruff man, he is an opinionated man, but he is a very good doctor."

Barton, still trying to process this unexpected moment, asks, "But, why are you willing to help me?"

Nurse Baird goes back to watching Smoke finish the apple, then responds, "The marshal told us who this vile man is, and what he did to your family. I am not as strong, in my saintliness, as Dr. Tilley may be. I lost a brother to such a man, and I still have the memory of the degree of relief I felt when they hung that evil murderer. Watching him swing didn't take the hurt away, it will always be there, I know. Maybe, in some form or fashion, I just understand what drives this tall man on the big, gray horse more than anyone else."

Barton, with a new appreciation for Nurse Baird, thanks her for understanding and wonders if Tomes is still in or around Prestonburg.

"He hasn't been back to the infirmary, I know that. I got the impression that he would stay in the area for a while, as he really seemed convinced that his information was reliable. You might check with Granny Ryan; the marshal tries to call on her when he is in town. Plus, she is around a lot of talking, gossiping and story swapping. If for no other reason, you look like you could use a good country meal."

Barton climbs into the saddle, turns Smoke toward the heart of town, leans forward, and says, "Tell Doc that, maybe, helping me dodge death won't be a bad thing someday." Nurse Baird waves as Barton and Smoke head for a visit with the feisty old lady who may be able to add to his growing account of tips and details.

Prestonburg was busy on this sunny but cool day. The streets, sidewalks, and store-front benches seemed to be occupied as Barton surveyed his surroundings. A couple of blocks from Granny Ryan's, the tall man decided to slide off Smoke and try to blend in with the assembly of citizens. Maybe, on foot, he and the big, gray horse wouldn't be as easily noticed among the people who had come to town for various reasons. Everything, from needing something to help with their daily lives, to just having a break from their daily lives by being around other people who, likewise, needed a fresh voice or face interjected into their routines.

Once arriving at their destination, Barton ties Smoke outside of Granny's eatery and walks inside. Seeing an available table in a back corner, the tall man walks over and sits down. As he waited for someone to take his order, he searches among the patrons, hoping to locate this mature woman that so many had spoken so hopefully of. Just as he was about to give up, an elderly lady walks through the kitchen doorway, carrying a coffee pot in one hand and a cup in the other. She walks over to where

Barton is sitting, places the cup in front of him, fills it with hot brew, then sits down.

"Hi, I am Granny Ryan. That's my name on the front door. That means I don't have to ask where I can sit. I have wanted to meet you, sir, for a long time. Didn't know if I ever would get to. I am an old woman. You are in a dangerous profession, and I didn't know if either one of us would live long enough for this to happen. Just indulge an old woman, if you don't mind, Mr. Anderson."

Barton nods his consent, although he knew it wasn't going to matter if he did or not. As he takes a sip of the hot coffee, his white-haired host calls a waitress over and instructs her to bring the biggest, freshest steak to the table. With his order now in place, Barton awaits, as his host looks him over. Then, she smiles, as she knows that any conversation will be very one-sided when it comes to her tall visitor.

"You walking in with the crowd may have fooled some, but I am a pretty sharp old bird. Plus, it's kind of hard to hide a big, gray horse like that one out there. After hearing Marshal Tomes speak of you so often and so colorfully, I feel like I know you. You are welcome here, anytime."

Barton, again, nods his head in a sign of appreciation. When a young girl brings the ordered meal to the table, Granny Ryan waives her hand, expressing her desire for him to dig in. As Barton takes the utensils, and cuts into the still steaming piece of prime meat, Granny shares what is on her mind concerning the man sitting across from her.

"I am a praying woman, Mr. Anderson. I have prayed for my friend, Marshal Tomes, many times. I have prayed for other lawmen. I have even prayed for you. Some people would say I can't be a religious person and ask the Good Lord to watch over someone who kills people as an occupation or calling. I said I was a praying woman, but I didn't say I was a perfect woman. You see, right or wrong, I feel there is a need for certain adjustments in society to keep things on a more even keel. And, lawmen aren't allowed to make those adjustments. It takes someone outside the realm of legalism, someone who has the ability to go right to the edge of justifiable, to lean over that threshold to get the job done, but never step over that line. I don't know who called you to this duty, whether it was the powerful men in Topeka, or Almighty God himself. I am just glad someone did, and I can sleep good with that confession."

Barton pauses from his eating to give his senior companion a look of appreciation for her insight and confirmation of his new life purpose.

Suddenly, their time of visitation and introspective is shattered by the sound of nearby gunfire, men yelling, and women screaming. Within moments of the disturbance erupting, the front door of the eatery bursts open, and the town constable stumbles into the room, gasping for breath and words.

"Bank robbery, Granny! The bank is being robbed! They say it's Coy Newton and some riders! They killed the banker and guard, maybe more! Marshal Tomes, the sheriff and a few more have them trapped in the bank! It's awful, Granny!"

The spirited owner of the eatery jumps up from the table, points her boney finger at the bumbling lawman, and angrily asks, "Why don't you have your useless behind up there, helping them get those outlaws out?"

The trembling constable turns toward the corner table and points at Barton. "Marshal Tomes sent me here, Granny. When Tomes was riding into town, he saw the big, gray horse outside and told me to come and get him!"

Rising from the table, Barton takes one last sip of coffee and heads for the front door. As he passes his concerned host, he gives her a wink and then whispers.

"Say one of those prayers, mam. Hopefully, someone is listening."

Barton walks out to where Smoke is standing, slides his Henry rifle out of its covering, and then places his hand under Smoke's chin, and says, "You stay here, I will be right back."

The bank is within walking distance of Granny's, and Barton takes his time in arriving where all the shooting is. By not running, he figures that he might not draw as much attention to himself, plus it gives him time to survey the situation. As Barton gets closer, he notices sporadic gunfire coming from the bank, across the street from where he is. Upon further observation, return gunfire is being delivered from a general store, a watering trough, and from upstairs at a hotel across from the financial institution. As to how many shooters on both sides of the street, Barton couldn't really ascertain, and it didn't really matter at this moment.

Whatever anonymity the tall man thought he was invoking by walking slowly down the sidewalk was interrupted by the sound of a bullet going over his head and the shattering of a window behind him. Putting his long legs to good use, Barton picked up his pace. As he neared the general store, running in an irregular pattern to throw off those shooting across the street, Barton heard a familiar voice yell his name.

"Barton, get in here before you get yourself killed!"

As he ran into the business, there behind a stack of seed bags placed against a front window, was Marshal Tomes. Next to the federal lawman was the county sheriff and another deputy. They were bunkered down, returning fire toward the bank. Once his tall friend found a place and got situated, Tomes filled in Barton on what they were facing. According to two tellers and a bookkeeper, who escaped out a back door when the shooting started, there were three outlaws still in the bank. One bandit, who was outside holding the horses, was shot, and killed by Tomes as he arrived upon the scene. The witnesses said that the banker and a bank guard had been killed upon Newton entering the establishment. As for those helping the lawmen, Tomes said there were two citizens in the upstairs of the hotel, a passing cowboy behind the water trough, two armed business owners watching the back door of the bank and the four of them in the store. Unfortunately, three volunteers got caught in the initial shooting, and were still laying where they fell. So, the challenge facing them was to get all the bank shooters neutralized, either through arrest or death.

No sooner had Tomes finished his assessment, gunfire started pouring into the store again, sending canned goods, feather pillows and bottled liniment in all directions in the storeroom. Upon their first chance, the guns positioned across from the bank returned fire into the temporary sanctuary of Newton and his cohorts.

This back and forth went on for twenty minutes, then after one volley of gunfire from the bank, the cowboy cried out that he had been hit and needed a doctor. Bad.

Barton, reloading his Henry rifle, turned to Tomes and reminded the marshal of a time they had been in this very same predicament not so long ago.

"How long are you willing to wait, and how many people are you willing to lose before we bring this thing to an end?" Barton asked.

"It's not as if we have a lot of options. They aren't in a grove of trees, but in a fortified brick building," Tomes answers with both frustration and curiosity in his voice.

As he puts another cartridge in his rifle, Barton rises to peek over the seed bags, lowers himself back down, thinks for a minute and then asks the sheriff a surprising question, especially considering the situation they were caught in.

"Sheriff, how thick do you think that front door to the bank is?"

The local lawman looks at Tomes for an explanation of his friend's inquiry. The marshal just shrugs his shoulders and nods his head toward Barton in a way to encourage the sheriff to respond, no matter how crazy his friend's query may seem.

"I would guess it's three, maybe four inches thick, but I am just guessing, I wouldn't want to bet my life on it, though."

Tomes, giving Barton a concerned looked, says, "Yeah, you may not be willing to bet your life on it, but I think this fellow may be getting ready to. What are you planning to do?"

Barton, asking Tomes for his pistol and placing it in his pants belt, looks at the bank and answers, "I have sixteen cartridges in this Henry rifle, that's sixteen chances of taking that door apart before I get there. If I do get through the door, then with my pistol and yours, I will have twelve chances to take out three murderous thieves. Once I get through the door, the rest of you come as fast as you can and do your lawman duty and arrest anyone that's still alive. Sounds like a plan, doesn't it?"

The sheriff looks at Barton with horror on his face, then proclaims, "Sir, you are absolutely insane if you are seriously considering doing such a thing!"

Tomes, slowly shaking his head and with a smirk on his face, responds, "No, he is not insane. He is Barton Anderson. Everyone, load up and get ready to give the front of that bank everything we've got as soon as he starts in that direction."

Tomes looks back at Barton, who is checking his guns one last time, and inquires, "Just one thing. What if that Henry rifle doesn't do a number on that bank door and you don't get in?"

Barton, faking a surprised look like he had never considered that outcome, says, "Well, you won't have to haul my butt near as far as you did the last time I was in a shootout, will you?"

Tomes laughs at the simple logic of the alternate outcome of his friend's action. After waiting for the outlaw's latest volley of shot to die down, and upon getting Barton's sign that he was ready, Tomes yelled out for all to hear.

"Give em' hell, men! Give em' hell!"

The thunder of simultaneous gunfire was deafening, but Barton didn't hardly notice as he was concentrating on making his own noise. As he ran as hard as he could, he worked the lever on his Henry rifle as fast as he could. Shot, after a forty-four caliber rimfire shot, hit the front door of the bank, wood chips and splinters flying with each blast. As he got to the door and fired the last rifle shot he had, Barton threw himself into the door. The entrance collapsed open due to the damage it had sustained from the rifle assault and Barton's weight. The tall man threw the rifle aside, pulled both pistols and shot two of the bandits without them coming close to hitting him. But he couldn't locate the third one immediately. With the gun smoke hanging in the air, it made it difficult for Barton to see clearly for the moment. So, he slid himself back against the nearest wall, cutting down the directions from which he could be attacked. Barton sat on the floor, desperately listening for any sound that would give him an indication of where the last bandit was. It seemed like it was taking forever for something to happen.

Then Barton sensed that there was someone behind the bank counter. Without moving his head, he transitioned his eyes to his left. As the smoke cleared, there Coy Newton stood with his gun pointed straight at his sitting target.

"I had heard you were looking for me, rancher. I have been looking over my shoulder for too long. Tonight I will sleep a little better, rancher!"

Kaboom!

Before Barton could even try for a desperation shot at Newton, he heard a shot that echoed in the bank building. The tall man figured that it must have been a precise hit, for he did not feel the impact or sense the bloody result. But when he looked back at the bank counter, Newton was not there.

Rather, the next sound that Barton heard was to his right, and when he spun his guns in that direction, he found Tomes standing where the front door had been, smoke still rolling out of the barrel of his Winchester rifle.

"Mr. Newton can sleep in hell tonight," Tomes declared as Barton got up and hurried behind the bank counter, where he found Newton lying and bleeding.

Barton knelt beside the dying outlaw, pulled him up by his shirt and, desperately, pressed Newton for an answer that only the bandit would know.

"The little boy you took from my ranch. Where did you bury him? He died from a rattler bite. Where did you bury him? Do something right, for once in your sorry life. Tell me where you buried my son. Where is my boy?"

At first, Newton didn't respond but just laid quietly as Barton continued to grab him by his shirt. Then the outlaw coughed and smiled. Barton was losing patience, and losing hope, for finding the last piece of the puzzle so he could lay his family's tragedy to rest.

Newton opened his eyes, looked at Barton, and then spoke. "If you got that information from Angus, then all I can say is that is one cold-hearted tale to tell the father of that boy. But that was Angus' way."

Barton, now confused and wondering if the outlaw was out of his mind, as Newton ran out of blood and life.

"What are you talking about? What are you trying to say? Is my son dead or not? Tell me now!"

After another fit of coughing and fighting for breath, Newton's last words shook Barton to the very bottom of his soul.

"Angus might be a cold-hearted bastard, but I can't do that to you. Your boy was bit by a rattler, got pretty sick, but the kid hung in there long enough for us to get him to Angus' sister's place in Lawrence. She said she knew a wealthy couple that would pay good money for a kid like that. Angus told her that he better get half of the cash she got from selling him. I couldn't believe it, people buying kids. Only Angus would have thought of that."

And with that shocking revelation, Newton took one last breath and died.

Barton's head was spinning, his heart was pounding, and his chest was feeling like it would explode. He stood up, turned, and looked at Tomes, who was stunned by the last words of the hardened criminal. Then the lawman walked over to his tall friend, put his hand on his shoulder, and said, "You get on that big, gray horse, and you ride hard. You ride fast. You ride until you find your son. The next time I see you, I do not expect you to be alone. Go, Barton, get out of here. Seth is somewhere out there wondering where his father is!"

Barton, picking up his Henry rifle, ran out of the bank, stood in the street, and whistled a high-pitched signal that only one horse would respond to. Within seconds, he heard pounding hooves approaching him. Without missing a beat, as Smoke ran beside him, Barton grabbed the saddle horn and let the big gray horse's momentum pull him up into the saddle. After placing the rifle into its sheath, Barton patted Smoke's neck, and with a new purpose in his life, proclaimed,

"Run, big gray, run! Seth is alive!"

Not the End, For the Search Begins.

About the Author

GK Beatty's life has not been boring. From a small town Kentucky farmboy, to a well-known radio personality, then becoming a Baptist minister, and now a published author.

Thru it all, one thing was common to each stop in the highway - writing. While the subject focus changed, upon arrival at each destination, the talent was always there to express what was going on in the "theatre of the mind".

Now, GK gets to live the dream, relive the memories and write about one of his greatest loves, the American Western. As he often states, "life is still good!"

Made in the USA
Las Vegas, NV
29 April 2023

71194106R10173